ALSO BY JIMMY DE SANTO

Weekend Warriors

American Muscle

Jimmy De Santo

A Chestnut Book

2013 **Chestnut Publishers** Mass Market Edition

Nazareth, PA

Copyright © 2012 by Jimmy De Santo

Published in the United States by **Chestnut Publishers**

ISBN 978-0-615-73502-3

Library of Congress Control Number: 2012954635

Cover Design: **Chestnut Publishers**

Printed in the United States of America

---

* With the exception of Rocky, who was obviously inspired by screen legend Sylvester Stallone and created in the hope that Mr. Stallone would inexplicably become aware of this book's existence, want to play Rocky in a film version (in a wink-wink, self-referential nod to himself), and subsequently make me a millionaire. Should such a pipe dream come to pass and Mr. Stallone should ever find himself reading *American Muscle*, he can contact me by leaving a comment on my website, jimmydesanto.com.

For my father.

I never knew how much I could learn holding a box of nails.

Prologue
1989

The leather radiates heat, but Jimmy Pedals' only choice is to sit in the '68 Oldsmobile 442 and wait. The ribbed upholstery singes grill marks into the flesh beneath his t-shirt, but he sucks it up. 'Cause on a job like this, you don't turn on the engine for that soothing breath of A/C.

You damn sure don't get out of the car.

Jimmy feels the nerves lighting up inside him like on race nights, when he eases his front tires to the line and awaits the signal. A glowing nausea the size of a fist, nestled in the pit of his gut, sending lightning flashes down the lengths of his extremities, threatening to take jittery control of his faculties.

It's *almost* like the moment before a race.

Not quite. 'Cause he *uses* that energy. Lets it nearly consume his very bones and organs before he eats it up, gets off on it. Takes it for a fancy dinner, brings it home and has his way with it.

Fucks the shit out of *that* energy.

This energy—this nervous sitting, waiting, not for a race but for four guido assholes to beat it back to the car after giving some unlucky fuck the old one-two in the back of the head—well, he can't take control of this energy. *This* energy just fucking owns him.

Which is what Anthony Pugliese asked of him a week ago yesterday.

If he could own him.

The don told him his resolution of a certain situation showed "creativity and balls," for which he offered Jimmy a permanent gig driving for the Pugliese family in New York. No more side jobs for the boss in Chicago, no more drag racing with Sonny for cash, a regular cut of the family payroll, respect, protection, all that bullshit. The kind of proposition you're really not supposed to turn down.

Jimmy wishes he'd had the "creativity and balls" to tell the boss to go fuck himself.

Because when the violent *crack* that ended that man's life echoes in his mind, he feels nothing. It's far more disturbing than if the memory reduced him uncontrollably to tears.

Plus, there's the matter of the ridiculous nickname he got stuck with in the aftermath.

Jimmy Pedals. Makes him sound like a goddamn florist.

Jimmy thinks about how, before the Don's offer, he used to cross the GW en route to an airstrip in Jersey or a stretch of vacant upstate highway to dust the competition in the 442, which he and his partner, Sonny, built from the tires up. Every time, he'd feel the same jolt, that good-to-be-out-of-the-city feeling.

But Jimmy knows that shit's gone forever now that he signed on with Pugliese for the long haul. And that's what's burning inside Jimmy Pedals' stomach as he sits parked where two wet, grimy alleyways form a *T*. His reluctant acceptance of this job sealed it: He belongs to Don Pugliese.

La famiglia. Family. For life.

The very thought raises Pedals' body temperature another exceedingly uncomfortable five degrees. His sweltering '68 adding insult to sunburnt injury.

So he does something he's never done on a gig of this kind. He turns on the radio.

Doesn't rotate the key far enough that the engine turns over. Just enough for the A/C to wash over him and the music to drive out those pesky thoughts of commitment and loyalty and family.

Except the radio raises his Stress-O-Meter from Severely Peeved to Downright Pissed Off. 'Cause he watches that fucker light up electric blue, and suddenly he's serenaded by some whiny glam metal bitch-man on one of Sonny's infernal CDs. Christ, Jimmy can practically hear the Aquanet perm and matching eye shadow in the guy's voice.

Sure, they're racing partners, but how he ever let Sonny, the crazy son of a bitch, convince him they should install a fucking CD player into a 1968 automobile he'll never understand.

Everything else in the car—every last fucking thing—is genuine Oldsmobile. Vintage. Torn from the wrecks of Oldsmobiles that died in battle long before their time. And Sonny, with his hard-on for metal music insists they put in a CD player for their long trips out of state.

Jimmy reaches for the knob, but his thumb and forefinger freeze on the button before he can silence Captain Hair Spray. Something hits him, holds him riveted in place. His guts tighten, and he feels his balls receding into his abdomen.

His whole body's telling Jimmy to pay attention. To what, exactly, he has no fucking idea. But the world has stopped and suddenly he's floating somewhere in a holy ether, above the car, above the four assholes he's waiting to drive to the safe house, above the sewer smell of that fucking alley.

Wherever it is he's floating, that music is still with him. Filling his head.

Except that cheesy, soulless fucking music is somehow heavier up here. More substantial. Sweet and mournful. A work of staggering beauty.

Makes him feel like he did the day he first laid eyes on the 442.

Jimmy hates CDs, owns only vinyl. And even those are mostly Springsteen. Can't fucking stand the pretty boys Sonny listens to. But this guy, with his goddamn roses and thorns and his cowboys singing sad songs? That empty-stadium echo on the strings like this guy with the broken heart is the last man on the planet?

Despite chord changes so simplistic a toddler could be playing rhythm, there's something about it Jimmy can't ignore. How this guy feels he's at the abyss of loneliness even though the whole world knows his name. All because *she's* gone, man. Whoever the fuck *she* was, she's gone. And now he's a legend, but that ain't what he wants. She made him feel free and now she's gone. And with her, that feeling of freedom. He's left with the crowd pushing toward the stage.

And they own his ass.

From wherever he's drifted, Jimmy returns to the car, feeling form-fitted to the seat. Could have been born there. Supposed to die there. His hand's still on the knob, and though the air conditioning has cooled the interior into the sixties, he's sweating more profusely than ever, his face gleaming. He tries to shake off whatever the fuck just happened. But it won't go.

So he turns the knob. Runs the volume all the way up.

And when he pulls out of that alley, alone in the 442, that pretty boy with all that hair and the broken heart drowns out the gunshots inside the apartment building.

Jimmy doesn't hear the wiseguys calling after him as they stand in his distant wake. And he damn sure doesn't see the ambush that follows.

Not that he cares.

Because he's got that song on repeat, and by the time the Lincoln Tunnel births him anew on the Jersey side—sun bouncing off the black-striped yellow of the car's bold finish— he's singing along to the chorus he learned along the way.

Fuck if he ain't getting that good-to-be-out-of-the-city feeling once more.

One
Grandpa's Car

It's always James.

Never Jim.

Don't even think about calling him Jimmy.

And this afternoon, James is taking his son, Kyle, out driving.

Kid's sixteen, a month away from his license, and James knows exactly what Kyle's doing as he flips the turn signal and hangs a steady left onto Maple. James doesn't say anything, just gives Kyle enough rope to hang himself as they pass a huddle of freezing cheerleaders gathered near the sign out front of Gower High—*Class of 2013 Snow Ball December 12th, 6:00*—waiting on parents to pick them up.

James looks past Kyle's disarming smile, his 10-and-2 hands, eyeballs the speedometer.

Yup. Speed limit's 25, kid's doing 43.

Teenage boys. You give an inch, they take the whole darn yard stick. And when girls are involved? Forget it.

"Take it easy, there, Andretti."

Kyle's smiling across the lawn at the shivery squad, some of them raising mittened hands, waving hello, so when he turns back to the instrument panel, he does so with an overly annoyed squint. Like, Dad, what's up with the cockblock?

"I'm doing, like, ten over."

"You're doing almost twenty over. Find another way to impress the ladies."

"There's nobody on this road."

"I'm pretty sure that doesn't change the speed limit," James says, not a big fan of teenage rationalization. "Cop pulls you over, it doesn't matter if you were doin' two over on a road nobody's driven in forty years. You're gettin' a ticket."

"There's no cops on this road," Kyle mutters.

"Just slow it down, huh?"

"Fine."

James feels a drop in momentum, but he can tell without even looking that his smirking son hasn't eased off enough.

"Slower."

Kyle does the patented teenage eye roll with matching shoulder shrug. "Come on, it's impossible to do 25 here."

"Actually, it's remarkably easy. You just take your foot off the gas until the trees aren't whipping by so fast."

Kyle shakes his head and does as he's told. Which is what Kyle usually does in the end, because—though he'd be loathe to admit it—he has a lot of respect for his old man. So he's never so big a dick it'll ruin James' day. Just likes to goad him a bit—like showboating behind the wheel of the Accord when he's supposed to be learning to drive—because that's the natural teenage response to a bona-fide hardass.

Which James Worthington just so happens to be.

Not that *James* would describe himself that way. Letting alone that he wouldn't see the description as fitting, he also gave up profanity in all its forms twenty years ago. Hasn't uttered a cuss more vile than "fart" in the years since.

He cracks the window, the glass receding with a muted hum, and sucks a lungful of frigid country air. It's about three degrees outside, but James isn't fazed. With that whisper of Mother Nature's naked breath tucked deep inside him, he may as well be on the beach in Tahiti for how good he feels.

Trees out his window, his own business to run, a kid who gives him less agita than one would expect. He doubts there's ever been a man who's lived a better life.

"Pop," Kyle wakes him from his reverie, "the window. I'm freezin' to death over here."

"It's good for you. Toughen ya up."

"Yeah, maybe if the car wasn't twelve years old. It takes like a half hour for this thing to warm up."

"All right, all right." James reluctantly complies.

"I don't see why we can't take Grandpa's car," Kyle says. "I mean, in the winter at least. The heat's gotta work better than this piece of junk."

"You don't find it a little, I don't know, ironic you keep begging me to drive a car you refuse to work on?"

"I help you with the 442 all the time," Kyle argues. "We just tuned her up last week."

"I practically had to drag you into the garage."

"That's because all you let me do is hold the wrenches, Pop. It's boring as shit. If you actually let—"

"Watch your mouth."

James knows it wouldn't matter if he let Kyle do *all* of the hands-on work. Cars just aren't the kid's thing. James keeps trying nonetheless, because he favors the same secret fantasy harbored by all fathers: He still hopes, even this late in the game, that his son will grow to manhood embracing some of his old man's passions in life. That junior will be, as they say, a chip off the old block.

Thus far, they're batting, like, .000 on that score.

Kyle likes to run track. James likes cars.

Kyle likes movies. James likes…cars.

"That's why you moan and complain every time I bring my toolbox up from the basement?" James asks. "It's not because you'd rather be spending time with Katie?"

"I've got plenty of time for Katie. I just don't see why I can't be the one doing the actual work when we—"

"Really? Plenty of time for your girlfriend? I seem to remember you sending her texts whenever you thought I wasn't looking."

Kyle's face scrunches with confusion. How the hell did his father know that?

"Just 'cause I'm under the hood doesn't mean I'm deaf and dumb," James tells him. "Look, you think you're entitled to drive a classic when you're not even responsible enough to pitch in on the upkeep. Until you show me you're more mature than that, she stays in the garage."

Any response Kyle may have been formulating, it never sees the light of day.

"Besides," James goes on, "I only hold onto that thing for sentimental reasons. It's all I have left of my father. Not sure I want *anybody* driving it."

"You labor over it like you're gonna take it to Daytona. It's a little excessive for a car you never drive, don't you think? Like you've got OCD or something."

"You'll understand when you're older."

"What, I'm gonna get OCD when I'm an old man, too?"

"There might come a day when I'm gone and you choose to honor my memory in a way that doesn't make a lot of sense to *your* son. Like I honor my father by taking care of his old car."

"Not much of an honor letting that thing collect dust in the garage."

"A layer of dust won't change the work I've put in. That car's in top shape."

"Maybe we should take it for a spin, just to make sure."

"Enough. It's a tribute to the legacy of my father. Someday you'll understand."

"Oh, I understand already. I plan to honor *your* memory by finally driving that car."

Be that as it may, it's in the Accord that they pull up to James' auto parts store. As soon as the engine stops, Lacy flips the "Closed" sign in the window next door, strolls toward them. She and James own stores in the same strip mall, been friends for years.

"Hey guys." She turns to Kyle. "Ready?"

"Lacy." James nods his hello.

Kyle offers, "You don't want to hang around a little longer? It's only quarter to five."

She waves him off. "Earlier I get home on a Saturday, the less bitching Kelly does. Besides, nobody's buying handmade furniture in this economy."

"Tell Kelly I said hello," James says.

Though Gower is a small town with antiquated values, the saga of Kelly and Lacy inspires little more gossip than the occasional unfunny *Cagney* and Lacy joke or a passing jibe about which one wears the pants. Her family has lived in town for so long, and the quality of her custom furniture is of such a caliber, that Lacy Penderhall remains a respected member of the community regardless who she beds down with.

"And you"—James turns to his son—"not too fast. You notice his foot getting heavier when he drives with you?"

Lacy evades the question. "He's been doing fine."

"Well, remember," he adds, turning back to Kyle, "Katie doesn't come over when I'm not home."

"Yes, sir," he mocks.

James says he'll catch them later and disappears into the store. Lacy watches until she's certain he's out of earshot.

"I love your old man, but, God, what a cockblock."

Kyle's like, "I know, right?"

"You tell him about last week?"

"Hell no."

"Good." She hops into the passenger seat of her F-150 as Kyle takes his place behind the wheel. "Since the cop didn't actually give us a ticket, I'm content to live the rest of my life without your father ever knowing you got us pulled over on my watch. He'd have both our asses for that."

"Maybe you should drive this time."

Lacy studies the keys in his hand. "Nah. You need the hours, right? But for Christ sake, you know where the cops sit. Slow down around the speed traps at least."

Behind a cardboard standee for car wash supplies, James listens to the entire exchange, and he can't hide his smile. Been a father sixteen years, and he's still amazed his son can't see right through him, directly into his sordid past, every time James comes down on him. If the kid knew a fraction of the stuff he was doing when *he* was sixteen, the whole authoritarian thing would scatter to the ground like the house of cards James is well too aware he's constructed. It makes him feel like the world's foremost hypocrite, but he has no choice. He knows all too well what it's like coming of age without that kind of guidance. How fast you're forced to grow up, how the experience burns you through to the bone. Changes you.

Which is why it's good there's someone like Lacy in Kyle's life. A responsible party who lets him behave irresponsibly. Cuts him some slack and doesn't ride him so hard for every little indiscretion. James sometimes fears his efforts to prolong his son's age of innocence have done little more than render the boy hopelessly naïve, left him clueless about the harsh ways of the world. Smothered the backbone right out of him. That even with Lacy's help sneaking around behind his father's back, Kyle might not be growing up fast enough.

He's probably worrying too much, but that's James.

Not Jim.

Certainly never Jimmy.

Two
A little Fresh Air Won't Kill Her

The following Friday, Beth's standing in James' kitchen, arms crossed in her heavy fall jacket, when she tells him, "This has gone on long enough. We're taking the 442."

"You too?" James says. "Everywhere I go lately, it's the same broken record."

Much like Kyle, Beth's been asking about that old yellow car since she met James ten years ago. Matter of fact, seeing him labor over that thing in the garage—tune it up, polish it to the nines even though he never drives it—sealed the deal between the two of them.

Beth never could resist a guy's guy in a grease-spattered t-shirt.

James had split with Kyle's mother just a year before, and he certainly wasn't looking for anything serious. But when Beth walked into his store, shopping for a new car battery and told him not to try to upsell her one that would last longer or bullshit her about warranties, James smelled city on her breath and was instantly smitten.

As hard as he's tried to put the city in his rearview mirror, women are one area where the whole country thing didn't take. Carol, his ex-wife, had been as country as they come—and that had been a disaster.

"James, it's the *homecoming* game," Beth insists. "You're the town's biggest fan, and everybody's gonna be there. If there was ever a time for people to see you behind the wheel of that thing, this is it."

"I don't care if anyone *ever* sees me drive that car."

"Really?" she challenges him. "You treat that thing like a second child, and you expect me to believe you have no intention of ever showing it off."

"If I did, don't you think I'd have taken it for a spin by now? Really, I only hold onto it 'cause it was my—"

"All right, all right, all right." She's heard it all before. "I'll make it simple. We're taking the Olds."

James crosses his arms before his chest, awaits the kicker.

"Or I'm leaving you."

Head cocked to the side in a parody of disbelief, James tells her, "Yeah, OK."

As if *that's* likely.

Her bluff called, Beth sighs and presses her chest against his, her breasts impossibly pert for a woman her age, kisses him lightly on the cheek.

"You got me. You know I wouldn't leave."

A smile steals across his lips and he wraps his arms around the small of her back. Once she feels him stiffening against her jeans, she pushes him away.

"But I'm suspending certain privileges unless we take that car out."

In a decidedly different tone this time, James says, "Yeah, OK."

He does, however, find his balls in time to lay down a few ground rules as they pull the heavy car doors shut, a tomblike silence engulfing them inside the garage.

"Just this once," he says. "We buy food during the tailgate, drink any soda, none of that comes inside this car. If we sit on the hood, we lay down a blanket first. And tomorrow morning, you spring for the car wash if a bird drops a doo on her or anything like that."

"A doo? Come on, James, this sarcophagus hasn't seen the light of day in twenty years. A little fresh air won't kill her."

James is undeterred. "And we leave at halftime."

He's usually the last one to leave the stadium. There was a game last season, the bleachers cleared during the first half when the skies opened up and drenched the field. There was practically no one left in the stands—even the parents had split for drier climes—but it was the playoffs, so the Grizzlies braved the storm.

And so did James.

But Beth is too pumped about the plump leather she's sinking into, the growl of a genuine Detroit motor beneath the hood, to do anything more than yes him to death.

The whole way to the field, James doesn't let the speedometer sneak past the teens.

"You must have been hell off the line," Beth chides.

"Get your feet off the dash."

His mood is as flat as his tone for the rest of the evening.

No matter what Beth does to coax him out of his shell, he remains surly and quiet. They walk a loop around the parking lot, past a bake sale, every kind of tailgate game from ladder golf to Ultimate Frisbee, but even the funnel cake she buys them doesn't put a smile on James' mug.

He just can't take his eyes off that car. Like if he leaves it unattended for longer than two seconds an unfortunate fate of monumental proportions will befall it.

Christ, he's like a child about it.

So, after a while, Beth gets fed up with the 'tude, and instead of trying to baby the baby, she starts busting his balls here and there when the opportunities arise. Like when a photographer from the local *Express Call* snaps a photo of some kids pitching quoits in the parking space beside theirs and then walks past the two of them perched on the hood of the Olds. They're polishing off a couple slices of pizza, James holding his over the side so as not to spill any, 'cause God forbid the grease should find its way through the burly cotton of the blanket beneath them and kiss the paint.

"Hey, check out this car," Beth hollers at the photog. "Get a load of this classic."

The newspaper guy shrugs good-naturedly and tells them to huddle together. In a flash, Beth's arms form an arc around James' neck, pulling herself in as close as she can get, half-moon smile plastered across her face.

James does his best to hide his grimace behind the pizza.

He's unsuccessful, as everybody in town knows the next morning. 'Cause that picture lands on the cover of the local section. Right between a shot of Mary Clark's bake sale-favorite apple pie and a stunning portrait of darling Lyndsey Mauer, the homecoming queen.

After that, James' car is the talk of the town. He must answer, like, thirty questions from thirty different customers about the Olds on his next shift at the store.

"It was my father's."

"It's a 390 with some modifications."

"Not a present for Kyle."

"Why don't I ever drive it? It's, uh, not insured."

"No. It is absolutely not for sale."

And his favorite question of all. The one he gets later that night.

"You see," Beth says. "That wasn't so bad, was it?"

As she brings their plates to the table, James rises from his seat and upends the whole fucking thing.

There's a bouquet on the wood top, and three place settings. All of it clatters to the floor as the table slams down, its legs poking up from the tile like fence posts.

Beth and Kyle stand there, stunned and speechless. They'd just put the finishing touches on the salad, Beth joking with the kid like some sarcastic older sibling. James usually loves to watch the two of them together, talking about their running—him with the track team, her with her marathons—loves that his son and his girl have a relationship. But after a day spent fighting off questions about a car he *knew* he should have kept in the garage, his patience has pretty much run its course.

James' finger comes up, points in their general direction, and they both prepare for, like, his head to spin around or for him to sprout horns and a pointed tail, so uncharacteristic is the outburst.

Instead, they hear a voice, deep and low. Very cold and very New York.

"That's enough about da car. Both of ya. From now on, it stays in the garage. Anybody asks ya anything about it, ya don't know nothin'. Ya got dat?"

Though her every instinct tells her to hurl the mixed greens right at the son of a bitch's face, Beth can't move.

It's like she just found a pile of snuff films in a nun's closet.

Kyle's experienced oddities like this over the years, quirks of his father's personality so inexplicable they're genuinely frightening. Like the incongruous shoebox he discovered in his father's closet years ago.

The one with the gun inside.

He convinced himself his father bought it for security down at the store, and Kyle never said a word about it.

Just as he says nothing now.

"Good," James says, taking their silence as compliance. "I'm going to bed."

When the sun comes up, James is his old self again. He doesn't acknowledge the previous evening's events. Closest they get to that is when he comes home from work and finds the leftover chicken in the fridge.

But even then all he says is, "This looks good."

After a few days, they all kind of forget the whole thing.

And no one mentions the 442 that continues to sit in James' garage.

Three
A Gangster and a Gentleman

"We found Jimmy Pedals."

Those are the first words Dominic Pugliese hears at the meeting. Not that those are the first words spoken at the meeting. Dom just isn't exactly in the habit of showing up on time for these things.

And he's like, gimme a fucking break with this old vendetta shit.

Dom's ongoing tardiness has become so old hat that Anthony Pugliese has stopped calling attention to it, pausing just long enough when his son—grown in body, but frustratingly naïve and adolescent in will—wades into the room to let him know his fashionably late entrance hasn't gone unnoticed. The don's brief silence says more than any reprimand from the big man could, and his crew—already harboring an unhealthy disdain for the don's son, who thinks his prima donna shit don't stink—gets the message about leaving business between the father and the son for the father and son to deal with.

Even if the big man ain't as big as he used to be.

In neither status nor stature.

The Pugliese have never truly recovered from the war with the Abruzzi that tore them down back in the '90s. A war they lost, though no member of the family would put it quite that way. They'll simply nod sullenly if you suggest they're a far cry from their glory days of the mid-eighties.

And as for the don's stature, the once-hefty bulldog hulk has been worn down by age. Nearing his seventh decade, the robust mass of his youth has been severely compromised by an inability to digest the foods he once loved so dearly. Gone are the pastas, the *sfogliatelle*. Even when he tries to put away a steak half the size of the monsters he once polished off with ease, he gets the liquid shits for three days.

The family limps on. The limping being one of the reasons Dominic Pugliese, the heir apparent as the don's only son at twenty-four, is less than enthusiastic about taking the reins.

But it ain't the only reason.

As Dom takes a seat at the massive oak table in the pool house behind the don's Long Island mansion, it gives him douche chills to think his father would rather he waste the financial headstart he was born with playing Gotti to a bunch of Pauly D wannabes than do something more constructive with the Bachelors in Business they both agreed he should get.

Dom's thinking, *Thug life was your only option, Dad, I get that. But it ain't mine.*

Though for a while he was happy to let his father believe he was down with the plan.

Like when the big man first started talking about college, describing it as a way for Dom to learn some of the cutting edge theories of the modern business world and return to the family to guide them in modernizing their financial holdings. Investments, the restaurants, the barbershop, whatever. Maybe, eventually, Dom could even be named *consigliere*, a position the family hadn't utilized since the market boom of the eighties.

Dom was like, business school, sure, sure, and the whole time he's thinking it'll buy him four years away from the family, where he can learn about *international* business, maybe find a job thousands of miles from anything his old man's got in store for him.

Of course, then the Abruzzi war found its way, literally, to Dom's doorstep, and he was forced to take more of an active interest in *La Famiglia*.

Fucking fluke thing. Dom's playing cards with his roommates in his George Street apartment at Rutgers when some button man from the Abruzzi clan busts down the door, starts blasting away with a fucking sawed-off.

Apparently there was some dispute over territory—couple of Abruzzi guys pushing dope in a Pugliese neighborhood. Angelo Curatola, one of the capos, took his crew and put the situation right—by peppering the Abruzzi soldiers with .45 slugs and cutting their legs off. A Sicilian message: Nobody walks on our territory.

Unfortunately for Dom and his poker buddies, one of the guys they cut into pieces was Carlo Abruzzi—the boss's eldest son. The thug charging through the apartment door, he was there to settle the score. A son for a son.

And to think, Dom had his buddies convinced he was no relation to those Pugliese guys in the papers. Even had them pronouncing his name Pug-LEE-see as opposed to Pull-YAY-zee to further distance himself from the media's favorite mob family.

But any hope of a normal life at Rutgers went out the window with Dom and his buddies just as the Abruzzi button man started blasting up the kitchen. If it had taken them even two seconds longer to scurry down the fire escape, Dom would've been another Pugliese headline. But since Dominic survived the attack, the only way for Don Pugliese to assure his son's protection was to make him an official member of the family.

They cut Dom's thumb, burned a playing card while a couple of guys prayed before a statue of some such saint, and it was a done deal. Dom became a made guy. As close to untouchable as a mob heavy can get.

So, here's Dom now, his college days behind him, still in line for the top job, listening to Angelo bring up some grudge that's older than he is.

Angelo—hair black and thick, greased the way he's been wearing it since his twenties, though he's getting on in age—drops some disheveled rag of a newspaper onto the table for all twelve or fifteen disciples in the room to see. Aside from Angelo and another pair of standbys from the good old days, the crew is appallingly young. Like they missed the casting call for *Jersey Shore* and chose mob life because they already had the clothes.

As they lean in, Dom, whose late arrival relegated him to a seat off in the corner, notices the rapt looks on their faces. There's a birthday party for a granddaughter of a cousin going on back at the house, but these wing nuts would rather be out here in a poorly heated pool house taking orders from an ancient, war-torn commander. And they're not just tolerating the situation, they're frigging elated to be out here.

Italian pride, they'd tell you.

Fool's pride, Dom would call it.

"One of our guys was fishing in the Poconos," Angelo goes on. "He picks up the local paper to read with his coffee on the boat, sees that."

The paper's folded back to the local section, faded and creased in about a thousand places like it's been studied to death. By the time the newsprint makes its way to Dom, he's beyond the point of asking why something that happened in a bygone era the soldiers of his generation have only heard legends about matters at all, so he buries his nose in the paper and can't tell at first which picture has caught everybody's attention.

There's the apple pie, the couple perched on the hood of a muscle car, and some teenybopper wearing a crown and sash. Dom's assuming the guy on the car is the subject at hand, but he doesn't look much like a gangster.

More like a farmer, actually.

"Some broad he found out there," the don muses after some quiet consideration.

"His name's in the caption, so there's no doubt," Angelo said. "The only question is what we do about it."

"That ain't a question," some baby-faced greaser in a too-baggy suit chimes in. Like most of the rest, he's dark-haired and tan, but he's easily the youngest guy at the table, even by the family's increasingly youthful standards.

Then Dom realizes he's looking at Nicky Sorrentino, Jr.

Little Nicky can't be more than twenty. Kid used to follow Dom around back in high school, figured that since they were part of the same "family" Dom was an in with all the older, cooler kids. Dom was always gracious, but the truth was, he couldn't have given a shit what the cool kids were doing. He was too focused on his grades, preparing himself for the college thing so he could get his ass away from the Pugliese.

"We kill him," Little Nicky continues. "I do it."

The table's quiet as the don lets out a breath.

So that's why the flames of the Jimmy Pedals beef, even though they burned cold two decades ago, are being fanned back to life. The way Dom heard it, the guy was a driver, not even a connected guy, who took off and left a crew in the lurch.

Big fucking deal.

A bunch of overweight guineas having to walk ten miles home after a hit.

Like a bad joke, really.

Except that one of them was dumb enough to get himself killed.

After that, the don never employed anybody who wasn't Italian. 'Cause when they went out looking for Jimmy Pedals, they couldn't exploit any of the usual angles they'd have pursued if one of their own needed to be taken care of. Guy had no family to strong-arm, no steady girlfriend to question or intimidate, no sense of honor or loyalty they could threaten.

Only a *medigan* could live such an unattached and meaningless life.

Best they could do was find the guy he used to go racing with. Sandy or Sally or Sonny or something like that. Another *medigan*. They laid into him, busted him up pretty good, but he didn't know anything. And they couldn't really threaten to kill him either, not over something like that. It wouldn't have been worth the heat it would've brought on the family.

The whole thing would still be a dead issue, Dom supposes, if the guy who got killed on that job were anyone other than Nicky Sorrentino, Sr., who left behind the infant son who now sits at the table demanding reparations.

Clearly, he's grown into an even bigger douche than his father.

While the old man's weighing his options, Dom thinks he sees an opportunity to resolve the whole thing right here and now. Worth a try anyway. After all, the Sorrentino kid used to look up to him when they were in high school.

"I say, with all due respect, Nicky," Dom begins, "that what's done is done. It's not in the family's best interest to pursue a vendetta that's two decades old."

Some of the guys at the table start nodding their heads. It's not the first time Dom's gotten involved this way, offering the peaceable, practical solution when his father would be more apt to strike out with unnecessary violence. And even though they think Dom's an arrogant prick, most of the boys at the table would rather have the rep of a mob soldier without all that messy bloodshed that usually accompanies the title.

"Hey, Dom," Nicky says, "all due respect, take a cock up the ass."

So much for high school.

The table erupts. Echoes of "Oh" and "Ay" all around. 'Cause you can't talk to a made guy that way if you're on the lowest rung. You can't insult the don's kid. And you definitely can't tell a made guy who also happens to *be* the don's kid to take *anything* up his ass.

The don raises his palms to quiet everybody down and tells Nicky his comment was uncalled for. Nicky looks like he knows it would be prudent to say nothing more. But in that way of the young, he can't hold back.

"Don Pugliese, what's done is done? I've been without a father since I was less than a year old. Nothing is *done* for me.

Everyday I have to remember that gutless piece of shit and how he got my father killed. He deserves to die. You owe me that."

Some of the guys at the table nod, others shake their heads. But everyone knows this is going to end one of two ways: Either the don gives the order, and Jimmy Pedals is a dead man. Or one of them is gonna have to drop Little Nicky to the bottom of the ocean.

They're all quiet as the don rises from his chair. It's kind of a sad sight to observe for how unsteady the guy has grown over the years. It takes a visible effort, holding onto both armrests, for him to straighten his back and walk slowly around the table to stand beside the seated Nicky, who doesn't rise—doesn't even look up at the don.

Not out of disrespect, they all know.

But because he's shitting his pants.

Anthony Pugliese gestures the kid to his feet. Standing, Little Nicky is almost a full head taller than the boss, but that doesn't matter. Despite his deteriorating physicality, there's a confidence, a well-documented and bloody history that surrounds the don like a visible aura. Nicky looks ten years younger than his actual age when placed next to the great man he turns to face.

The don wraps a palm around the back of the kid's neck, and Nicky Sorrentino straightens up, his limbs trembling. The don shakes his head and smiles, kisses Nicky on one cheek before pulling him into an embrace.

When Pugliese pulls back, he says, "And are you up to this? Not just this job, but being brought into the family in this way?"

The kid decides a single definitive nod would work best. Either that or he's still too shit-scared to manage anything more.

"*La Famiglia*," the boss tells him, "is for life."

As the kid nods again, the boss sneaks a look at his son that Dom does not fail to notice. With a light pat on Nicky's cheek, the boss nods, the order given, and he heads back to the house to enjoy the rest of the party.

Though he's closest to the door, Dom's the last one out of the pool house.

His father catches up with him later, as he stands waiting for car service beside the unmanned guard post at the front gate.

"Goddammit Dominic, what are you doing?"

"Waiting for my ride."

"Cute. I'm talkin' about you coming in late, talking out at the table. Shoulda put a stop to it years ago, but I thought you'd outgrow it. Whatever hormonal bullshit you're going through—youthful rebellion, whatever—it ends now."

"I just offered an opinion."

"Any other man were to behave like that, we'd be sending his widow a mass card."

"What are you saying, Dad?"

"I'm saying let's stop dancing around this, shall we?"

"Dancing around what, exactly?"

"Don't kid yourself you're gonna end up working in a cubicle, Dominic."

"I'm doing fine with the job, Dad. The one you got me."

"I did that to make you happy. I didn't think you'd be the only Pugliese crew member who would actually *report* to his no-show job on a daily basis. Between the job and the girlfriend, I can feel you slipping away. Why didn't you invite her, anyway? It was a family thing, we woulda like to see her."

"Come on, Dad, you know how Ma and the other girls make her feel."

"They're just disappointed you're marrying *medigan*, that's all. They'll get over it."

"They hate her."

"Hey, you talk nice about your mother. And why you wasting half the afternoon waitin' on car service? I bought you the Mustang to make it easier for you to come and see us. You won't even drive it."

"Letting the Jimmy Pedals thing go was the right call."

The don sighs, so exhausted he feels it in the marrow. "The problems we face, *La famiglia*, cannot be solved with Band-Aids and ice cream. Going easy on this piece of shit would only make us look weak. Make *me* look weak. I can't believe my own boy would make such a suggestion just to spite me."

"Spite?" Dom's flabbergasted. "If you think that's why I said we should spare a man's life, you should step down now, Dad. Save what little might be left of your soul."

The don raises a palm like he might smack. Instead, he grips his son's shoulder, his weathered hand startlingly heavy as it clenches Dom's deltoid. "Nobody makes me look weak, Dom. Not even my own son. The order I gave, it had to be done. Someday, responsibilities like that, they're gonna fall on you. When that time comes, believing you can fart sunshine and make the world's problems vanish is gonna destroy this family. And no one will ruin this family under my watch. Not even my boy. I won't allow it."

"Then maybe I'm not cut out for the big job."

The don raises a bony finger. "I'm not gonna tell ya again: Watch your mouth."

But Dom can't. "A soft touch woulda worked here. We *should* let this guy go. It's ancient history."

The don takes a breath, nods slowly, getting the words ready. 'Cause the kid don't wanna fuckin' understand. "All of my territories in Queens I gave up for you. Don Abruzzi would take nothing less to let you live. It nearly destroyed us. But I'd do it again in a heartbeat. You're my son, and you're the only person I want in charge when I'm through. Now, you're gonna have to accept that, and you gotta get right with what we do in this family."

Anthony can practically see the smartass comment hanging from his son's lips, and he spares them both another go-round. "You're blood. That's that."

He claps his son on the back of the neck. Much harder than he needs to. Doesn't kiss his boy as he turns toward the house.

Shaking in the cold, Dom watches him fade away.

Four
Little Miss Mansion

"You've gotten a lot better," Lacy tells him as the headlamps swing an arc into Kyle's driveway. It's the usual routine: Kyle drives James to work, Lacy lets him drive her truck back home so he can log his hours.

"Thanks." He shifts into park. "Twenty-six days I can go for my license."

"Ah, the way you handle my rig, manual transmission and all, I think you're ready now."

Kyle wants to play it cool. Like, of course I'm ready. Who fails their driver's test? But he asks, "You really think so?"

Lacy makes a circle with her thumb and forefinger. "At least as ready as Little Miss Mansion over there in the bushes." She nods at the side of the house, where Katie sits low in the darkness of her Jetta. "Hiding like that, she looks ready for all manner of things."

Busted, Kyle smiles with embarrassment. Not because he and Katie have been caught sneaking around, but because he'd rather not have to consider a woman he's known since he was in diapers processing thoughts of what he and his girlfriend will be doing while alone in the house.

"Come on with the mansion stuff, Lace. Not all rich people are evil. Go easy on her."

"Likewise, stud."

Kyle reddens and turns away.

"Don't sweat it, Romeo." Lacy chuckles. "I won't tell Captain Conservative. Just don't get yourselves into any trouble, OK?"

*   *   *

The "Little Miss Mansion" jibes are dead wrong. It ain't about the money.

Though as he rams his tongue down Katie's throat, the two of them lying atop his bed, Kyle can't shake the suggestion.

It could *easily* be about the money, and it probably looks like it is—God knows she comes from plenty of it—but, though he and his pops aren't exactly rich, they're far enough from destitute that Kyle's never had to give financial security much thought. Whatever they've needed over the years, James has always managed to come up with the cash.

So it wasn't the smell of money that caught Kyle's attention. It was more the fact that Katie wasn't attracted to the smell of it. Which is not to say she doesn't like the stuff. Or that she's above accepting it as her parents shower it upon her in place of the love they reserve for their jobs, their vacations, their cars, their massages, their electronics, their...

Well, the list of selfish pursuits they rank above their only child goes on and on. But their money? That they make readily available.

New wardrobe every Spring and Fall? Katie ain't complaining. Spring Break trip to St. Thomas? She's down with that. In lieu of the kinds of afternoons Kyle spends working on the old car with his dad—hell, her folks couldn't even be bothered to take her out driving when she had her permit, just threw her into Driver Ed and called it a day—Katie gets presents.

And she gets left alone. 'Cause if you want to make the kind of money Katie's parents make, you gotta put in the hours. Which is why she meets no resistance sneaking over to Kyle's place whenever she feels like it. If Dad's at the office, he can't raise an eyebrow, ask who exactly she's going to see and whether or not his parents will be home.

If asked, she'd grudgingly admit that her parents would be there for her if she suddenly needed them. Eyeballing their watches as they came to her aid, counting the seconds until they could dive back into their respective piles of paperwork, but they'd make themselves available.

The only thing is, Katie's never really needed them. Or their money.

Katie doesn't really need anybody.

Certainly doesn't need the proverbial pat on the back.

Coach offers her cheer captain, she's like, gee, I'm honored, but no thanks. AP Euro test for college credit? Not for me, I just took the class to challenge myself. She doesn't need accolades to prove she's accomplished something. Without parents to root her on, she's developed intrinsic motivation.

Kyle loves her for her quiet rebellion.

Which is why she feels so guilty about blueballing him the way she's been.

See, Kyle's a virgin. Katie, not so much.

She wishes she could have saved herself for the love of her young life, but Katie wasn't always as evolved as she's become over the last year or so. There was an earlier boyfriend, he drove a Mercedes, had a chin like Brad Pitt, told her he loved her, blah, blah blah…

So she can't give Kyle something she'd really like to.

You live, you learn. It's a lesson she'll be sure to teach her daughter someday.

And the real irony is she gave it up for a guy who represents that whole Rolex-and-fake-tit lifestyle from which she's trying to distance herself, yet she won't give herself to the boy-next-door who really deserves what she has to give.

And, boy, has she got a lot to give.

She may not get their attention, but she's got her parents' WASPy blue eyes and blond hair. Their perfect smiles and soft skin. Mom's curves and Dad's statuesque musculature. But Katie finds that whole side of her—the physical façade she's already used (in moments of weakness) a time or two to her advantage, winning over teachers and employers with the slightest bat of an eye—so shallow and repugnant, she doesn't want Kyle anywhere near it.

And it's a shame, too. 'Cause it would be sweet and it would be good, and they'd both enjoy it so.

Besides, poor kid deserves it. He's waited long enough.

Just look at him, his kisses getting harder and harder as he slides his tongue against hers like he's attacking an ice cream cone. His eyes pinched in concentration, thinking if his lips touch hers in just the right way from just the right angle she might tremble and melt and finally give him what he wants.

Not that she's a casual observer in all this. His efforts do quite a bit for her too. Those kisses, raw and experimental as they are, succeed with a vigor and enthusiasm that make up for the lack of polished skill. And his hands on her body—*God*, those same rough palms he uses on that car. She knows he hates when his dad makes him help out in the garage, but just the thought that he's used those fingers to turn wrenches and dial timing belts into the perfect, purring rhythm—she feels herself softening beneath his touch, fearing her body will take over and tell him yes before her words can stop him.

As those fingers find the eagerness emanating from between her thighs, as if her juices have telegraphed a psychic signal, she feels the snap of her jeans being pulled open and her back arches in surrender as he guides her pants and cotton panties down low enough that he can reach inside her. Eyes closed, her neck rises and a gentle moan escapes her throat.

Unfortunately, it only lasts another ten seconds.

That's when the alarm on Katie's cell phone goes off.

Beth will be there any minute to take Kyle driving.

They both go rigid. Kyle keeps his hand in position, fearful he'll never find his way back there again. Katie rolls onto her side, forcing his fingers loose so she can topple off the bed and hop her jeans back up. Kyle resists an urge to slap himself on the forehead.

He can't make himself move out of the bed, but Katie's already shrugging her coat on. 'Cause Beth ain't the lenient surrogate parent Lacy is.

Especially where Little Miss Mansion is concerned.

Five
Shit or Get Off the Pot

Like a formality, a perfunctory detail that required his attention before Dom could continue his silent sulk, he made love to Maria. Upon climax, he slipped out and walked naked to the window of the high-rise condo they share uptown.

In the darkness, she can just make out his profile, bathed in the moonlight soaking through the blinds. She watches him—pensive, a million miles away—as if in the two minutes since he reached ecstasy inside her he's somehow forgotten the act even took place.

"I'm sorry," Dom tells her.

"What is it?" she asks, sitting up in bed.

"Do you remember when we met?"

"Of course."

It was the summer before his final year at Rutgers. The Abruzzi war finally over, he signed up for a study abroad program, needed to get the fuck away from the family, the life he'd been forced into. When it ended, he spent two weeks backpacking across the European countryside. No directions, no map, no plan. Ten days into the trek—filthy, unshaven, smelling like the ass end of God's country—he saw her.

Middle of nowhere, short, inky hair stark against skin of vanilla cream, thong-clad and rolling around on an Indian blanket. Wandering across the Irish hillside, he stumbled right into her photo shoot.

"They cleared seven acres just for you. Just handed it right over."

"Fired me the next day," she reminds him.

The photographer had tastefully implied that without a proper blow job he'd be incapable of fulfilling his duties on the shoot. It's practically standard procedure in the industry, and most models eagerly oblige.

But Maria is not most models.

"And you just rolled with it," he says with admiration. "Went right on with your life."

"What else could I do?"

Dom faces her. "That's what I've been asking myself all night."

Maria wraps herself in the bed sheet, joins him at the window.

"What happened today?" she asks. "At your father's house."

Though Dom doesn't make a habit of sharing family business with her, Maria would have to be an idiot not to know about the Pugliese. Since Dom knows this is decidedly not the case, he hasn't kept her in the dark. Something hits the papers, Dom doesn't deny it. Particularly unsavory details get reported in the gossip rags, Dom doesn't pretend it's just sensationalized fiction.

There's no point in playing coy. Maria's a smart cookie.

Dom would even admit she's a brighter bulb than he. He killed it at Rutgers, but he broke his ass doing it, whereas big ideas seem of endless supply to Maria. Lack of book learning aside, she received a worldly education, something far more practical than the smorgasbord of academia served up in a Liberal Arts program. Coming from where he does, Dom's always thought himself street smart, but Maria dwarfs that too.

He only knows the streets of New York. Maria's walked streets in every country imaginable.

"My father came across an old business associate," he explains. "Someone who used to work for him a long time ago. This guy, he was involved in a business deal with the family, and he didn't hold up his end of the bargain. Someone got hurt as a result."

Maria nods slowly, piecing together what the business analogy might actually mean.

"So now my father thinks settling up, after all these years, is the right thing to do. Shit, it's worse than that. He's put some…some frigging kid in charge of the whole thing. Guy's no older than twenty."

"About the age you were when you met me," she muses.

"Yeah. Remember how young and stupid I was?"

"Yes. I do."

His smile rises to meet hers.

"It's not funny, though," he goes on. "This is the kind of thing that destroys a family. You let your emotions muck up your common sense. Start getting sloppy. It's the impulsive posturing my father will never learn is ineffective."

"Is this…old business transaction that insignificant? Could the family just let it go?"

Dom shakes his head in disgust.

"It's ancient. And minor. If we go after this, we may as well start going after guys who may have taken an extra dollar or two from the tip jar in one of my father's restaurants—back in the 1980s. Fuck, Maria, how the hell am I gonna take the family from what it is now to what it needs to be? Since I've gotten out of school, they've moved *backwards* for Christ sake."

They're quiet a while, Maria offering no solution. Dom shakes his head dejectedly while she works her palms through the knots in his shoulders.

"We can still do it, you know," she tells him.

"No we can't."

"I've got enough in the bank. It doesn't matter if he cuts you off." She grins. "I'll be your sugar momma. We can live anywhere in the world."

Dom's shaking his head. "My father would find me."

Which they both know isn't likely. Even if Anthony Pugliese had the inclination to track his son overseas, he doesn't have the resources. Not after the Abruzzi war.

The real reason Dom doesn't run off with Maria is he simply can't do it. Though it's a heritage that often sickens him, Dom was born Italian-with-a-capital-*I*. He was born mafia. And he can't bring himself to walk away from it completely.

He can see Maria cocking her head like, come on. So Dom takes another approach.

"With everything I learned in school, I can steer this family in the right direction. Run it clean. I know I can. I just have to tough it out until the time is right."

His voice lacks conviction. Truth is, his doubts as to whether or not that's still possible have been eating away at him as of late.

"OK then," she tells him. "I guess it's time to shit or get off the pot."

"'Shit or get off the pot?' The girl I met in Ireland never knew such a phrase existed. You've been in New York too long."

"My point exactly. Either we make good on this phantom promise of a fairy tale life in some far corner of the world or you make a play for the reins of the family."

"Make a play for the reins?"

Frustrated by his sudden inability to do anything more than repeat her, Maria abandons the massage, pushing him away. "You can't say goodbye to the family, then you run it your way, and you do it now."

"Maria, how am I supposed to—"

She smiles and leans her face less than an inch from his. "When life lets her guard down, you kick her in the fucking balls."

She's granting him her blessing to do whatever's necessary. And once he's on top, it'll be his show to run.

Boy, Dom's right.

She *has* been in New York too long.

Six
Nicky Sorrentino Says Hello

Going over the night's receipts, James sees headlights out of the corner of his eye, looks up to see Beth's Jeep Liberty pulling in, Kyle behind the wheel. When they don't immediately get out of the car, James assumes (correctly) that Beth's chewing the kid out for something. He laughs and shakes his head.

Better Kyle than him for a change.

James is punching numbers into a calculator when the boy finally walks in. He doesn't look up as he says, "Saw Beth pull out of here in a hurry. What'd you do to get her steamed?"

Kyle shrugs, feigns ignorance. Doesn't tell his father it was a lecture Beth felt compelled to unleash after she caught Little Miss Mansion pulling out of the Worthington driveway when James wasn't home.

Beth isn't half the hardass James is—never had kids of her own to worry about—but she's got to draw the line somewhere. Plus, she hates being taken advantage of. So if Kyle was fucking Katie on her watch, that's unacceptable.

"Wasn't me," Kyle says. "I think she had a bad day at work."

James looks up, sales receipt in one hand, pen in the other. "It's Saturday. She didn't work today."

"Maybe she had a bad day 'cause she *didn't* work." Kyle smiles like he's oh-so-clever. "You know what a workaholic she is."

James says, "Right," and turns back to the calculator.

There's a life-size cutout in the front of the shop of a woman in a red, white, and blue bikini hawking some new brand of car wax. She's holding buckets, looking playfully shocked and appalled like someone just sprayed her with a hose, soaking wet from her bangs to her bare feet. Kyle studies it while he waits for his old man to finish up.

James is nearly done counting out the last of his three registers when headlights dance across the plate glass. He squints, trying to decipher who has business with the Gower Strip Mall an hour after closing.

"It's just Lacy," Kyle announces.

"What the heck is she doing here?"

Kyle doesn't see as how it's much of a question. Her furniture shop is right next door. But since it'll get his father back to the count so the two of them can get out of there for the night, he offers to go outside, see if she needs help with anything.

"Forgot to set the damn alarm," Lacy tells him.

"You could have called us. We would have set it for you."

"Kelly was in one of her moods anyway. Good excuse to get outta the house."

Kyle nods, notices Lacy's killed the engine and locked her car. Clearly, she plans on staying outta the house more than a little while. He waits until she's safely in her store before walking back to his dad's place. Without the hum of Lacy's engine, there's barely a sound to be heard in the cold Pennsylvania countryside. Just the rustle of settling gravel beyond the furniture store, down at the far end of the plaza where the storefronts end and the retention pond begins. Almost like somebody shuffling his feet against the cold.

Kyle breathes steam clouds into the night, peering into the darkness. Sees nothing. Figuring it for a raccoon, he heads back into the store.

"Pop, we good?"

James is behind the counter, spinning the dial on the store safe. "What's up with Lacy?"

"Trouble in paradise."

James snickers. "Been there." He places a small bag of the night's income inside the safe, closes the weighted door and spins the dial again. "We're good," he says, grabbing his ski jacket.

Kyle's elated. Palm goes to the handle on the front door immediately. But James stops halfway to the entrance, says, "Crap," and snaps his fingers.

Kyle's eyes roll heavenward, and he groans. "What?"

"I don't have any cash on me." He looks back toward the safe, then looks to his son leaning hard against the front door. "Heck with it," he decides. "I'll hit the ATM outside."

On the sidewalk he hands Kyle two sets of keys. One for the Accord, one for the store. "OK, secure all three locks, jiggle the handle to be sure. Then warm up the car and pull around for me."

"Got it."

On his way to the ATM on the far side of Lacy's furniture store, James calls back, "And make sure you jiggle the handle."

"Anal much?" Kyle mutters to himself.

Standing before the ATM, James punches 4-9-4-2, the numbers that correspond to the letters of his son's name. Corny, he knows, but Kyle was the first four-letter word that came to mind when he opened the account. After all, James gave up most four-letter words years ago.

The headlamps of the Accord light him from behind, his shadow long against the ATM. Because he's been to this machine a thousand times and could remove his cash with his eyes closed—and because he's a man with no vices who still needs to feel like a bit of a wiseacre—he presses the button for German when he's asked his language preference.

Doesn't know any German, just has every screen memorized to the point where the words don't matter. Long as the machine doesn't spit his currency out in Deutsch marks, James can pretend he's learning a new language.

Top button, Withdrawal from Checking. Bottom button, Enter Different Amount. Two, Zero, Zero on the keypad—those numbers are engraved in the metal, they don't change.

He gets a little message that he knows translates to Please Wait While Your Transaction is Being Processed. So James is waiting, shoulders up against the winter breeze, whistling some nameless tune when he feels someone walking up behind him. He's about to turn and ask Kyle why he's braving the tundra now that the car is warm when he hears a click.

It's been a while since James has kept company with a gun-toting crowd, but he knows the sound of a revolver's hammer being thumbed back when he hears it.

Not wanting to make any sudden moves, he shows the guy his profile, tries to diagnose the situation, see exactly what he's in for. He barely makes it that far before the guy says something, gruff and serious, and James knows the guy wants more than his wallet.

'Cause what the guy says is "Jimmy Pedals, this is for Nicky Sorrentino."

Then Jimmy Pedals turns all the way around, spits at the guy's feet, and says, "Fuck Nicky Sorrentino."

Seven
Dead in Two Fucking Seconds

On the radio, Taylor Swift is singing about some dick that dumped her when she was fifteen. Or maybe Katy Perry is. Kyle can't tell the difference. He gives the song three seconds before he's flipping around the dial again, trying to find a tune that doesn't completely suck. Nothing but pop bullshit from top to bottom. He works the seek button from the low nineties all the way up and is about to start again when he notices some dude in a black trench coat standing behind his father at the ATM.

And he's like, where the hell did he come from?

Kyle looks to his left, his right. He knows he can be oblivious to stuff that doesn't concern him, but he's pretty sure he would have noticed another car pulling into the lot.

Other than Lacy's old Chevy, there isn't another vehicle in sight.

And why's the guy reaching out toward his father?

Then, with the radio tuned to a station putting out nothing but soft snow, Kyle hears the click, and the gun's silver plating reflects his headlights.

His heart races. And not just in his chest. It's hammering, like, everywhere in his body. Through his arms, in the back of his throat, his temples. Sweat moistens his brow, palms go slick on the wheel.

His father's about to get shot, and he's powerless to move.

All he can do is watch as James turns and—shockingly— hawks one on the guy's shoes.

The mugger's posture changes completely, like his spine's been switched out with a steel rod.

And Kyle knows his old man's gonna to be dead in about two fucking seconds.

Before he realizes what he's doing, he reels his arm back and punches—literally *punches*—the Accord's horn. Holds his fist against it in a long, high whiny wail.

As if in response, James dives to his right. It's a maneuver born of panic and instinct—logic-be-damned—and even if by some trick of fate he does clear the path of the impending slug, the guy's got five more loaded up behind it, and they'll all strike home while James is cowering on the ground.

But coming at the same moment that Kyle lays on the horn, James' evasive action proves moderately effective.

See, the guy's aiming for James' heart, but the nasal cry of that horn turns his arm to jelly, and the gun dips as he pulls the trigger.

The bullet tags James in the side instead, going through his love handle on the left before tearing through his back and dinging into the cash machine.

The pain is like somebody lit his abdomen on fire.

From the inside.

With a dozen blowtorches.

In the middle of the desert.

The next time he's watching a movie and somebody walks away from a gunshot wound, tearing a piece of cloth from his t-shirt, tying a nice, neat bow around the bullet hole—well, James is just turning that flick right the fuck off.

He's screaming. Unbridled, untamed shrieks that he couldn't control if he wanted to. And he doesn't want to. He's in fucking pain. He's fucking scared. He's swirling inside himself, everything around him turning to liquid, the car horn tearing into his brain. He's so out of his head with agony, he forgets about the guy with the gun. The kid in the trench coat stepping forward to place the revolver's muzzle against his forehead and empty the five remaining shots into his brain.

Then he thinks the pain is causing delirium. Because for a second he sees Lacy leaping off the hood of his Accord like a wrestler from the top rope, swinging what looks like a caveman's club.

Turns out it's actually the leg from some custom table she was putting together in the shop. A big fucker, room for twelve. Whatever spat drove her from the house, it ends up working out pretty well for James.

And as for the flying leap, she just happens to be a little bit taller than the kid in the trench coat, which makes it appear, from James' vantage point, that she's jumping off the hood of his car. That, coupled with the sudden rapid blood loss James is experiencing, makes it seem she's some primitive ancestor descending upon his attacker when she swings that giant fucking hunk of oak against the back of the guy's skull.

Kid drops like he's got legs of straw, his scalp striking the ATM as his body crumples.

Lacy keeps her weapon high, breath coming in quick adrenaline-gasps.

Then she sees the guy's hand twitch. Could be a spasm, could be he's reaching for the gun he lost on his way to the pavement.

Either way, Lacy closes her eyes and brings the table leg down in an arc, all the force of her artisan hands behind it. The splintering crunch leaves no doubt that if the first shot crippled the guy, this one outright killed him.

The horn finally dies, and Lacy turns toward Kyle.

"Holy shit," he says, stepping out of the Accord.

She's still breathing hard, can't say anything.

Kyle cries out for his father, rushes past Lacy and the pulpy remnants of the mugger to cradle James in his arms. His dad's still semi-conscious as Kyle takes hold of him. Long enough to offer his son a dazed look before passing out, going limp in Kyle's grasp.

"Lacy," Kyle shouts, "my phone's in the car. Call 911. Tell them there was a…a…"

But Kyle lacks the words to describe exactly what the hell just took place.

Eight
A Matter of Heart

Dom hasn't been on his father's boat, the *Mother Mary*, in a decade.

Until Dom turned sixteen and focused his attention solely on his studies, he and the old man used to spend their Saturday mornings fishing. A couple of city boy goombahs, neither of whom could swim, up at the ass crack of dawn, toting a cooler stuffed with sodas and Ma's meatball sandwiches. The old man was even cool with junior downing a few brews while they were out on the water. 'Cause his boy was on the verge of manhood, and it was male bonding time, right?

Until Dom got too big for his britches, told the old man he was tired of the boat.

Now the don only takes the boat out when he's gotta discuss a family problem that's too hot to be addressed anywhere near a potential police tap.

Plus, there ain't a problem can't be dumped over the side of the old man's yacht.

Which is why, as Dom stands on her deck watching his father and Angelo—serious looks on both their faces—he checks for chains or cement, any weighty instruments that could drag his young bones to the depths of the sea.

Not that the old man's gonna drown his only son, but why the fuck are they out here?

The chop rocks the hull, lapping sloppily against the sides. It's the only sound as Angelo stands beside the don's deck chair, both men draped in bulky winter garments topped with wool hats. The old man's wearing sunglasses beneath a sunless sky. Angelo's glaring at Dom, half a smile creeping up his face. Dom's trying to stand perfectly still.

Thinks if he allows himself to move, he'll start shaking all over, for fear and cold.

"As it turns out," his father begins, "in regard to Jimmy Pedals, we probably shoulda followed your path of least resistance."

Dom's thinking, *OK, OK, that's good. So why the hell am I freezing my balls off on a boat on Long Island Sound in the middle of fucking December?*

"But the tardiness, the halfhearted interest in the family business—all your unrestrained comments that contradict whatever I say, from the Jimmy Pedals thing to what we should order for lunch. Maybe your mother's right. Could be that *medigan* girlfriend's got you wrapped around her finger."

The girlfriend thing lands like an anchor in Dom's stomach, but he says nothing.

"And that's the dilemma I find myself in at the present moment," his father continues. "Part of me wants to smack ya— maybe worse—for your insolence, but I can't exactly do that if you were right, can I?"

Dom sucks a cold breath into his lungs, asks, "What made you change your mind about Jimmy Pedals?"

The don glances up at Angelo, lets his lieutenant take up the slack.

"We gave the thing to the Sorrentino kid," Angelo says. "You were there. He was supposed to have it done by yesterday."

Dom can't halt a reflexive smile. An I-told-you-so grin. "The kid couldn't do it," he says.

"That's the thing," Angelo tells him. "We don't know. Nobody's heard from him in three days. Could be he couldn't do it, could be he got pinched—"

"Could be he's dead."

"Could be. Anyway you slice it, kid, we got a mess needs cleanin'. We just don't know how dirty until we follow this kid out to the sticks and diagnose the situation."

"Which is how I've decided to handle this tension between you and me," the don chimes back in.

Dom feels his asshole clenching in anticipation.

"You and Angelo will mop up the Sorrentino mess. If the kid didn't get the job done, the two of you will. Angelo will provide the muscle and experience, but he'll take orders from you." The don taps a finger against his own temple. "See, your brain is good. That noodle is what I'm counting on to keep the Pugliese thriving after I step down. It's your heart that's questionable, Dominic. I send you on a job where one conflicts with the other, it'll be good practice for when you're in the big seat and you need to make decisions you wish you didn't have to."

"Let me get this straight. You agree with me now that we should let Jimmy Pedals live, yet you're asking me to find him and kill him?"

"I'm askin' ya to do the smart thing here. Whatever you decide that is. Assess the situation, make the right decision—even if that's the hard decision." The don spears the air between them with a bony index finger. "And it probably will be. All we know, guy could be responsible for the deaths of *two* family members now."

So Dom still has some say in the matter.

He's grateful for that much at least.

He looks to Angelo. "Your opinion, how ugly is this gonna get?"

Angelo's face twists in consideration. "If I had to guess, I'd say Sorrentino's probably in the clink somehow. Just a matter of time before he talks. Strange town, no familiar faces. Hell, out in the country, God knows how they persuade a guy to give up his buddies. Kid's young, he'll crack."

"So, we gotta kill him too? So he can't talk?"
"That's the most likely scenario, yeah."
"While he's sitting in a jail cell?"
Angelo shrugs. "I've worked harder jobs."
Well, his father's right about one thing:
Dom's heart ain't gonna be in this one at all.

Nine
A Friendly Game of Poker

James opens his eyes, surprised that heaven looks so much like the Brooklyn Botanical Gardens. He's even more surprised the universe has decided to recycle him to a better place after his ticket got punched by that little punk from the Pugliese. Though he spent twenty years putting as much distance between James Worthington and Jimmy Pedals as time and space would allow—a transformation so complete, weeks would pass where he'd actually forget they were the same person—he was never fool enough to believe his repentance would score him an invite to the party upstairs.

"Oh, thank God."

It's the first angel he's ever heard speak, and her voice is beautiful but unexpectedly human in its cadence. Though it's borderline blasphemy—something he'll have to remind himself to avoid now that he's dancing on the top floor—he thinks for a second the voice sounds a lot like Beth's. Then a saintly visage sweeps in from his left, a blur of fabric and red hair, and he thinks, Christ, she looks like Beth, too.

And he has to remind himself again about the blasphemy.

As sensation returns to his body, he feels a moist tickle upon his cheek as the angel buries her face against his, weeping and thanking the Lord repeatedly.

So James knows something's up. 'Cause however he managed to get himself added to the Good list, there's no way they'd be this excited to see him up here.

"Don't you ever leave me like that again," Beth tells him.

His eyes go wild, circling about the room. There's Kyle and Lacy and…

"Beth?" he asks. "I'm alive?"

"You bet your ass you are." She's sniffling all over him now, wiping at her face as she loosens her grip and leans back to take in the very sight of him. "I knew you had it in you."

His vision clearing, James counts bouquet after bouquet. Bushels of yellow and red and white flowers, baskets of candy, stuffed animals brandishing "Get Well" signs. It surrounds them like some synthetic forest or…

Or the Brooklyn Botanical Gardens.

Beth sees him pondering the hospital room, tells him the support they've received over the past twenty-four hours has been incredible. He half-hears her, looking for a bare space between bouquets, finding none.

He's in the hospital one night, and the whole town pitches in for a showing like *this*?

Unbelievable.

In New York, forget it. He'd have been dead in the street three days before anyone got around to dealing with the inconvenience of his corpse.

"Fuck me," he says.

The air goes out of the room.

No one can believe the word that just escaped his lips. As long as any of them have known him, James Worthington's never uttered a syllable harsher than "heck."

He sees the muted shock in Beth's eyes, shakes his head like he's got water in his ears. "Gosh, Beth, I'm sorry, I—"

But she's laughing before he can finish the apology. It proves contagious, everyone in the room picking up the refrain.

Everyone but James.

Giggling through his nose, eyes shot through with red, Kyle takes a step forward and grabs his father's hand. On the other side of the bed, James sees Lacy ruffling her tangle of shoulder-length hair, as gray as it is stringy and tough.

"Pop, you all right?"

James turns to Kyle and nods slowly, as if unsure. There's a distance in his eyes, like he's working through a complex math equation. Trying to remember the steps.

"Yeah," he tells his boy. "I'm all right." But his brow tightens when he looks to Lacy. And the vision of her clubbing the Pugliese soldier to death resurfaces.

Through pursed lips, James offers his gratitude.

She waves him off. "Just in the right place at the right time."

James squeezes his son's bicep, nods up at him. "And you, sounding the horn. Some smart kid I got."

Kyle drops his eyes, a little embarrassed. Tells his father, "Nah, I froze. Shoulda got out of the car and done something."

"You did good," James tells him.

"I'm just glad you're OK, Pop."

Turning to Beth, he raises a hand to her hair, feels the plush red curls between his fingers. She closes her eyes, softening to his touch.

"Missed you, babe," he whispers. "You haven't replaced me yet, have you?"

"I was gonna give you another half hour."

There's some clatter in the hallway, the door handle turning open. James doesn't want to, but he tears his eyes away from the people who love him, sees a doctor and the local sheriff. As the doc approaches the bed, the sheriff recedes into the background, waits his turn.

"Mr. Worthington," the doc in the white coat says, "I'm glad to see you're feeling better." He introduces himself—some Indian name James probably couldn't repeat—and slips a cuff around James' upper arm, tests his blood pressure. Taps the IV, jots something down on his clipboard. Presses the stethoscope to his chest, nods approvingly. Tells James his vitals are strong, that shortly they'll be running further tests. Describes how the bullet missed his stomach by less than an inch, passed right through his back. Lost a lot of blood, but they seem to have that under control. Only concern now is possible infection.

James hears none of it. He's looking back and forth between Beth and Kyle, shaking his head in disbelief over the beautiful family he doesn't deserve.

One that has no idea the havoc he's invited into their quiet, unassuming lives.

As if he senses James' mind turning toward his criminal past, the sheriff steps to the bed. Once the doctor disappears through the doorway, he affects a sense of decorum, removing his hat and holding it before his belt buckle in both hands.

"Damn glad you made it through, Mr. Worthington. How you feeling?"

From the bed, James nods.

"Listen, if you're up to it, I need to take a statement. Already got one from Lacy, but I didn't want to trouble Kyle with it until you came around. Thought maybe I could take yours and his together. Get it over with in one shot."

When James looks to Kyle, the boy shrugs.

"Sure," James says. "That's exactly how I want to spend my first waking moments."

"I'm sorry, Mr Worthington, but it's procedure."

Resigned, James nods, smiles up at Beth, says, "Honey…"

She leans to kiss his forehead, beams at him. Tells the sheriff not to take too long, and he promises he'll take as little of their precious time as the law requires.

Once Beth leads Lacy out into the hall, the sheriff waits until the door locks home before hanging his hat on a hook and sliding a chair toward the bed. He rolls the dinner tray until it's hovering over James' chest. Then he slips a deck of cards from his breast pocket, nods at James and starts shuffling.

They share a conspiratorial smile.

"Well, *Mister* Worthington, how much you think you won off me last week?"

"Wasn't much, *Sheriff*." James tries to recall, props himself higher on his pillow, groaning at the effort. "Ten bucks maybe. Hank bore the brunt of it, I think."

"Well, whether I'm behind or ahead, I can't recall the last conversation we had didn't take place over a hand of cards. Wouldn't feel natural."

"OK, Garrett. Deal 'em."

"Then we'll get to this business of your getting shot out front of your store." Cocking an eyebrow at Kyle, Garrett asks, "You know how to play this, kid?"

Kyle's still dumbstruck by the sudden casting off of formality. "Um, is it Hold 'Em?"

Sheriff Sanders winces as if he's been slapped. "No, kid. I make it a habit not to play anything Ben Affleck plays. Tell you what, we usually play stud, but if you want in, we can play draw."

"OK," Kyle says. He pulls another chair up to his father's bed as James cuts the cards on the tray table. "What's the buy-in?"

"That's the spirit," Garrett says. "But I think"—his eyes linger upon both of them—"we'll keep this a friendly game. That all right by you two?"

Knowing the sheriff ain't just talking cards, James takes a moment before he agrees.

Garrett shucks the cards into three piles, fans his hand and waits on Kyle to his left. The kid hands over two cards, and Garrett deals him replacements.

"Angie driving you completely nuts this week or just partially?" James asks.

"Completely. But you know Ang."

"I know married life," James says. "Gimme three." He slips the new cards in with his others. "Wasn't for me, that's for sure." When Kyle looks up, James smiles demurely, as if to suggest it wasn't all bad between him and Kyle's mother.

"Dealer takes one," Garrett announces, trading for a single fresh card. "So what have you boys got?"

The question's in regard to their cards, but the sheriff's tone is broad. If there's anything more they'd like to lay down, he'd love to hear it.

Kyle shows a pair of threes; James, two pair—eights over deuces.

Garrett sticks out his lower lip in admiration.

Before laying a King-high flush on the tray table.

"Well, look at that. Guess my luck's turning around. Who knows? Might even get you boys to tell me exactly what the hell happened out at the store last night."

Ten
The Sheriff's Office

Angelo leaves the don's kid waiting in the Mustang, enters the station house, the wood soles of his designer shoes clacking against the petrified cold of the front steps. The exterior is chintzy beige stucco and wood siding. Very plain, very country. The only indication that the building even functions as a police station is the fancy silver crest beside the door labeling it the Gower Sheriff's Office.

Without that, the place could just as easily be another convenience store.

Or a fucking barn.

Inside, he finds one cop on duty—a broad working a switchboard so quiet it don't really need working. One hallway with four alcoves jutting out at each end, like a capital letter *I*. That's it. That's the whole fucking place. It would fit neatly inside the bathroom of some of the joints where Angelo's been detained.

The lady cop looks over from her desk—a glorified table with communications equipment stacked on top—shows him a suspicious expression. He ain't surprised. Probably been a while since someone walked through the door wearing something other than coveralls and shit-crusted work boots, let alone a three-piece suit. And his fucking complexion? The way he'll sound to her the second he opens his mouth? Around here, they probably figure every eye-talian for mafia anyway, so there's little chance of him disguising his background.

Especially if they already got Little Nicky cooling his heels in an interrogation room.

Best to make the inquiry quick, scram before Janey Law starts asking questions he'd rather not answer.

"May I help you, sir?"

He can just make out the name on her badge from where he's standing.

"Yeah, Officer…Lindaberry," he reads, "I'd like to speak with the person who's in charge here." Does his best to sound affable, loose. Like he's not here for anything more important than a parking ticket or a PBA donation. "Chief of Police, Lieutenant, whoever that might be."

Gotta be the boss.

'Cause there ain't no point trying to bribe some lowly flatfoot if it turns out they got Little Nicky in the stir and someone has to lead Angelo down a hallway in plain view, flagrantly "leave" a door unlocked.

Only the guy in charge has that set of keys.

"This is the Sheriff's Office."

"Yeah," Angelo says, hooking a thumb behind him, "I read the sign out front."

She stares back at him, deadpan. "Man in charge would be the sheriff."

Angelo straightens his suit coat at the lapels, restrains an outburst. *Smarmy small town bitch.* "Right, right. Makes sense. He around? Can I speak with him?"

Turning back to her unlit switchboard, she tells him, "He's out taking a statement."

"Any idea when he might be back?" The frustration starts bleeding through his voice.

"Like I said, he's taking a statement. There's really no telling. Could be ten minutes, could be two hours."

And then the bitch picks up some harlequin romance, plants her elbows on the desk and starts fucking reading. Right there, right in front of his fucking face.

"That's fine. I'll just hang around," he tells her, hoping it's the last thing she wants to hear. That she'll radio the sheriff just to get him out of her hair. "Take my chances on it being ten minutes and not two hours."

But she just cocks an eyebrow that says he can wait for the rest of his life if it so suits him, just so long as he shuts up and lets her get through a chapter or two.

Angelo finds the daily paper on a nearby table, takes a seat by the window. Through the glass he sees Dominic huddled inside the idling Ford, and he exhales heavily. Knowing when the shit goes down, Dom won't have the balls to pull the trigger. Bad move, the boss putting all of his eggs in Junior's basket.

The kid looks antsy in the car, trying to make eye contact with Angelo. His expression broadening in a what's-up gesture. Angelo shakes his head—more in disappointment than response, like he's telling Dom to calm the fuck down and be patient—and takes a closer look at the paper.

Doesn't even make it past the cover. 'Cause right there, above the fold, are all the answers he could possibly want.

Beneath pictures of an ATM draped in yellow police tape and a still of "Local Proprietor, James Worthington," the headline reads, "Local Man Shot in Apparent Robbery Attempt."

Scanning the text, Angelo gets the gist of the situation. He runs a thick finger over descriptions of Pedals getting ambushed while withdrawing cash, taking a bullet to the midsection. Getting rushed to Stroudsburg General, twenty minutes north. Angelo learns that his "assailant"—an as-yet-unidentified individual—was killed at the time of the robbery when another local patron, Lacy Penderhall, responded with brute force, striking the gunman down with an implement from her furniture store.

Angelo snorts laughter about that last part.

Fucking Sorrentino. Killed by a fucking wicker chair or some shit. About as competent as his dipshit old man.

Angelo folds the paper under his arm, walks out with the only copy at the station house.

The receptionist doesn't bat an eye. Never even looks up from her Fabio book.

Outside, he piles into the passenger seat, slams the door before too much of the heat can escape, warms his hands before the vents.

The kid's looking at him like, well?

"Remember those signs we passed on the highway for Stroudsburg? Turns out we gotta double back. Little Nicky got the job halfway done, then he got himself killed. We gotta finish things up."

Eleven
All a Blur

"Think I got you this time, Sheriff," Kyle says.

"Let's see 'em."

James is sitting this one out, folded his hand as soon as he saw the cards. He watches as Kyle's set of tens loses to Garrett's full boat.

"Shit."

"Kyle," James scolds.

Garrett laughs mildly, gathers the cards, starts shuffling.

"Brought your A game today," Kyle says.

"I always bring my A game," Garrett tells him.

"Left it home last Tuesday," James mumbles.

"Aw, Angie was giving me a hard time about something or other. Couldn't focus. But I always come to play when I'm on official duty." Garrett's studies them both. "So you didn't recognize this kid from anywhere? The gunman, I mean."

"Well, my memory's a little hazy," James tells him. "By the time I got a look at him, I had a bullet in my abdomen. But I don't think he was anybody I knew. Besides, isn't that your department? You know, IDing suspects, stuff like that?"

"We're working on it. Kid had no wallet, no credit cards. Prints have yet to trigger a match. We'll know more within the next twenty-four hours. Just expedites the process if someone directly involved can shed some light. How 'bout you?" He juts his chin at Kyle as he flutters the cards between his palms.

Kyle shakes his head. "Never seen him before. Didn't look like a local guy. Clothes were too fancy. Hair style wasn't right. Too greasy."

"Hey," James interjects. "What's gonna happen to Lacy now?"

"Lacy?" Garrett asks.

"Yeah. She gonna be in any kind of trouble for…for what she did?"

Garrett leans his head to the side, weighing a response.

"Well, it ain't like she ran a red light, James. She killed a man. And that's an ugly deal regardless the circumstances. It *is* as clear-cut a case of self-defense as I've ever seen, though. It'll be on the County DA to press charges after I file my report. I know him pretty well—we played ball together back in high school. I'd say he's a reasonable fella who's likely to see the situation for what it is."

James knows what Garrett is more or less telling him. In rural PA, high school sports are gospel, which means if the sheriff played ball with the DA, they may as well be brothers. And the DA will lean in the direction Garrett steers him, putting Lacy in the clear.

"Either of you see where he came from? The shooter. Lacy didn't come out until the situation escalated, so she missed that part. See a car drop him off, anything like that?"

"My eyes were on the ATM machine the whole time," James says. "Seemed like the guy just appeared out of nowhere."

"That about right?" the sheriff asks Kyle.

He nods, but then he stops, his face contorting in sudden realization. "No. He was there a while. When I went out a few minutes earlier to check on Lacy—Remember, Pop, we saw her pulling in after hours, didn't know what was up?—I heard something moving around on the gravel down at the end of the strip. I just figured it was a raccoon or something. But he must have been there waiting."

"That makes a certain sense," Garrett says. He's watching James over a pair of Queens, feeling like he's got another hand won. "That ATM doesn't get a lot of traffic. Could have been waiting a while for someone to happen by. Patient little bastard. He say anything to you?"

James starts rolling his head back and forth slowly, like he's struggling to remember.

Really, he's trying to sell his bluff.

'Cause he can quote for the sheriff exactly what the kid told him before he opened fire, but there ain't a chance in hell he's spilling that. It don't matter how good of friends he and Garrett have become since Jimmy Pedals became James Worthington.

"No, nothing at all."

"That *doesn't* make sense," Garrett says.

"Why, you know a lot of chatty thieves? Kind of guy breaks into your house, wakes you up for a cup of coffee and some small talk before he makes off with your TV?"

"No, but I also don't know a lot of guys who like to shoot *before* they get your wallet. That's risky. Our friend learned that lesson the hard way."

"Actually"—Kyle looks up from his cards—"I think the guy did say something."

James nearly shits himself right there in the bed. Inside, he's chanting a feverish litany of *Shut up, shut up, shut up*, but he can't signal the kid without the sheriff seeing.

"Oh yeah?" Garrett asks.

"Yeah." Kyle's beaming with pride. "I didn't hear what it was, but my father spit on his shoes."

"Spit on his shoes?" Garrett turns back to James. "Guy's holding a gun on you, you spit on his shoes?"

James shrugs.

"Ballsy, Worthington. Guy must have said something to piss you off. Don't recall what it was?"

James raises his palms, cards in one hand, says, "Nah, it's all a blur. I don't even remember spitting on the guy. Doesn't even sound like something I'd do."

"I'm with you on that score," Garrett says.

"But if Kyle says I did it…I guess something just came over me."

Kyle's nodding enthusiastically. "He did. He spit right on the guy's shoes. It was like what they say happens in times of extreme stress. The adrenaline surge, like, turns you into a whole different person."

Fuckin' A it does, James thinks.

"Call," the sheriff says.

Kyle shows nothing. A Jack high.

The sheriff lays his Queens right on top.

James folds. Lays his cards facedown on the cheap faux-wood of the table tray.

"James, all these years we've known each other, and you won't even show your hand?"

His concentrated glance tells James cards are the last thing on his mind. In the look they share, they each let the other know they're fully aware there's far more to this ATM robbery than either is acknowledging.

But in the end, the best Garrett can do is get James to flip over a busted straight.

Twelve
Who's the Boss?

Dominic slides back into the driver's seat, turns to Angelo.

"You won't believe this," he says. "That cop we went looking for in Gower? He's sitting in with Worthington right now."

"No shit," Angelo says. "You find anything out?"

Dominic only had to pass through the cold for a minute walking from the hospital back to the car, but he pauses to warm his hands in front of the heater, grateful—perhaps for the first time—for his father's gift of the fully-loaded, brand-new Mustang. One with heated seats and a digital temperature readout.

"Couldn't get too close to the room without attracting attention. There were a couple of women waiting outside for the cop to leave. I told a receptionist I was a friend of Worthington's, asked her what she could tell me. Said she could only divulge information to the immediate family. She did, however, say that since she's been getting so many calls from friends of James Worthington, she supposed she could let it slip that he was gonna be just fine."

"So we wait for the sheriff to leave, pay Pedals a little visit." That settled, Angelo reclines his seat, cozies up for a nap.

"For what? Guy doesn't know anything. He's gonna make it through, I say we let it go."

Angelo smiles, doesn't bother opening his eyes. "You fuckin' kidding me? Suppose he could identify Sorrentino? You heard your old man. We can't leave any loose ends."

"How would that be possible? Sorrentino was barely even born when Pedals took off. Far as Worthington's concerned, he got held up at an ATM by some nobody. End of story."

"Right. And when Sorrentino's prints come back? What then? Your old man gave the order, Dom. Boss's instructions ain't exactly an interpretive thing."

"I heard my father loud and clear. I seem to remember him saying something about me being the brains and you being the muscle. That you're supposed to take orders from me."

"He also said I'm along for the ride 'cause I got experience. Experience says you don't take a chance lettin' a guy like this live. It also says you don't cross Don Anthony when he gives you a direct order."

Dom tries another tactic. "Fine. But your plan's shit. What are we waiting *for*? Soon as that cop leaves, the women are going in. They looked like they'd be there a while. And I think his son was in the room, too. Gonna be days before he's alone."

An exhausted sigh parts Angelo's lips. "You get anything from the two broads?"

"Get anything?"

"Yeah. Did you overhear them talking about anything we can use? Like, maybe ya overheard 'em discussin' their dinner plans, talkin' about when they were leavin', how long they'd be gone. Anything helpful?"

"Yeah, I heard one say, 'Lacy, do you want another cup of coffee?'" Like, sure, Angelo, that's real fuckin' helpful.

But Angelo ratchets his seat upright in a hurry. "You sure about that?"

"Yeah." The words leave Dom's mouth drenched in sarcasm. "One was gonna bring the other a cup of coffee. I'm pretty sure."

"What'd she look like?"

"Who?"

"The Lacy broad."

Dom's face is a scrunched grimace of confusion.

"Spit it out, kid."

The significance lost on him, Dom gives a description of Lacy Penderhall as best he can from the second-and-a-half he happened to glance at her.

"Good. You think you'd recognize her if you saw her again?"

"I guess I could, yeah."

"Keep an eye out."

"For the woman?"

"Unless Jimmy Pedals steps out on the lawn to do jumping jacks, yeah, the woman."

Thirteen
This is Katherine Tyler

Katie's trying to steer the Jetta with one hand and rub Kyle's back with the other. She's doing an OK job keeping the car on the road, but with Kyle she's lost.

He's crying in the seat next to her. Unabashed sobs from a teenage boy. In front of his girlfriend. As long as she's known him, he's never shown such vulnerability, and she doesn't know what she can do for him.

It's heartbreakingly cute, the tears running silently down his cheeks, glistening in the lights of passing cars. She wants to pull over, hold him close, whisper that everything will be OK. But she knows drawing attention to the raw emotion he's bared will only embarrass him.

And they say teenage *girls* are hormonal.

Kyle hadn't seemed this way when they left the hospital. Though she'd only gone there to see how Mr. Worthington was doing, Kyle's old man had insisted she take Kyle home. Said his son had a math test to study for, and he had to be up for an early morning run with the winter track team.

Kyle, who'd been all smiles perched at his father's bedside, was crestfallen. Couldn't believe his father was dismissing him for responsibilities as trivial as a test he could make up later in the week and a routine two-miler. As if he'd lose his wind and his position as top runner if he missed a single morning's training.

"Gotta honor your commitments," James insisted. Then he turned to Katie, offered a gracious smile. "Really appreciate you stopping by. Very respectful. It means a lot. Now take this kid home and make sure he gets some sleep."

James has never been less than sweet with Katie. Really admires the way she carries herself. But she'd have to be blind not to notice the occasional bewildered expression he can't fully restrain.

Like, *this* girl's with my son?

Beth uttered a barely audible groan Katie pretended not to hear. Whatever James sees in the girl, it's lost on Beth. Much like Lacy, she can't get past the big house and the brand new car, the salon-perfect hair and acrylic nails.

When they get home, Kyle flips on the light in the family room, sits on the couch without removing his winter coat. He's twisting his hands in his lap, staring blankly at the carpet. The tears have stopped, but neither of them has said much since leaving the hospital. Katie shrugs out of her coat, drapes it over the sofa and sits beside him.

Rubbing his thigh compassionately, she says, "He's through the worst of it, Ky. The not knowing. He's gonna be fine."

Kyle nods, sucks a breath.

"You saw him back there," she goes on. "He's already back to his old self."

Kyle's choked response comes in a jerky, breathless gasp. "It's just...you never realize...I never stopped to think about it...you don't say it, you know."

She doesn't. It's a grief-struck ramble, Kyle probably not even sure what he's feeling or saying. Running her hand through the thick wave of his brown hair, she waits, lets him find the words he's stumbling toward.

"I should have been better to him. I mean, the car? Every time he wants to work on that thing, he's just asking to spend time together. And what do I do? I fucking bitch and complain. I don't even know why. Most guys, their fathers come home from work, drink beer and go to bed. I mean, look at your parents."

The words haven't fully left his lips before he wishes he had them back.

"Sorry," he breathes.

"No," she says, stung but understanding. "It's OK. That love/hate thing you have with your dad, I wish I had that kind of relationship with my parents. He loves you. It's all right."

Kyle's still not convinced. "He's never missed a single one of my meets. I run all year round, and he's there every time, home or away. Gets someone to cover for him at the store, and he's there. And how do I repay him? I treat him like some overbearing asshole I can't stand."

"Well, he *can* be pretty strict." She grins, trying to coax a smile out of her boyfriend.

But Kyle's having none of it. "He's a good father. He deserves better."

Katie nods. "Then it's a damn good thing he's gonna be all right, Ky. You'll have plenty of time to make it up to him."

They pass a long moment quietly.

"Come on," she tells him. "I'm putting you to bed. You need to get some rest."

Kyle complains all the way up the stairs. He doesn't want to sleep, can't sleep, shouldn't sleep. Not with all that's happened.

But it's late, Katie tells him, and they both have school tomorrow. Best thing he can do for his father is give him the peace of mind that his son will be all right in the aftermath of the accident. Keep up the daily routine to show James he hasn't been scarred for life.

"How am I gonna run tomorrow morning? How can I take a test or even sit still in my seat? Hell, how can I brush my fucking teeth?"

"You'll be fine. You just need to calm down."

And that's when she closes the bedroom door and slips her blouse over her head.

Kyle stands speechless, watching as she reaches behind her, unclasps her bra. Like shed skin, it dribbles down her shoulders, over the tops of her breasts, to the floor.

He just stares, doesn't know how to react. Isn't sure what's going on.

In the eight months they've been together, they've fooled around a lot. Bedrooms when parents weren't home, in Katie's parents' pool 'cause her parents are *never* home, the back of her car since she got her license. He's held her in more ways than he can remember, touched her time and again, seen her in bikinis, cheering outfits, underwear.

But she's never undressed for him. Not like this.

She tells him to go to the bed.

Without question or comment, he walks backward, sits on the edge of the mattress beneath his poster of a badass Ryan Gosling doing his best Clint Eastwood in *Drive*.

She follows him, places a palm on his shoulder. With her other hand, she works the zipper on her jeans, starts guiding them down her hips. Supporting herself against him, she tugs them off, one leg at a time.

When she stands tall before him, clad in nothing but lacy red panties, he knows she's waiting for him to do something, but his heart's beating so loud in his ears, he's not sure what. She takes his wrists in her palms and leads his hands to her hipbones. Together they slide her underpants past the knobs of her knees, low enough that she can step out of them.

And then he's looking at her.

Katie.

All of her.

As God intended.

She hears the deepening of his breath and it makes her smile. It's flattering even though she knows he'd have the same virginal reaction to the sight of any naked woman.

Still, this isn't just any naked woman in Kyle's bedroom.

This is Katherine Tyler.

And no matter what happens between them after this—next week, next year, ten years down the road—Kyle Worthington will never forget Katherine Tyler.

Not after tonight.

He raises his hands over his head when she grabs at his shirt and slips it over his arms, pulling the undershirt with it. He's bare-chested in the soft light, and though she's seen him this way on more than a few occasions, she feels a greater appreciation for his physique—all muscle and sinew, hard and trim from his long runs—because she's about to experience it in a way she never has.

Her hands drop to his waist and she goes to work on his fly, popping the button and working the zipper as he leans back onto the bed, hears the slow release of each metal tooth as the bedroom's cool air tickles his freshly exposed flesh, and the pants come down.

When Katie snickers softly, he looks up from his back and sees his raging hard-on poking through the fly in his boxers. He chuckles as she slides his checkered underwear down his legs.

But then, with both of them naked, the coming intimacy a foregone conclusion, a hot rush of fear pulses in his chest. Kyle's suddenly frantic, paralyzed with the terror of a thousand potentially horrifying outcomes.

Premature ejaculation.

Pregnancy.

What if he's horrible?

What if someone walks in?

Where exactly does he put it?

But then she's on top, her hand warm around him. As she takes him inside, settling herself upon him, he feels a hot, wet resistance, and all worry—all conscious thought—dissipates completely.

Which is precisely what Katie longed to do for him the moment he shed his first tear.

Fourteen
Proving Herself

It's quiet enough in the parked Mustang that Angelo can hear the vibrations of another incoming call inside Dom's pocket.

"Either call that broad back or turn the phone off already."

Dom would argue—he's the one who's supposed to be giving the orders, after all, and he's getting more than a little tired of taking shit from an old, bloated guinea—except that Angelo is right. It's the third time Maria's tried to get a hold of him since they crossed state lines, and he can't keep ignoring it.

But ignore her he does.

Again.

Until he can figure out what to tell her, Maria's going to have to wait.

Angelo just shakes his head at one whipped fucking kid. Maybe they should have stopped by her place on their way out of the city, dug his balls out of her purse before hitting the road.

They're parked on some rural turn-off from the numbered two-lane that runs through Gower. Three isolated houses on a short stretch of crudely-paved roadway. They've been there twenty minutes—drove straight over from the hospital, trailing behind the Lacy woman Angelo had taken such a devout interest in—and Dom has no idea why. The only explanation Angelo gave while they tailed her pickup was, "Loose ends, kid. Loose ends."

From the darkness beneath a maple tree across the street, the two of them sit listening to the hush of the 'Stang's heater and the muffled tones of an argument inside the house.

"Hey," Angelo asks. "Does that sound like she's talking to a broad in there to you?" His face lights up like a kid who's been given a fistful of candy. "You think maybe Lacy's a...uh...you know..." Angelo spreads two fingers in a peace sign, waggles his tongue between them.

Dom hangs his head in world-weary disbelief. "It's 2012, Angelo."

"Yeah, I know, kid. Whole fucking world's gone gay. Didn't know it had made it out to the sticks, though."

Angelo shrugs at the kid's sour expression. Then he rocks his girth forward, pulls a .45 from his waistband and a silencer from his jacket pocket.

"Angelo, what the fuck is that for?"

"Muffles the sound of the gunshot."

"I mean what the fuck are you doing?"

Angelo works the silencer onto the barrel, lets the question fall dead between them.

"Seem quieter in there now? Maybe they went to bed," he says absently. "Nah, some of the lights are still on. Hey, maybe they're not sleeping at all. Maybe they're...you know." He pumps his fist in the air, offers Dom a perverse smile.

And Dom decides it's time to exert his influence, remind the lummox exactly who his father placed in charge. "You're not going in that house."

"I'm not, huh?" His eyes are on the split-level.

"No." Dom raises his voice. "You're gonna sit right here and tell me what the fuck we're doing out in front of this house."

"That a fact?"

"Angelo, my father gave me the lead on this thing, and I'm telling you—"

A copy of that morning's *Express Call* lands in Dom's lap.

"Here," Angelo insists, "read that."

From beneath a wrinkled brow, Dom reads the headline.

"You got any further questions, oh-fearless-leader, I'll be in the house cleanin' up Sorrentino's mess."

"Hey, wait—"

"Just fuckin' read the thing, college boy."

And with a firm slap on the cheek, Angelo's out the door.

* * *

It's not that Kelly feels Lacy didn't do the right thing.

Actually, she thinks her partner was brave as hell saving James and Kyle the way she did. She just hates that Lacy had to be the one to do it, to put herself in that kind of danger. That's the way it's always been with Lacy. Her whole life, she's been on the offensive, ready to give the world a black eye, too tough for her own good.

Or at least for Kelly's own good.

'Cause she's been scared shitless ever since Lacy took a table leg to that mugger. Can't shake the fear of "what if." Can't chase from her mind the haunting fantasies of Lacy being gunned down outside her store.

When Lacy walks through the door, back from the hospital in the deep heart of the night, she finds Kelly slumped on the couch, the air thick with dread and frustration. She shakes her mop of hair before Kelly can even open her mouth. "You should have been in bed hours ago."

"How am I supposed to do that, Lace?"

"You turn off the lights, close your eyes, sleep happens. It's like magic that way."

"So is the art of imagination. You know what I see when I close my eyes?"

Lacy exhales so hard it's like air bursting from a blown tire. Yeah, she knows what Kelly sees. She also knows she's bone-tired and doesn't have the patience to handle her lover with kid gloves again.

"You should get some sleep. Staying up thinking about me, worrying, that's only gonna make you feel worse."

"I'm just supposed to block it out? Go on with my life like you didn't pick a fight with an armed man?"

"Let it go. It's over. Why dwell on it?"

"It could have ended a lot worse. Have you considered that?"

"It absolutely would have ended a lot worse if I hadn't done what I did."

"What happens next time? Or the time after that?"

"Really? We have a terrible gun control problem in Gower now? I'm gonna turn this into a pattern of behavior? Go around looking for guns to jump in front of?"

"It already is your pattern of behavior. It always has been. You don't have to go around proving yourself every chance you get."

"Proving myself." Lacy laughs. "Talk to James, see if he thinks that's what I was doing."

"It's what you're always doing." Kelly springs from the couch as Lacy tries to shoulder past her into the kitchen. "You've lived in Gower your whole life. This whole town knows who you are. They're comfortable enough with you that you don't have to come on so strong. Not every word out of your mouth needs to be a threat or a challenge."

"Last night wasn't about me. A man was in trouble and I came to his aid. A good man you and I have known for years. Whose kid we babysat in this very house. And he was about to get himself killed. What was I supposed to do?"

Kelly hangs her head, muttering hysterically that she doesn't know.

"All these hours you spend thinking about what could have happened, you don't think about what it would be like for me if I had to live knowing I let the two of them die right outside my store."

Kelly drops onto the couch, defeated.

"I'm going to bed." Lacy says it as softly as she can through her sorrow and exhaustion, and she turns down the hall hoping

Kelly will forgo the couch and join her in a slumber they both so sorely need.

But before Kelly can follow, the front door crashes in.

Whirling, Lacy has just enough time to see the fear in Kelly's eyes before Angelo puts a bullet in her chest and one through her head.

Two shots, silenced—*puft, puft*—and Kelly's body shrinks into itself on the couch.

Lacy wants to run to her partner, will her awake with the touch of her hand.

Instead, she switches instinctively to crisis mode. When shit hits the fan, that's how Lacy Penderhall's always responded.

Just as the fat Italian in the dark suit turns the pistol in her direction, she dives around the corner, into the hallway off the kitchen. On her hands and knees, she scrambles across the cold, hard tiles toward the staircase.

With the goon blocking the only exits, she'll have to take her chances on the second floor. Maybe kick out a screen, leap from a window. Or try to lose him in the dark of the house, slip past him to the front door.

Yet as she makes it to the first step, she hears the heavy breath and heavier footsteps of the gunman behind her, and she freezes there on the staircase like some house fly caught in a spider's web.

Only time in her life she's ever considered surrender.

Because she thinks of Kelly, knows if she submits, they'll be together again. The only person with whom she's ever let her guard down.

When she rolls onto her back, he's hovering over her, aiming the silenced barrel of his .45 in her face.

"Sorry, toots."

She closes her eyes and breathes her lover's name.

For the last time.

Fifteen
What My Father Wants

Dom looks up from the paper, stares at the dark expanse of road before him. He just got to the part about Lacy killing Nicky Sorrentino.

"Oh, shit!"

He rips open the car door, makes a run for the house. His shoes have barely touched the frozen lawn when Angelo tramps through the front door, steps into his face.

"Get back in the car," he tells the kid. "We're finished here."

And Dom knows he's too late to help the women inside. "You just...just...both of them..."

"You read the piece, kid. She killed Little Nicky herself. Had to be done."

"And the other one...?"

"She seen me soon as I come through the door. What was I supposed to do?" Angelo brushes past him, indignant that he has to explain himself to the don's prissy heir.

Dom swallows down an urge to vomit, steadies himself on weak legs. "Angelo, you're finished here."

"Yeah?" he calls back without turning. "Says who?"

"This ain't your gig, it's mine. By my father's orders. I don't need you. I'll finish this my way."

The burly wop turns back. "What are ya, Frank fuckin' Sinatra? What does that mean? Your way?"

"Doesn't concern you. I'll take care of it. My father put me in charge."

"Doesn't concern me. Right." Like he's getting the idea.

Except that he's not.

That becomes clear when Angelo's palm closes around Dom's throat.

"You got no idea what your father wants, kid."

Dom grabs at Angelo's wrist with both hands, but it does no good. He feels the hard side panel of the Mustang against his back as Angelo pins him on the hood, his heels barely scraping the pavement below. Angelo watches the kid's face go all cherry tomato, clenching his fist tighter around his windpipe.

Then he lets go. The kid rolls off the hood, lands awkwardly on his side, rubs at his neck.

When Dom finds his feet, Angelo places a palm against the kid's chest, holding him at attention. "Your father didn't put you in charge so you could play Mr. Fuckin' Rogers and end this thing peaceful, Dominic. He wants to see blood on your hands. *Your* hands. See how you handle it. *If* you can handle it. He ain't gonna let you come home until Worthington and his son are fuckin' dead by your hand."

Dom stares a long while.

"Breathe, kid. I don't know what delusions you were under when you came out here, but this is what we do."

"She didn't know anything." The kid's voice is a barely audible rasp.

"What's that?"

"Lacy. We could have let her go. Her, the other woman in there. Why?"

Angelo shakes his head, can't believe the kid still doesn't fuckin' get it. "Broad killed one of our own. Piss-ant piece of shit that he was, Nicky Sorrentino, Jr. was a member of the Pugliese. That ain't somethin' we ever let go."

Dom's attention drifts to the house. "I should go in there. Cover our tracks, clean things up a little bit." Actually, he wants to make sure the bodies are left in some kind of half decent condition. Even if he has to sort through the carnage with his own bare hands. Those women would still be alive if he had half the balls or know-how he'd given himself credit for when he left Manhattan.

"Nah, nah, it's all right, kid." Angelo raises a gloved hand. "No prints. Gun's untraceable. I *have* done this before, you know."

Climbing into the passenger seat, Angelo closes the debate. Dragging his heels, Dom sits down beside him.

"OK," Dom says. "I guess my old man sold me a line of shit to get me out here. Since you're the one who's really running the show, what do we do now?" Though whatever it is, Dom's sure he doesn't actually want to hear it.

"Pay a visit to Worthington over at the hospital, try to take him and the kid in one fell swoop. Oh, and for Christ sake, send that girlfriend of yours a fuckin' text already."

Sixteen
WWJD

When James wakes Monday morning, his head is clear enough he can marvel at the potency of his pain meds. Until now, they've kept him so effectively sedated he's been able to ignore the implications of the dirty life he abandoned twenty years ago colliding with the one he's been shaping and polishing ever since.

Of course, it might not be the drugs.

Could be, surrounded by gift baskets and teddy bears, he just can't bear the thought of a life outside of Gower. Doesn't want to think about what a botched hit might mean to his life here as James Worthington, pillar of the community.

But, when Garrett pays him a second visit, face dour as melted wax, he knows full well before the sheriff opens his mouth that he's got to do some fast thinking.

"James, you feeling all right?" The sheriff closes the door, drops into a chair beside the bed. "You OK to talk a minute?"

James nods slowly, as if he can't imagine why Garrett has returned. Best bet for the time being is to play dumb, keep pretending this was all a random act of violence.

Like, gee, Sheriff, I don't know what else I can tell you.

"Not gonna do either of us any good to beat around the bush with this, so I'm just gonna come out and say it." The sheriff wets his lips, wishing he didn't have to go on. "Last night sometime, Lacy Penderhall and Kelly Carlisle were murdered. Shot to death. We found the bodies this morning."

"My son," James says.

So first James takes a bullet by an ATM, the mugger opening fire before actually *mugging* him. Now, Lacy's lying on a slab at the town morgue and his concerns turn immediately to his son.

Garrett would have wagered as much.

"Now why don't you tell me what you've gotten yourself mixed up in before anybody else gets hurt? Kyle, Beth, anybody."

But James isn't interested in telling old stories. He scrambles frantically to his feet, yanking tubes and cords from his nose and forearms.

"Slow down, now," Garrett says.

"I have to see my son."

"My brother's the resource officer down to the high school. I had him pull Kyle out of class as a precaution."

"I have to see him."

The sheriff stands defensively. Friends though they may be, if Worthington thinks he's leaving, he's sorely mistaken. "Whatever trouble you're in, James, you need to tell me right now."

Kicking his legs into a pair of jeans, James doesn't answer.

"Damn it, James, where do you think you're going?"

James pulls a Polo over his head, jumps into his shoes without untying the laces.

Garret says, "I'm not talkin' to you as a poker buddy now. I'm ordering you as Sheriff of Gower to tell me what the hell is happening."

James has a wild thought that maybe it'd be easier on him if he did come clean. Let the authorities handle the Pugliese problem. James didn't kill anybody, after all—at least not as far as Garrett needs to know to resolve this particular situation—and there must be some statutes of limitation on the prosecution of his misdemeanors from twenty years ago.

But he dismisses the notion. There's no way Garrett, who was born in a barn and raised beside a cornfield, can solve a vendetta forged in the streets. Even James Worthington, who's lived with hay in his hair for the better part of his life now, is gonna have trouble on that score. He's not sure if he knows how to deal with men like the Pugliese anymore.

"Jesus, James, didn't you hear what I said? Lacy and Kelly are dead. They'd still be alive if you'd have leveled with me yesterday. This has gone far enough." Garrett lays the heel of his hand atop the butt of the revolver in his hip holster.

Facing the door, James catches the gesture from the corner of his eye.

"You said my boy was pulled out of class."

"Twenty minutes ago."

"He's all right? You're sure he's all right? Where is he now?"

"He's fine. Sitting with Dermott at the high school. Whaddya say we talk about this, huh?"

James weighs his options. But every scenario he envisions starts with the same problem: James Worthington is a good man who always does the right thing. Which means the only way out of this room for James Worthington is in the sheriff's custody. That's what a good man would do. They'll go down to the station, sort through the details, and his and Kyle's lives will hang in the balance while Gomer Pyle and his country police force take on the Pugliese.

That's what James Worthington would do.

Jimmy Pedals, on the other hand…

He wheels around, trailing a right hook that catches the sheriff on the jaw, knocks his hat off, spins him to the ground unconscious.

James crouches beside the downed man, the skin folding against his bullet wound, pain radiating across his stomach. He fetches a papery pillow, props the sheriff against the wall.

"Christ, I'm sorry, Garrett. You just don't understand what we're dealing with here. And I don't have the time to explain it to you."

Then he's out the door, making a break for the exit.

Seventeen
A Liability Thing

Life changes on a fucking dime.

That's what Kyle Worthington thinks as he sits, head in hands, in the resource officer's room at Gower High.

Two days ago, his father—he of the mild manners and unassuming demeanor—was shot in front of an ATM in a neighborhood that makes Sesame Street look seedy.

Last night, he cried in front of his girlfriend like a whiny little bitch.

Then he lost his virginity.

This morning he was frantic, heading for school, fretting over a period two math test for which he'd neglected to study. He'd been readying the I-was-at-the-hospital-all-night excuse as he fended off a thousand or so questions about his father's shooting and how "badass" the whole thing was.

Until he was suddenly being escorted out of period one English by the resource officer and the school psychologist.

All they told him in the hall was they needed to speak with him, and the nerve-sweat that broke from Kyle's brow made his previous test anxiety feel like a mild case of gas by comparison.

'Cause they don't send the school psychologist to get you unless it's something serious.

Like they've discovered your drug problem or someone you love has died.

His dad. Gotta be.

The infection set in, there was nothing they could do. Kyle just knows it.

But he's too scared to ask any questions, so it's not until the three of them take seats—the psychologist behind his desk, the resource officer perched on its edge, Kyle in a chair across the mahogany—that they break the news about Lacy.

Kyle feels horror. Sheer, nauseous horror over so gruesome an act perpetrated against so sweet a woman. A woman he's known since he was a child. Who cared for him, took him to movies, listened to him when he had problems he couldn't bring to his father.

And now she's gone. Like the passing of a summer breeze.

But that horror, that emptiness, is offset by a certain guilt. As bad as this is, Kyle's tempted to utter a prayer of gratitude that it wasn't his father.

"May I be excused?" Kyle asks as the tears bubble up. Bad enough he wept in front of a girl he's spent the past year trying to convince he's one cool dude. He isn't about to lose it again in front of a cop and a teacher.

Deputy Dermott Sanders gives Dr. Strong a concerned look, but the school psychologist nods emphatically, tells Kyle to take as long as he needs. They'll be waiting for him when he's finished in the bathroom. Kyle wonders what role the resource officer is supposed to play in all this. Maybe it's a liability thing. Like if the psychologist breaks some bad news and a student goes all suicidal, the school can't get sued because they took the proper precautions.

Whatever the case, Deputy Sanders watches him all the way to the restroom and waits in the hall for his return.

*   *   *

"That guy look like Worthington to you?"

As if waking up in a car isn't bad enough—what with the sore back, the drool drying on his chin, the sleep-sweat matting his hair—Dom's gotta wake up to the alluring sound of Angelo's voice.

"What time is it?" he asks, easing the driver's seat to an upright position.

Angelo flicks his eyes at the dashboard clock before turning back to the guy in the jeans and the collared shirt stumbling across the parking lot.

A Polo shirt in fucking December. And the guy's in a real fucking hurry.

"Ten-thirty. He look a little underdressed to you?" Angelo raises his eyebrows at the man who may or may not be James Worthington. Then he sneaks a sip from a Styrofoam cup.

"Where'd you get coffee? Did you bring me any?"

With his free hand, Angelo turns Dom's face in the guy's direction. Holds it there until the kid leans forward, takes a look.

"I don't know. Could be him, I guess."

"What kind of car does Worthington drive?"

"I thought he drove a yellow 442."

"That one ain't in the lot. You know if he's got another one?"

"I don't know."

They watch as the guy in jeans makes his way to a white Honda Accord.

"Let me see the picture." Angelo flaps a palm at Dominic.

It takes him a few seconds, but Dom fishes from his pocket the folded clipping from the newspaper article about the homecoming game. The one with the picture of Jimmy Pedals on the hood of his 442 with the pretty redhead.

Angelo grabs it, his face scrunching in evaluation. "I don't know. Looks a helluva lot like him."

The white reverse lights of the Accord blink on. Dom's shaking his head, rubbing his eyes, trying to disconnect himself from his dreams.

"Why would he be leaving?"

"I don't know."

"They wouldn't let him leave already," Dom says. "And wouldn't somebody be here to pick him up? He's had people with him the whole time we've been parked here."

Angelo cocks his head. All good points. "Maybe we should follow him just in case."

"Sure, why don't we kill *everybody* in Pennsylvania while we're at it. You know, just in case."

"Smartass."

Angelo watches the guy for a clue. The car spins out of its parking spot, faster than necessary, and the guy's fiddling with his cell phone, barely watching the road as he tears out onto the main drag.

"Certainly in a hurry," Angelo says.

"You ever met anybody who wasn't in a hurry to leave a hospital? It ain't him."

"You sound pretty sure."

"Well, I also thought I was the brains of this operation, so what the hell do I know, right?"

"All right, all right, quit your cryin'. I'm probably just buggin' out 'cause I haven't slept. Take over the watch so I can catch a few winks." Angelo takes his time wadding up his coat, fluffing it like a pillow, getting it just right before he leans back in his seat and shuts his eyes. "Don't forget, you see the kid go in to visit his old man, you wake me up. You got it? Probably won't be until the school day's out. Once we got them both together, that's when we move."

Eighteen

An Agonizing Five and a Half Minutes

A hundred times James has asked his son, "Why would I waste time texting when I can just call the person?" But now, as he turns out of the hospital parking lot—phone angled awkwardly in one hand, steering wheel in the other—he'd have to admit there's a time and place for everything.

Even texting

'Cause he can't exactly call Kyle and chat him up if the kid is sitting beside the brother of the sheriff James just cold-cocked.

Of course, as he tries to find the *D* button, he almost punches a red light, has to jam the brakes as the cross traffic nearly tears his front bumper loose.

So James' feelings on texting are still pretty mixed.

*   *   *

Kyle sits atop the toilet lid in the stall farthest from the door, crying through his laced fingers, a whole mess of badness swimming 'round his head.

His father. Lacy. The two men waiting for him down the hall.

He has a ridiculous fleeting thought about his math test, wonders what the protocol is if Sanders or Strong discover he's about to miss it. Would they make him take it?

As if in response, the phone in his front pocket vibrates.

do not tell him its me, the screen reads.

As if the cryptic message isn't bizarre enough, he checks the sender, sees it's his father.

James Worthington has never sent a text message in his life.

Kyle wipes his moistened cheeks. Goes to work with both thumbs. Taps out, *what r u talking about*

It's an agonizing five and a half minutes before the phone vibrates again.

can u get away from him
who
sanders
im alone in the b room

Or at least he thinks.

Looking through the bathroom door, Dermott Sanders couldn't see much, so he's wandered inside.

Though he doubts Kyle's in any actual danger, he's been assigned to watch him, and he can't exactly do that if the kid's gonna spend the rest of the afternoon dropping a deuce. He walks from stall to stall, trying to find the kid, make sure he isn't trying to hurt himself or anything.

You know, liability.

And when Sanders hears the subtle vibration of the phone, he makes his way to Kyle's stall, knocks lightly with a knuckle. "Everything all right in there?"

Kyle sits up rigidly on the toilet seat.

"Fine. I just need a minute to compose myself. I had to answer a text."

"Girlfriend?" Sanders is half-kidding.

"Yeah, you know how they are."

Shaking a beleaguered head, Dermott steps back into the hallway.

he is waiting 4 me, Kyle texts his old man.

window

Slowly, so the lock doesn't click and the door doesn't clang, Kyle pokes his head from the stall, looks to the wall that borders the west lawn. A row of old fashioned beveled windows—the kind you unlatch and push out—are set too high near the ceiling for him to reach. After a long look at the open entrance door, Kyle punches a few keys, hits send, and tucks his phone in his front pants pocket.

Then he moves quickly, grabbing the rubber wastebasket—full of tissues and wadded paper towels—upending it and placing it against the wall.

Just below the row of windows.

*   *   *

going now, the text reads.

And James nods as if Kyle's beside him in the Accord.

He's pulling into the school parking lot when he realizes he has no idea where the bathroom is. No clue where he should go to grab Kyle and get him the hell out of there.

But then he sees his son, sweatshirt snagging on an open window frame as his feet dangle toward the ground. James bangs a left down a long line of student cars and swings the Accord around to the curb as Kyle lets go and falls three or four feet to the sidewalk, landing swiftly on his Nikes.

"Come on," James shouts as the passenger window rolls down.

Kyle freezes in a half-crouch, freaking the fuck out. On the one hand, it's his father beckoning him away from the school. On the other, he just ditched a cop and crawled through a bathroom window.

And he's got a fucking test next period.

"Kyle, get in the fucking car!"

Not one to defy his father—especially now that his father's apparently mastered the art of profanity—he bolts for the passenger door. James sees him coming, kicks her into gear so Kyle's got to open a moving door and climb into a car doing ten miles an hour.

The door closes as James burns the tires, rockets the two of them out of the parking lot.

Neither knowing what in the hell lies ahead.

Nineteen
Road Trippin'

As they carve their way through town, Kyle asks his father what's going on.

When James, busy smacking a palm against the horn and swerving around a Mini, doesn't answer, Kyle opens his mouth to ask again. Louder.

This time, his words are lost beneath a squeal of rubber as his father swings the car to the right, barely tapping the breaks as they come through a four-way intersection. At least two of the cars left in their wake have to stop short at the cross streets, their drivers shouting expletives and laying on their horns as the Accord flies by.

After that, Kyle thinks it best to just grab the oh-shit handle and fasten his seatbelt.

It's not until they pull into their driveway and James springs from the driver's seat and sprints into the house that Kyle thinks it prudent to start asking questions again.

Well, maybe.

'Cause in addition to driving like he just signed a contract with NASCAR, James Worthington's been cussing like a motherfucker the whole way home. Random *shits* and *fucks* spewing from his mouth like profane spittle. Plus, he's cutting people off, flipping the bird, screaming out the window. And most of the other drivers, they're staring back with dumbfounded eyes.

Because they *know* the guy raging behind the wheel.

That's James Worthington. The guy that sells hot dogs at the concession stand at the football field. The guy that fixed my carburetor. The dude that donated $500 to the Gower SPCA.

Kyle's just getting out of the car when James reemerges from the house in a big goddamn hurry.

"Dad, what's g—"

James tosses him a set of keys. "Start the car."

"It's still on. You never turned it off."

"Not that car."

"Pop, we've only got one…" But then Kyle takes a closer look at the keys in his hand. Simultaneously, their heads roll toward the yellow and black behemoth across the garage.

"Look, there's no time for specifics," James says. "We need to get out of town. I'll explain on the way. But that piece of shit"—he hooks a thumb at the Accord—"will only slow us down."

Kyle fights back a smile. Despite the onslaught of shit that's hit the fan, he's ecstatic to finally be driving Grandpa's car. "Where are we going?"

"Just start it up and wait for me. Gotta grab a few things before we go."

"I'll pull her out, wait for you in the driveway."

"No." James is emphatic. "Just start the engine, and make sure she sounds OK. I'm the only one who drives that thing."

*   *   *

Twenty years.

Twenty goddamn, motherfucking, cocksucking years.

If you're not in the clear after two decades, then it must be true what they say—*La Famiglia* is for life.

The shoebox reeks of mildew and mothballs. But the cylinder on the old .38 spins as smooth and true as she did in her heyday.

James slides open his bedside drawer, digs for the balled up socks—the ones with the yellow stripes at the top that he hasn't worn since he was a New Yorker. Unraveling them over the bed, he watches six bronze bullets trickle onto the comforter, bouncing off the tightly-made bed like popcorn.

With the sweep of a palm, James gathers them up, slips them one after the other into the chambers. Then he flicks the wheel closed, thumbs the hammer and sights over the barrel.

Push comes to shove, she'll get the job done.

Passing through the kitchen, he notices the picture Beth cut from the newspaper and stuck to the fridge just before James flipped the table. The one of them sitting on the hood of the 442.

And somehow he knows that's how they found him.

Unable to control himself, he grabs a sticky note and a pen, scrawls an enraged message and pins it to the front of the picture. Hell, even if he's wrong, that picture *could* have been the way they found him. Not that Beth or anybody else will ever see the note, but it makes him feel a little better to put his anger in writing.

Until he finds Kyle in the driver's seat of the growling 442.

James watches his son rev the gas pedal over and again, getting a feel for the timing, the power of the 390 beneath the hood. Learning its language, grinning like a bastard as he becomes one with the car. Oblivious to his father standing by the door.

Kid's got no idea what's coming. And there ain't a chance he's ready.

"Move over," James yells over the engine.

Startled, Kyle climbs across the middle console, makes room for his father.

Behind the wheel, James presses his foot against the pedal. Once, twice. The roaring purr of the modified block fills the garage until the vibrations tickle their ears, tighten their throats.

"What you did today," James tells Kyle, "running out of the school, climbing through that window—that was good. Caught you by surprise, but you did what you had to do. You took matters into your own hands, despite what you'd been taught was right."

Kyle shrugs. "I just did what you told me to."

"Think you can keep it up?"

"Jumping out of windows?"

"Doing what I tell you to."

This is where Kyle would ordinarily roll his eyes and take out his phone. But this time, he nods meekly. "I think so."

It'll have to do.

"Good." James pulls his lap belt across, winces as it tightens over his wound.

"You all right?"

"I'll live."

"So what do we do now?"

James takes one last glance at his son before shifting into first.

"We drive."

Like a blur of sunshine, the Olds sails out of the garage, and James guns it out of the driveway and out of Gower.

Twenty
Worthington's House

"How many miles you doing today, Beth?" the clerk at the flower shop asks when she comes in bundled for the cold, bathed in an incongruous sweat. Skintight Under Armour beneath a Marty McFly vest, topped off with a beanie and a pair of cotton-ball earmuffs like puffs of snow matting her red hair.

"Not sure. At least six. It's kind of a spur of the moment thing."

She's not currently training for a marathon or a mini or a 10K or anything like that. She just decided to knock off work early to visit James, got the itch to bang out a run first. Figured she could squeeze in a few errands while she was out, passed the flower shop less than a mile from James' place, thought she'd pick up a bouquet for the house, brighten it up a bit for his return home.

She'll walk the rest of the way, catch her breath, put the flowers in a vase before she jogs back home to change and drive out to the hospital. While she's at James', she'll fill his duffel with fresh clothes. Maybe pick up some personal touches for his last day in the hospital. Even if he only has twenty-four hours to go, a picture or two of her or Kyle might bolster his spirits.

'Cause he did seem a little off yesterday. The change was slight, but when you know someone as intimately as Beth knows James, you notice the little things.

Like his use of the F-word.

What the fuck was that about?

*   *   *

The Jetta idles to a stop in the Worthington driveway, Katie finding it odd that the garage door is wide open and that old yellow car is gone. After she calls out for Kyle or James and checks the entirety of the first floor, she hangs her jacket over the back of a kitchen chair, sits down to check her phone. She's sent Kyle two unanswered texts already, and she's about to thumb out a third when she takes a second to recap everything that *supposedly* happened today.

You can't trust the talk amid the halls of Gower High, but it was practically verified as fact in the cafeteria that Kyle was yanked out of class during first period. The conspiracy theories behind why, however, rival that of the Kennedy assassination.

Turns out he was the one who really shot his father.

He was in on the robbery.

He's suicidal.

Got caught jacking off in the bathroom.

If the school psychologist and the resource officer really were involved though, there must have been an especially compelling reason. In fact, the only time she's ever seen the school shrink outside his office was on Teacher Appreciation Day when the secretary announced that free donuts were available in the front office.

When the school day ended, Katie waited for Kyle by the willow tree in the courtyard where they meet each day either to drive home together or simply to share a kiss before Kyle has to get to practice, but today he didn't show. First time since they started dating.

Katie knows there's gotta be some logical explanation for Kyle's whereabouts. But his house proves surprisingly tight-lipped on the subject.

* * *

After Angelo spotted the guy that looked like James Worthington hopping into the white Accord, he couldn't sleep no matter how hard he tried.

Instead—underslept and overcoffeed—he identified five more James Worthingtons over the next two hours.

And five more during the hour after that.

All guys leaving the hospital of their own accord, fitting a general description of Worthington. And each time he swore with increasing certitude and indignance that this guy was *definitely* James Worthington. When he finally pointed at someone who looked damn near sixty and grabbed for his gun, Dom volunteered to go inside and scout out the hospital.

Figured if he didn't Angelo would end up storming the place, shooting his way up to Worthington's room, killing anyone unlucky enough to be standing in his path.

That, of course, would not include Worthington's son, who, despite the school day's conclusion, never showed up.

Getting in is no problem. Like when he'd gone in the day before, as long as it's visiting hours and you don't look like a complete degenerate or an obvious threat to public safety, you just ask the receptionist about the person you're there to see and they wave you through.

Getting near the room, however, turns out to be a total bitch.

What with the three cops standing in the hallway outside.

Dom lowers his head and passes them by, waltzes to the vending machine, makes like he's purchasing a Snickers.

But what he's really doing is listening.

It's not that hard because the only other people around are a paraprofessional behind the counter to his right and a decrepit old man slouching on the sofa behind him.

Actually, listening attentively only becomes difficult when it's the sheriff's turn to talk.

And that's only because Dom's gotta struggle not to laugh.

Turns out Jimmy Pedals slugged the guy, knocked him the fuck out, and snuck out of his room. Pulled his tubes, changed his clothes, hustled the hell out of there.

Dom can't believe Angelo's paranoia was justified. One of the dozen guys he spotted in the parking lot probably was Worthington.

The sheriff tells one deputy to hang around and search the floor, question any of the staff or patients who may have spoken to Worthington earlier in the day or maybe even saw him on his way out. Then he tells the other deputy to come with him, they're swinging by Worthington's place on Scenic Drive. He admits it's a slim chance, but James might stop home before he takes it on the lam. If he's not gone already.

Dom knows if he tells Angelo, the old wop is gonna make him drive over to Worthington's house on the double, try to get there before the cops.

Force him to kill anyone they find inside.

But if he doesn't, Angelo's just gonna see the cops hit the lights and cruise out of the parking lot anyway. Twitchy bastard's gonna figure out they're going after Worthington. Which means there's no avoiding a trip to the guy's place.

Dom can only hope James had the sense not to dawdle before hitting the road.

*　　*　　*

Before Beth even realizes who it is standing by the kitchen table, she's on a tirade. "What the fuck is going on? Why is the house wide open? What's the Accord doing parked in the middle of the driveway with its doors open?"

Katie looks up from the Worthingtons' kitchen table.

Thinks, *Of all the people who could have walked through that door…*

Fuck, she'd rather have surprised a burglar.

Beth's all disheveled from her run, eyes beady green dots beneath a brow furrowed like pale leather. Flyaways jutting from her ponytail. And the litany only heats up when Beth realizes it's none other than Little Miss Mansion making herself right at home. "What are *you* doing here?"

"I can't find Kyle."

Beth's a statue. Hard glare, hands on hips. "Did you see him at school?"

"We drove together this morning, but he didn't meet me after. Heard some wild stories."

"What kind of stories?"

Katie shrugs, reluctant to share teenage gossip and hearsay with the queen of the cynics.

Beth gestures toward the garage. "And all this?"

Katie shakes her head, mystified. "I checked around. There's nobody here."

"Where's the car?"

Another shrug.

"Anything else missing?" Not quite accusatory, but with the usual unfounded suspicion she directs toward Katie.

"Not that I could see. All the TVs are where they should be."

Beth walks to the sink, drinks tap water from a glass. "Should you just be sitting there? I mean, with nobody home."

"*You're* here."

Beth glares over the rim of her glass. "I have a key."

"Pretty sure you didn't use it to get in."

Beth takes another sip, leaves the glass in the sink. She removes the flowers from her backpack, lays the bouquet on the counter.

"Kyle's not answering his phone."

There's probably nothing to that. Beth's been around Kyle often enough to know how ineptly teenage boys prioritize. Kid hasn't learned if your girlfriend calls, you answer the damn phone, no questions asked. Took her a while, but she eventually got James straight on that one.

"I'm going to take a look around the place. See if I can figure out what's going on." Beth makes it as far as the refrigerator.

Sees that the newspaper picture of her with James now has a sticky note adhered to it. "What the hell?"

"'Told you this was a bad idea,'" Katie reads over her shoulder.

Snakelike, Beth flicks her eyes at the girl she didn't know was hovering behind her. "It's James' handwriting."

But it's not possible. She was here the day James was shot and the picture didn't have a note on it then. Either James can telekinetically pin rude sticky notes to pictures in far away places…

Or James was here.

Again, Beth tells Katie she's going to look around.

When she's gone, Katie takes a harder look at the picture and the note. Doesn't seem significant to her. She leans against the counter, drums her fingers against its edge, antsy as all hell now that it's just her and Beth in the place.

Absently, she grabs the flowers and retrieves a tall vase from the cabinet. Turns the faucet and leaves the container to fill up while she fetches a pair of kitchen shears from the butcher block.

The blades are closing around the ragged stems of the bouquet when she hears the inner garage door open. Dropping the scissors to the counter where the flowers fall atop them, Katie turns, fully expecting to see her boyfriend.

Instead, some fat guy with a greasy tan is pointing a gun in her face.

"Be a doll," he says, "and turn off the water."

Twenty-One
The Weaker of the Two

Toweling cool clean water from her face, Beth hears muffled voices in the kitchen. Two guys talking to Katie. Probably James and Kyle.

But as she's about to open the door and demand that James tell her just what the hell is going on, the phone in the pocket of her black Lycra vibrates. Instinctively, she digs it out of the skintight fabric. Sees James' name and number on the screen.

Which begs the question: Who's in the kitchen with Katie?

Beth listens closer to the voices, one doing more talking than the other. A mirthlessly jovial tone that tells her whoever's voice it is, he's no friend of Katie's. Some pervert with a sick sense of humor judging by the devious way he laughs at his own jokes while the others fall silent. When Beth nudges the door open and presses her ear closer, she can make out most of what's being said.

"…must be the little guy's girlfriend.

"…wannabe sixteen again…

"…seen him?

"…pair like that…lucky bastard."

Guy's about as amusing as a rapist in clown makeup.

Beth risks opening the door a little wider and peers out with one eye. A middle-aged fat guy and a skinny kid not much older than Kyle. Maybe college age. Both dressed fancy, too swarthy to be native Pennsylvanians.

And, of course, they're both carrying guns.

As much as she hates to, she hits the ignore button on her phone.

The young one has his back to her, and the older guy's showing his profile, standing next to Katie against the counter. If Beth can move fast enough, she might be able to surprise the little one before they realize she's there. But only if she can rush him before the big goon sees her approaching. The way he's facing, turned half in her direction, it'll be a helluva race.

And Beth's always up for a good race.

She searches the half-bath, curses the Spartan décor. Nothing that could double as a weapon. There's the cover to the toilet tank, but when she hoists that bitch, she discovers it's one heavy fucker, and there's no way she's swinging it at anybody, let alone carrying it silently into the kitchen to stop these guys from robbing James' house.

Or hurting Katie.

She supposes there's that, too.

Inside the closet, she finds more of the same. Lightweight plastic containers she wouldn't waste her time throwing at a rat. Deodorant, soap, shampoo. A copy of *Sports Illustrated* atop a stack of towels.

Then, in the back corner, she sees something resting on the tile floor, sticking straight up like it's begging her to take hold and swing for the fences. Her fist closes around the wooden handle. The weight solid in her hand, the leverage enough she can attack from a safe distance. Help her put the college guy down so maybe she can get her hands on his gun.

What little she's seen of him, she knows he's the weaker of the two.

*   *   *

Here's something Dom definitely didn't learn in college: What do you do when a coworker is about to rape and kill an innocent girl?

Given the way he's set his .45 on the counter and moved behind her to press himself against her tightly-swaddled adolescent ass, that's clearly what Angelo's got on the brain.

"So, you givin' little Worthington any of that sweet hoochie-woochie you display so nicely?"

Dom's gun is pointed somewhere between the floor and the girl, kind of floating there aimlessly. He looks on, disgusted, as Angelo's interrogation starts to sound increasingly like a club scene on *Jersey Shore*.

"All that blond hair…" Angelo presses his nose to a handful of it, closes his eyes. "Can't be any Italian in you."

The poor girl cringes, stares down at the flowers, says nothing.

Angelo unhands her and steps to the side, looks leeringly into her eyes. "You want some?"

"Do you know where we can find James Worthington or his son?" Dom asks.

Angelo shoots him a hard-eyed look. Like, hey, I was getting somewhere over here.

Girl's so relieved to hear a *human* voice that she takes a deep breath and actually offers a reply, though her eyes never leave the flowers. "I came here looking for Kyle. I don't know where he is."

"Kyle," Dom repeats. "He's the son?"

Katie nods at the bouquet in front of her. Still won't face them.

"Maybe you know a way we can get in touch with him, sweetie?" Angelo says, moving closer to her once more. Her eyes remain locked on the multi-colored blossoms as her head turns reflexively away from his garlic and parmesan breath.

"Maybe you have his number?" He moves closer still. "Maybe you wanna give it to me?"

Dom sees her eyes close, watches her hands ball into fists at the edge of the counter, gripping the Formica with tense, sweaty palms.

"What do you say?" Angelo asks. "You wanna give it to me?"

One of her tiny fists closes around the stems of the bouquet. An emotional crutch to seize upon. Anything to distract from the repulsive creep nestling against her.

At least that's what Dom thinks at first.

Until he catches the glint of metal beneath the flowers.

Instinctively, he raises his gun. But before he can do anything more, he hears a sweep of air, feels a dull, rubbery *thwap* against the side of his face.

* * *

Katie's doing her best to look traumatized.

Let them think she's gone into shock while she sneaks her hand toward the scissors.

But then her plan goes to shit.

There's a swift slap behind them—the sound of the young guy falling like dead weight on the linoleum—and the old brute turns away from her.

He starts with an angry, "What the...?" But when he sees his partner flat on his ass, pressing his free palm against a bloodied cheek, Beth lording over him wielding a bathroom plunger like a Louisville Slugger, he falls into uncontrollable laughter.

"You see that?" Angelo asks no one in particular. "Kid got clobbered by Martha Stewart. You all right down there, kiddo?"

Dom isn't hurt so much as he's stunned and embarrassed. The rubber face of the plunger stung him, nicked his cheek beneath the eye. He's blinking away tears, rising from the floor. "Yeah," he mumbles, "I'm all right."

But before he can recover, Beth starts toward the fat guy, plunger cocked over her shoulder.

Angelo laughs again. And turns for his .45.

That's when Katie brushes the flowers aside and swings the scissors into the left side of his chest.

The laughter degenerates into a primal scream. Fast.

Pulling against the grips, fighting the tension of gristle and bone, Katie yanks the bloodied end free and thrusts the blades between his ribs once more. Swinging it like an ax, turning her whole body this time, putting all of her weight into it.

The shears disappear halfway up the handles as the white shirt beneath Angelo's suit jacket wells up red.

"MOTHERFUCKER!!! HAAAAHHHH, SON OF A BITCH, FUCK, COCK, CUNT!!!"

Dom looks up from the floor, sees Angelo dancing around, clutching the implement protruding from his chest, trying to shake off the pain and pull the thing free. Dom's frozen in place. Both he and Beth marvel at the sight of the big Italian thrashing about the small kitchen, each of them forgetting the respective weapons in their hands.

Katie's not as impressed.

She retrieves Angelo's .45 from the counter, surprised by the sheer heft of the automatic. It's, like, really fucking heavy. Nothing like what she's seen in the movies. Feels like she's trying to lift another cheerleader into the air, but somehow she musters the strength to point it roughly at Angelo's chest.

"Stand still, asshole," she commands, satisfied with the brass in her voice, though her heart's racing beneath.

Though blood darkens his shirt down to his waistline, Angelo's so infuriated with the sight of this little cunt holding his own gun on him and telling him what the fuck to do that he just loses it.

He lunges at Katie, arms outstretched before him.

Terrified of what the maniac might do should he manage to get his hands on her, Katie squeezes the trigger.

Which leads to two problems.

One for Katie, one for Angelo.

First, just as Katie was surprised by the sheer mass of the handgun, she has no idea what to expect from the recoil. Turns out it feels something like being struck by a car and sent back on your ass, totally and completely out of control. And when her tush hits the linoleum, she loses both her wind and her grip on the handgun, which slides across the floor toward Dom and Beth.

As for Angelo, at first there doesn't seem to be a problem at all. Katie pointed the gun at his chest, but she compromised her grip to wrap her dainty index finger around the trigger and lost her aim completely, the gun dropping by inches in her hands. Which means Angelo doesn't get shot in the chest.

It does, however, mean he gets shot a little lower.

And therein lies the problem.

When the bullet makes contact, his balls are forced out through his asshole.

Angelo lets out a long, dry squeal as he slumps against the cabinets. He manages one horrified look at what Katie's done to his manliness before the blood boils between his lips and his head falls to the side.

Dom can't believe it. Seeing Angelo fucking erupt, he loses it like the prissy college bitch his father's heavies have always thought him to be. Drops his piece and rises slowly to his feet, hands raised in surrender.

"Please," he tells Beth, "I'm not with him."

Beth's still trying to process the fact that Little Miss Mansion just shot a gangster through the dick when she realizes the other little shit is begging for his life. She catches the part about the two of them not being together, and she cocks an eyebrow, tightens her grip on the plunger.

"I mean, we are," Dom pleads, "but I was just trying to stop him. Please. I don't want any part of this."

The giant rubber nipple lands right between his eyes, and he falls on his stomach, uttering an effeminate "Ow!"

Then Beth swats him again and again around the shoulders and atop the back. "Shut up, asshole! You stay the fuck down there!"

And Dom does. He doesn't move a muscle, even though the plunger stings like a bitch.

"Guh," Katie utters, finding her feet, gasping for breath.

Beth squints a puzzled look.

Another struggle for breath, another muffled "Guh."

Except this time Katie points at Angelo's .45, smoke still rising from the barrel. Beth bounces the rubber end of the plunger off the back of Dom's skull twice more for good measure.

An exasperated "Fuck!" is his only response.

She moves across the floor, crouches for the .45. She too is surprised by its heft. Then the look of it reminds her of something. Turning back toward Dom, she kicks his .38 over toward Katie, who picks it up as she stumbles to her feet. Beth throws her arm around the girl's shoulders and ushers her toward the door.

They don't make it three steps before turning toward one another mutually disgusted. Katie shrugs free of Beth's grasp. No matter what they just survived, the whole sisters-in-arms thing ain't happening.

Twenty-Two
Don't Go Away Mad

When James' call goes to voicemail after six rings, he barely resists the urge to smash his phone against the dashboard.

"Look, if you get to call Beth," Kyle tells his old man, "I'm calling Katie."

But when Kyle pulls his phone out, James snags it, rolls the window down and wings it into the gray thicket beside the eastbound lane of route 80.

"What the fuck?" Kyle demands.

"I told you, you can't tell her where we are or where we're going."

"I don't even *know* where we're going. I just want to tell her I'm OK. She texted me twice to find out what happened at school. Seriously, Pop, what are we doing?"

James takes a slow breath, stares at the endless stretch of highway before them.

And starts talking.

They're nearing the Lincoln Tunnel by the time he's told his son everything.

Well, not everything.

James doesn't think Kyle needs to know all of his old man's worst mistakes. Just the ones that pertain to their having to run for their lives.

So now Kyle knows James was a wheelman for the mob. That he was never a member of the mafia, but that he pulled jobs for different families in New York and Chicago. James gives him the routine about how he never wanted a life like that but it was the only choice he had. He didn't grow up with the advantages Kyle's got, and living in the city was all about survival. Taking whatever opportunity presented itself and making the most of it. Even if it meant getting your hands dirty. If it kept food on the table, it was a good deal.

Tells him about the last job, the one he bailed on when the radio came up and he realized he couldn't be Pugliese's bitch. The job that left the family pissed enough to track him down twenty years later and take him out.

Kyle's quiet as they enter the dimly lit tunnel. Doesn't say anything until they're halfway through.

"Did Mom know about all this? Is it why she left?"

"You think she'd grant me full custody if she did? No, your mother got it stuck in her head she was gonna move to the slums, devote her life to that social work she was so passionate about. We agreed that wasn't the best place for you."

"You *agreed*? What'd you do, pull your gun on her?"

"Jesus, who do you think I am?"

"I really don't know anymore."

Sighing, James admits, "Fair enough. How'd you know about the gun?"

"Found it in your closet when I was a kid, playing hide-and-seek."

"How come you never asked about it?"

"Not sure." Kyle shrugs. "It was so strange, a guy like you having a gun. It was easier to just put it out of mind. So what was the song?"

"What?"

"The song you heard that made you drive away."

James shifts uncomfortably in his seat. "What's the difference?"

"What was it?"

James looks at Kyle with resignation. No more lies.

Like he's admitting to ogling naked pictures of his sister, James tells him the title.

"Guns N' Roses?"

"Poison."

Kyle's nodding. "That CD in the garage. The only one that isn't Bruce."

"You saw it?"

"Last time we were working on the car."

"There was just something about the sound of it while I was waiting in the car. It was soft and sad, the guy's crying about his girl cheating on him. He's gotta move on, figure out what his life's gonna be without her. It…I don't know…It spoke to me."

It starts as a quick snicker, but before long, Kyle's laughing so hard he can't talk.

"What?" James grumbles, his stomach wound suddenly throbbing.

His son's sentences come across in fragments broken by hysterics. "Your…life changing epiphany…was inspired…by Poison?"

"So?"

"Brett Michaels…from Celebrity Apprentice?"

"He wasn't doing that yet. What do you want? I was vulnerable."

"Some guy in makeup and hair extensions comes on the radio and you change your whole life?"

"He still had his real hair back then."

Kyle's laughter gets the better of him. He can't even breathe now.

"Great. I finally come clean with you, tell you something I've never told anybody else in my whole life, and this is how you react. It was a turning point. If I hadn't heard that song at that particular moment, I might have stayed with the Pugliese. Probably be dead right now."

"Hey, don't go away mad," Kyle tells him, "just go away."

"Very funny. That's Motley Crue, not Poison."

It's a good three minutes before Kyle's laughter passes.

Clearing his throat, James asks, "What about you? How you holding up? They... uh...told you about Lacy?"

Kyle doesn't answer right away.

"I cried when I heard. But now, I don't know. I mean, I'm sad. It just...doesn't seem real. None of this does. I mean, you, driving for the mob? Come on. It's like a movie or something. *The Transporter.* It's ridiculous. Why are they coming after you now anyway? You think it took them twenty years to find you?"

"Could be. These families are more muscle than brain."

"I'll say. Come and kill a guy just because he drove off on them."

"Well...there was a little more to it than that."

Kyle leans closer. It's the kind of undivided attention James always wished Kyle would pay to auto repair or schoolwork. James would be thrilled with the kid's sudden ability to focus if it weren't his father's youthful indiscretions that had peaked his interest.

"Early on after I left the city, I checked in once or twice with a few guys from the neighborhood. Guys I could trust. Wanted to see how hot my situation was. That last job, the crew was supposed to go in and...*talk* to a guy who was late on his loan payments. They sent Nicky Sorrentino, a fucking animal. He puts the guy down.

"But it turns out, sloppy as he and the other guys are, they come running out looking for the car, they don't bother to check around the guy's apartment first. His brother was hiding in the shower. With a shotgun. He follows them out, Nicky takes both barrels in the back.

"Sorrentino was a dick, but he was a made guy. My fault he went down. Not the kind of thing they give you a pass on. They may have waited this long for a reason. The kid at the ATM, before I spit on the ground, he told me it was about Nicky Sorrentino."

"I *thought* he said something."

"His voice, his eyes, I'm pretty sure it was Sorrentino's kid. I never met him. Just a baby when I knew his father. They might have waited all this time so he could be the one to do it. Sick fucks."

Kyle's shaking his head in disbelief. Seriously, this is his life now?

"That's why we had to get out of Gower," James says.

"But why are we heading *into* the city?" Kyle asks. "Shouldn't we be running *away* from the Pugliese family?"

"I gotta find out how bad it is."

"Pop, they tried to kill you. I'd say it's pretty bad."

"It's possible Sorrentino's kid was working alone. Not likely, but there's a chance. I need to find that out. If it was just him, we might be in the clear."

"Was he a…made guy too?"

"Probably."

"Won't they be twice as pissed at you now anyway? Even if he was working alone. He's one of their guys."

"I might be able to convince them it's in their best interest to avoid further bloodshed."

"How can you do that?"

James rubs his thumb against his index and middle fingers.

"Pop, we can't even afford to buy me a car, how we gonna offer these guys money?"

James looks at his son, drops his eyes as if he's been caught with his pants down.

"I knew it!" Kyle says. "No way you saved enough money doing tune-ups and oil changes to buy the store. I knew you had money stashed away somewhere."

"From my former life. One nice thing about mob families, they pay very, very well."

"How much we talking here?"

"Enough."

"And you were gonna make me share the fucking Accord?"

"What was I supposed to tell you? 'Here, son, here's twenty-five grand that fell off a truck?'"

"Honestly, Pop, if you wanted to give me twenty-five grand, I wouldn't have asked a single question. So now we just go right to the family and ask how we can make things right?"

"No, there's somebody else we can meet with first. He might know how fucked we are. If the situation's too hot, we don't make the offer."

"What'll we do then?"

"We'll run."

Twenty-Three
An Old Friend

James pulls up to a yellow curb and throws the Olds into park.

"Dad, we can't park here."

But James isn't listening. He can't take his eyes off the auto repair shop sandwiched between high rises on the swanky uptown street. The place is small but clearly successful—its four bays are filled with Jags and Beemers. James is pretty sure he spies a Porsche in there too.

So Sonny seems to have done OK for himself.

That's good. James always wondered what became of him. Hoped his sudden decision to leave town didn't have any repercussions on the poor guy. He heard through a mutual friend—not a city guy, but someone they'd met racing on the circuit down south—that Sonny bought a place uptown. That he was working on cars for a living.

But even after the guy told him where, James hadn't pictured it quite like this. It's fucking elite, and Sonny—well, he couldn't balance a spoon on his nose, let alone his checkbook. Certainly not the ledger for a place that pulls this kind of business.

James sits back in his seat before opening the door, making sure he can feel the cold weight of the .38 pressing against his spine. Sonny had nothing to do with the families, wasn't fast enough off the line to draw their attention, land a driving gig. But the money for a place like this doesn't fall out of the sky.

"You're just gonna talk to this guy, right?"

Absentmindedly, James nods. It's not terribly convincing. "Just keep it running and don't move from this spot."

"Pop, it's a tow zone. What if—"

"Anything happens, just lay on the horn. I'll hear it and come running. It's vintage, got a unique sound."

"Let me guess, 'Living on a Prayer.'"

"Glad you're enjoying this."

"Pop, who is this guy?"

James hesitates, as if he lacks the words to describe Sonny.

"An old friend."

But he was so much more than that.

They owned the car together. Though "own" is a funny word to use for somebody whose concept of chipping in for the cost of gas and repairs is constantly repeating, "I'm good for it," and then not actually *making* good for it. But it was the two grand Sonny borrowed from his uncle that afforded them the busted-ass heap of metal they eventually fashioned into the monster-of-the-two-lane-blacktop that was the 442, and as such, James counted them equal partners.

James did the driving, Sonny handled the mechanics.

Though his heart didn't march in time with the low growl of the engine as James' did, Sonny knew his way around a car, could diagnose a problem like it was nobody's business. And though he never drove, Sonny never missed a race. His job was keeping her tip-top so James could go out there, tear ass, bring home a fortune.

Two hungry street kids with no prospects, angling for a way to make an (almost) honest buck, they scoured junkyards, dug through skeletal heaps of Detroit muscle looking for the right car. '65 Mustangs, '67 Impalas, old Chevys from the fifties. The sight of each sent Sonny bounding into the air, exclaiming, "That's the one," every goddamn time.

James didn't like what he saw. "Just don't feel right," he kept telling Sonny.

And Sonny couldn't fucking believe it when, after all the time they spent in the scrap yards tearing through car after car, they passed a bombed-out wreck parked on someone's driveway wearing an orange For Sale sign and James made him double back.

Lighting a cigarette and sweeping his blond-brown hair from his eyes, he jutted his chin at the rattletrap carcass of a '68 Oldsmobile.

Said, "Now we're talking."

"We looking at the same car?" a profoundly perplexed Sonny asked. 'Cause they must have seen a hundred cars in better shape than that piece of shit.

The bitch of it was, through the red paint fading grayish-pink, the brown muck caked over the windows, the rust you could punch a fist through, James couldn't explain it. The best he could do was nudge a radial, jet black and shiny, with the toe of his boot and say, "It's in the tires."

James just had a feeling. And when it came to cars, no one questioned James' instincts.

Still, Sonny balked at dropping two grand on a car that oughta be included in an ad for tetanus shots simply because "It's in the tires." So, he was skeptical when he popped the hood.

But when the low morning sun bounced off that bronze and copper 390 block, he had to smile.

"Zero-to-sixty in 5.4," James prodded.

But Sonny was already sold.

It took them two months of round-the-clock labor to get her there. Sixty-odd days combing through more junkyards, reading the classifieds for any loose parts someone might be selling or giving away. They logged so many hours in the auto parts store, the clerks knew them by name.

Slow, meticulous, fucking expensive. But they spared no dime, no trip regardless the distance. In one case, they hopped an overnight train to Florida 'cause some guy from the neighborhood kept his *goomar* down there and swore he saw a pristine Oldsmobile carburetor from the old days collecting dust in some scrap yard.

And Sonny was damn glad he listened to James when they took her out on her first run on some abandoned airstrip in Jersey. James smoked a '71 Camaro so badly the guy may as well have been parked on the line when the 442 crossed the finish.

It was Win Win Win Win Win after that.

Wherever they went—and they'd go fucking everywhere on the east coast where gearheads were racing—they finished tops. Be it the Jersey circuit where they spent most of their time, upstate where they cruised the mountains, even down south for beach runs in the Carolinas. People saw the bumblebee yellow and black rolling through the morning mist and they just, like, handed the money over.

They'd heard the legend or they'd seen that monster in action.

They knew they were fucked.

Good as it felt, though, it wasn't about winning. It was about how they built that thing together, carved a masterpiece out of the grimiest, least-likely raw materials available. Two kids, poor-as-shit, constructing their very futures. Giving themselves a fighting chance at a life fate had done her damnedest to deny them.

It was about the trip. The travel. Getting the fuck out of the city.

Every time they cruised through the Lincoln tunnel or hopped the Tap-An-Zee or crossed the GW, James would take an audible breath, ask Sonny—every time without fail—"Son, how fucking good does it feel to be out of the goddamn city?"

Seriously, he'd be out of the city, like, point-two seconds and already he felt free.

How fucking good is it to be out of the city?

Every damn time.

And it was Sonny's hands alongside his own on that car they raised from the dead, piece by piece, that made all of that possible.

Twenty-Four
Joe Mafia

Inside, James asks after the manager. A big guy in a mechanic's smock nods toward the back before returning to the undercarriage of the Z4 he's got up on the lift.

There's a wood-paneled door marked with a black and gold placard that reads, "Office." Subtle and unremarkable. A quiet place for the man in charge to sit back and count his money. Walking among the buzz of wheel guns, shouted requests for tools, the loud hum of a classic rock station, James checks around before opening the door. No one seems particularly interested in what he's doing.

The simple portal opens to a much nicer hallway. White walls, wainscoted and brightly lit. Straight ahead, a staircase leads to additional offices, probably an apartment for late nights. James finds what he's looking for to his right. Another door, this one with a frame of glass at eye level. And inside, seated behind an oak desk at the far end of a very long office, James sees an older, fatter version of the pimply-faced kid who helped him build the road machine.

A ring of light gray hair encircles his otherwise bare head. Guy used to wear it long, teased-out like the members of the bands he loved so much. When guys on the street would call him a fag for dressing like a Long Island girl, Sonny'd wrestle 'em onto their stomachs, make 'em lick the pavement. A wild son of a bitch in loud Hawaiian shirts and rock tees.

And now he looks like Jimmy Buffet.

Jimmy Fucking Buffet.

James isn't even sure he's got the right guy until he notices the framed centerfold on the wall behind him. Nudie mags being as ubiquitous as they are in auto garages, he's got to squint a closer look at first, but what he sees identifies Sonny more accurately than a DNA test.

Julie McCullough, Playmate of the Month, February, 1986.

As obsessed as they both were with the Olds, their love affair was nothing compared to the fixation Sonny had on Julie.

She was big shit for a few years, what with her spread in *Playboy*, a fairly successful stand-up comedy act, and a stint on *Growing Pains*.

Yeah, *Growing Pains*.

James remembers it well. More than once they missed a midweek race because Sonny wouldn't leave his apartment until *Growing Pains* was over. God forbid the races cut into Julie time.

James takes a closer look through the glass, studies the man beneath the poster. The pimples have healed, leaving behind a pockmarked mask of flesh like a bomber jacket. James considers his own appearance—the still-sandy hair, hardened thighs from his occasional runs with Beth—weighs himself against the damage he sees before him.

Commends himself once again for quitting city life when he did.

When he walks in, Sonny's leafing through the *Times*, reading glasses tipped low on his nose. With a snort, he peers over his spectacles, narrows his eyes at the door.

James isn't sure which drops faster, the newspaper or Sonny's jaw.

"Son of a bitch."

"Sonny."

"Jimmy fucking Worthington." Sonny rises to his feet as fast as his girth will allow. "Been a long time."

Neither moves. Sonny's blinking, like he can't believe what he's seeing.

Or, James thinks, it could be a nervous tell.

Like Sonny's heard talk of James catching a bullet out in the sticks, and now he's deciding whether or not to pick up the phone, give Don Pugliese a ring.

"Well, shit, sit down." Sonny waves at an armchair across the desk. "Tell me why the hell you haven't given me a call in two fucking decades? I mean, I know you always hated the city, but twenty goddamn years?"

James takes his time getting to the chair, reading Sonny, what he might know. "I can't stay long."

"Whatever." Sonny turns toward a file cabinet. "Let's have a drink. You wanna drink? I got some Scotch back here in one of these drawers."

"Sonny—"

"Jim, whatever you're gonna say, we'll get to it. But I need a fucking drink before we go any further. This is like an acid trip or something, you showing up this way. It's shitty Scotch, but I know it's back here somewhere."

"No time."

Sonny feels the gravity in James' voice, sits back down.

"I'm sorry about the way I left," James starts. "That I didn't have a chance to talk to you first. Back then, the guys I was involved with…you must have heard what went down."

"I heard some stories. Heard some stories indeed."

Sonny leans forward, his voice deepening. Jimmy wants to be serious, he can do serious. "What I didn't hear, since you're in a mood to forego pleasantries and speak frankly, was why you left me high and dry the way you did. Really, man, a racing circuit ours for the taking and my partner disappears with the car. Just vanishes."

"I had to get outta the city. They'd a killed me. Like I said, I'm sorry."

Sonny snorts. "Hey, no sweat, pal." Waving his hands around the office, he adds, "I scraped by."

It is a helluva nice setup, but James thinks maybe he hears some unchecked sarcasm in the remark. He continues unabated.

"Recently, someone I used to work for—a long time ago— sent a representative to get in touch with me. You hear anything about that?"

"Jim, I ain't exactly Joe Mafia, here. Cut this shit with the 'people I worked for' and the 'representatives.' Tell me what the fuck is going on."

"Nicky Sorrentino's son tried to kill me."

Sonny's eyebrows pop. Either it's the first he's heard of it or he's pretending it is.

"Came to my store in PA and cornered me at an ATM. I need to know if it was a sanctioned hit or not."

"Holy shit. I mean, Jesus fucking Christ. What happened?"

James rises to reveal his wound, sees Sonny tense up before he's even out of his chair.

"A little jumpy, Son."

"Sorry. It's a lot to take in is all."

Slowly, James untucks his shirt. Careful not to reveal the .38 in the back of his waistband, he rolls the cotton blend high enough to expose a bandage like a sheet of notebook paper.

"Fuck me. That hurt?"

"Only when I breathe."

"And the Sorrentino kid?"

James shakes his head. "He won't cause me any more trouble. But I need to know if the family will."

"Like I said, I don't run in that circle. Even back when we were young, it was you they came to. The driver. I was just the grease monkey. Shit, I'm still just a grease monkey. I run a respectable business. Everything's aboveboard. Even the small-timers from the old neighborhood, I lost their numbers when I made the move uptown."

"Some move. Growing up, you never had two nickels to rub together."

"I always knew cars," Sonny says with a shrug. "Came into some money, put everything I had into this place. I've been clean ever since. Whatever happened to her anyway?"

"The Olds? She's parked out front."

"No shit. Still a fucking beast off the line?"

"Unbeatable."

"Goddamn." Sonny's eyes glisten in reverie. "Hell, you've got time for one drink, right?" He hops to his feet, turns back toward the file cabinet. "We'll put our heads together, see if we can't think of somebody who can help us. You can tell me all about that kid of yours, let me take a look at the 442. She's probably been missing my touch."

As the top drawer squeals open on rusty wheels, James stares through Sonny's back.

Says, "How'd you know I had a kid?"

Twenty-Five
Glad it was You

There's a slight pause before Sonny resumes his search for the booze.

"It's the city, Jim," he says off-handedly. "Word travels."

But there's an uncomfortable rigidity to Sonny's posture now.

"I thought you lost everybody's number?"

"I guess there was maybe one or two contacts I held onto. You remember Frankie—"

"Nobody in the city knows about my son."

Sonny deflates, his shoulders sinking to the middle of his chest. Leaving the drawer open, he turns a pained expression on James. "Oh, they know, Jim."

"The Pugliese?"

"Found some picture of you in the paper a week or two back. You and the car."

"Shit," James growls. Adds "I fuckin' knew it" under his breath.

"Look, I had no choice."

"No choice about what?"

"You left me with nothing, Jim. Took the car, more than half our racing money. Even the fucking CD I left in the player. I had no way to make a living. No idea if you were ever coming back."

"Go on."

"So there I am, a dumb shit street kid who's been making good money racing cars, now I gotta go back to the streets, scrape and scratch to stay alive? Made me sick just thinking about it."

"What did you do?"

"You know they came to me? After you left? The Pugliese. Sent those two bruisers, Angelo and the other guy looks like a movie star. You know the one. I think he's retired now, haven't seen him in the neighborhoods."

"Rocky."

"Yeah, yeah, Rocky. When I tell you they beat me within an inch of my life thinking I knew where you were, I ain't exaggerating. Rocky hadn't called Angelo off, he'd have finished the job."

Sounds like Angelo and Rocky. Back in the day, their routine was of the classic good cop/bad cop variety.

James Worthington wants to feel guilty about this. Jimmy Pedals knows he shouldn't.

"What the fuck did you do, Sonny?"

"What did I do? I went to work. With you gone, they needed a driver, settled on me. Despite my rep, I think they were hoping some of what you had rubbed off on me. They set me up with a souped-up Charger. Wasn't nothing like the Olds. Not even close. But it kept me outta the poor house. I never woulda had to worry about that if you hadn't started running jobs for them in the first place. If you hadn't left me with empty pockets, no way to earn a buck."

"That's how you bought this place."

Sonny nods. "They're my partners. They own half."

James hangs his head. "So what now? They burst through the door, shoot me full of holes?"

"You see me call anybody since you got here?" Sonny sounds almost insulted. "We go back a long way, you and me. Pulled ourselves out of the gutter together. That means something. Fuck, Jim, that means a lot. I wouldn't turn you over to them, even if you did fuck me."

"So the hit was on the books. They do want me dead."

"Oh, they want you dead, Jim. The price on your head? Forget about it."

Sonny turns and reaches into the open drawer. "I think we oughta have that drink now, figure out our next step."

But Jimmy's already figured that out.

He puts a bullet in Sonny's back.

It's not till Sonny wheels around—and James fires a second bullet into his chest—that he knows for sure it was his piece and not a bottle Sonny was going for.

The gun thumps its way to the carpet, Sonny raising a dying palm amid the dissipating smoke. Though it isn't smart, James kneels beside his friend, takes his hand in his own.

The hands that built the 442.

"Didn't wanna do it." Sonny struggles for breath, licks dry lips. "They'd have found out you stopped by. I let you walk out alive, they'd have killed me for sure. Thought at least if I did it myself…"

Growing up where they did, they never kidded themselves they'd grow old. Even for all the Pugliese family's offers of protection—that kind of work was a long, slow death sentence.

La Famiglia is for life. Only one way out.

Better your oldest friend punches your ticket than some guinea of the week.

"Glad it was you," Sonny gurgles.

It'd be an easier sentiment for James to accept if he weren't the one left to live with the other's blood on his hands.

"We got old, Jim. Fuckin' old."

It's the last thing Sonny says before the light leaves his eyes.

*   *   *

James finds the 442 idling where he left it, his son sitting behind the wheel.

"Uh-uh," he says.

"Come on, Pop."

"Your permit doesn't apply in a different state. And this is not the time."

"My *permit*! Dad, you used to work for the mob—"

"Move over."

Defeated, Kyle slowly exits the vehicle. Makes a big show walking around to the passenger side. Taking his time, hands jammed deep in his pockets.

'Cause it's really an appropriate time to pout like a three-year-old.

Climbing into the driver's seat, James speaks tonelessly. "We gotta get out of the city. There's an atlas under your seat, tell me how far it is before 80 hits 81."

Kyle sulks, says nothing.

"You do realize that giving me the silent treatment now could actually get us killed."

Huffing a breath, Kyle takes an eternity to retrieve the atlas, starts turning pages like he's trying to tear them from the spine. "That's back the way we came. *Past* the way we came. Why we going back that way?"

"Because there are no gangsters that way. Just do what I tell you. That was the deal, remember?"

"What happened with your friend?"

"That was a dead end," James tells him.

Leaving Kyle to wonder about the burnt stench of cordite on his father's clothes.

Twenty-Six
For Facebook and Stuff

When one of James' long-time employees tells them he hasn't seen the boss in days, Beth and Katie trudge hopelessly back to the Jetta, having expended the last possible lead either of them could come up with.

Hospital staff said James vanished. Track coach hadn't seen Kyle all afternoon.

And let's not even revisit the incident at the house.

Amazing how life can devolve into a total clusterfuck in under an hour.

Katie's in the driver's seat, hands strangling the steering wheel. Beth's seated beside her, face pinched like she's trying to solve an advanced calculus function.

When Beth grabs her phone and hits send, Katie tells her, "I've tried that, like, three times already. They're not answering."

Beth ignores her, counts the rings.

After three, she hears James' voice instead of the pre-recorded "You got James Worthington, leave me a message and I'll get back to you in a quick" she's been getting all afternoon.

"Beth?" James asks.

She makes it through "James, what the hell is going on?" before her brain and tongue start wrestling for the title belt. "I go to the house, everything is wide open, the yellow car is gone, we almost get killed by a couple of degenerate goodfellas, I call the hospital, they tell me you're not there—not that you've checked yourself out, just that you're gone and they don't know why—Katie tells me Kyle got into trouble at school—"

"*What* happened at the house?" he jumps in. "Are you OK?"

The rise of panic in James' voice is flattering, but it does nothing to allay Beth's fears. "Katie's pretty shook up, but we're all right." From the driver's seat, Katie shoots her a look of annoyed disbelief. 'Cause Beth's *way* more shook up by all this than she is. "Who the fuck were those guys?"

"She's with you?" James asks. "Katie's there right now?"

Kyle chimes in, reaching for the phone, saying he wants to talk to his girlfriend. James leans closer to the window, raises a frustrated palm for Kyle to wait.

"Yeah, she was at your house looking for Kyle. James, what's going on?"

"Kyle's with me. We don't have time to talk about this. Just get out of Gower. Head west and take Katie with you."

"Head west? What the hell do you mean, head west? Tell me what's going on."

"Beth, we're in trouble. All of us. Those men, back at the house, they're not gonna stop till they find you. You need to get out of there. Now."

"I don't think so, James. At least one of them won't be coming after anybody."

"Wha-What do you mean?" James stammers. "He's dead? You killed him?"

Beth's self-assured smile dims slightly. "Well, Katie did."

James blurts out, "Katie. Holy shit."

And Kyle gets antsy again. Starts in with the whole what's-going-on-let-me-talk bit.

"Your girlfriend killed a member of the Pugliese," James tells him, stunning the kid silent. He returns to Beth. "There were other guys there, at the house?"

"One. We were kind enough to let him go."

"Fuck, it's worse than I thought. They'll never let you off the hook now that you took out a family member."

"Family member? What—"

"You haven't gone to the police, have you?"

"No."

"Good. Whatever you do, don't contact Garrett Sanders."

Beth saw enough shit go down back in Philly to know when a situation is so well-fucked involving the cops would be a poor decision.

Like when you've blown a guy's nuts off and left him lying in your boyfriend's kitchen.

But she's not taking it on the run until she gets some answers.

"James, what's happening?"

"Where are you right now?"

"In front of your store. We came looking—"

"Do you have a car?"

"We're in Katie's Jetta. But James—"

"Beth, head west. Just start driving."

"I'm not going anywhere, James."

"Beth, listen to me, there's no time for—"

"I wanna know what's going on."

Her voice is steady, definitive. James knows her well enough to know she ain't kidding. She'll sit in front of his store all day if he doesn't tell her what she wants to know.

"All right." James wets his lips. "Beth, I used to be a bad guy. A real bad guy. Some other bad guys who I was bad to, they're coming after me. Me and everybody who means anything to me. Which means you and Katie are in immediate danger and you need to move now."

"Always knew there was more to you than the Boy Scout you pretend to be."

When Beth smiles, Katie rolls her eyes. They don't have time for any lovey-dovey shit.

"OK," Beth continues. "I'll do what you say, but just so we're clear, you're gonna be doing a lot more explaining the next time we see each other. No more of this vague, 'bad, bad, bad' shit. I want specifics. Got it?"

"Yeah." Though he can't promise her there'll be a next time. "I'm turning my phone off. I can't risk it. We won't be able to talk for a while. But, Beth, I love—"

She folds her phone shut before he can finish.

"Well?" Katie demands.

Beth taps the phone pensively against her chin. "You're rich, right?"

Katie sits back as if she's been slapped.

"Any chance you've got a laptop?"

"What is this, some kind of working class test? Like you get to hate me more if I do?"

"A laptop, Katie. Do you have a fucking laptop?"

Thin-lipped, Katie tells Beth that she does. "But what was all that stuff about heading west?"

"Yeah, we're not gonna do that," Beth tells her. "Where's this laptop?"

*   *   *

Turns out the laptop is in Katie's bedroom closet, which is where the girls find themselves fifteen minutes later.

"It was a Christmas gift," Katie explains as she pushes aside shoeboxes and digs through endless piles of cashmere sweaters in a closet you could park a car in. "I only used it once or twice, for Facebook and stuff. I didn't really need it. My desktop computer works just fine."

'Cause Katie's so not about the bells and whistles.

Of course, all Beth sees is a pampered princess who isn't sure where she put her two thousand dollar piece of technology.

"Wait." Katie takes a knee. "What's this?"

As if Beth's been in Katie's closet before.

"Probably just some Tiffany necklace you forgot about."

Wedged between an armoire and a plastic crate of photo albums, there's a thin black canvas bag, roughly the size of a coffee table book. Katie unzips it, finds a silver Apple staring back at her. "There it is."

"Your parents have Wi-Fi?"

Katie's way ahead of her. She's already turned the laptop on and brought it over to the bed. A king-size four-poster beneath a satin canopy. "Not much battery left," she says, clicking away at the keys.

"Go to the Verizon website." Beth's got her phone to her ear, waiting for someone to pick up. "Yeah," she tells the customer service rep, "my husband lost his phone, and I was hoping you could turn on the GPS so we can figure out where he left it. I'm sure it's in the house somewhere."

Katie's staring at the homepage Beth asked for.

"James Worthington," Beth says. Then she rattles off James' phone number. "His pin number?" From her grimace, Katie can tell Beth hasn't got a clue. "Uh, he's not really good with record-keeping. We can't seem to find that. What else can I give you? Date of birth, social? We really need to find this thing. My husband uses it for work."

Katie hears her spit out what sounds like a social security number. Then she thanks the woman, tells her she's been a big help, and hangs up, tells Katie to step aside.

In less than a minute, they're looking at a red dot on a map.

"What's that?" Katie asks.

"That's where we're going."

Katie takes a closer look, realizes they're staring at a spot in northern Jersey.

"That's not west. I thought James said we should go west."

"He did," Beth says, examining the laptop case. "But *I'm* saying we're gonna follow the dot. 'Cause that's where James is."

"And Kyle," Katie says, suddenly totally on board.

"Is there a car adaptor in here somewhere?"

Katie shrugs like she's just been asked to solve a Rubik's Cube.

"Forget it. We'll make do." Beth looks around the room, as if suddenly remembering where she is. "You wanna leave a note for your parents or something?"

Katie swats the suggestion away with the back of her hand. "They're in the islands. St. Martin, St. Thomas, one of the saints."

With a shrug, Beth tucks the laptop beneath her arm and ushers Katie out of the room.

Some kind of life, Little Miss Mansion.
Some kind of life.

Twenty-Seven
A Very Special Guest

Don Anthony Pugliese is so enjoying spending time with the young woman across his desk that it is with great reluctance he checks the call ID when his phone rings. But when he sees Dom's number on the screen, he realizes that's *exactly* the person he wants to speak with.

Sometimes, God truly does smile upon the wicked.

He rocks back in his tall plush office chair and picks up. "Dominic," he practically sings into the phone. "My boy. Been a couple days. How are things progressing?"

The don clenches his teeth as Dominic lets loose, tells him everything.

Little Nicky.

Lacy and her partner.

How James and his kid, the two girls from the kitchen, are all in the wind.

And, of course, Angelo. Dom works his way up to that one, knowing it's gonna break his old man's heart.

Don Anthony can't believe it. A standup guy who worked for him since they were Dominic's age, and some fucking cheerleader put him in the ground.

But the don brushes that aside. It's a skill you learn fast if you're gonna run a family like the Pugliese. Compartmentalizing. 'Cause he can't deal with the shit explosion Nicky Sorrentino, Jr. set in motion if he's preoccupied mourning the loss of an old friend.

"Well." He says it almost as a test of his voice. A quick diagnostic that reveals none of the weight sorrow would place upon a weaker man's vocal cords. "Sounds like you've got a lot of work to do."

"Dad, how am I supposed to make this right? It's gone too far. We should just cut our losses, cover our tracks. Be done with the whole Worthington thing."

It's what the kid's been saying since the first time Pedals' name came up.

Christ, has his son always been such a pussy?

Wanting a college education is one thing. Makes you smarter, adds a layer of legitimacy atop the smear of corruption. But that's kid stuff. Eventually, you gotta grow up.

And Don Anthony's boy will be a man by the end of this.

Or he'll be dead.

As far as the don's concerned, those are the only honorable options.

"It's funny you called when you did, Dom." Don Anthony shifts unexpectedly into a cool, casual tone. "I got somebody here with me you're probably gonna want to talk to."

The don hands Maria the phone, watches her nervously answer Dom's questions.

"I'm OK…They haven't hurt me…I only came 'cause I was looking for you, but then—"

Don Anthony grabs the receiver, sardonically appalled by his son's concerns. "Dominic, you think I would snatch your girlfriend, an innocent, off the street? Threaten her? Hurt her? Jesus, there's disrespect and then there's…this. You're breakin' my heart over here. Like she told you, Maria came here on her own. Said she missed you, hadn't been able to get you on the phone. Apparently, that's highly unusual."

He turns to Maria, doesn't cover the receiver, makes sure Dom can hear the question he asks. "What was it you said? You've never gone a whole day without hearing each other's voice?"

Pissed, but too terrified to do anything more, Maria nods bluntly.

"Yeah," the don's back on the line, "she told me your secret to a healthy relationship. Make sure you talk at least once a day. No matter where you might be or what's going on. Even if she's flashin' her can across Europe on one of those modeling gigs. Really sweet, kid. Really sweet."

"I swear to God, Dad, if you touch her—"

"Oh!" his old man bellows. "What did I just say? Hell, I even offered to let her stay here for a while. You know, until you get back."

The message in the don's voice is clear. You hold the contract on Jimmy Pedals, I hold your girlfriend until he's dead.

"No." Dom struggles against his own quavering voice. "She walks out of there. Now. You let her go, I'll do what you want."

"I don't know, Dom. I don't like these words you're using. 'Let her go'? Like I'm holding her against her will? And I'm not sure you're clear on what I want you to do."

"Angelo told me."

"What did he tell you?"

"You son of a bitch—"

"Watch the way you talk to your father!"

"Fuck you, Dad. You didn't send me out here to be the brains, you gave me the button on Jimmy Pedals. Me specifically. Your own son, and you couldn't even tell me the whole truth."

"What did you think you were gonna do out there? You'd tag along and Angelo would do all the dirty work? You're better than that, Dominic. You have to be. Time to live up to your name. There's only one path for you. I'm sure if I took the time to explain it to her, Maria would agree."

Hearing only half the conversation, Maria isn't sure what it is she would agree with, but reading the old man's lurid eyes, she knows it'd be prudent not to ask.

Just as Dom knows it would be the greatest mistake of his life to refuse his father now.

"Soon as she leaves," he tells the don, "I'll take care of it."

"Tell me where you are. I'll send a couple guys to help out."

"I wanna hear the door closing behind her."

The don grits his teeth. It's like battery acid on his tongue to be ordered around this way. Shrugging at Maria, he tells her if she doesn't want to stay, he won't twist her arm. As quickly as age will allow, he rises, takes her by the wrist, leads her out of the office.

"Let me talk to Dom," Maria says.

More orders. It's all the don can do not to break her neck. "He said he'll call you later."

"Put him on." She plants her feet in the doorway so the don would have to physically drag her through the arch.

He places the cell to her ear, wishing he could just bounce it against her fucking skull.

"Dom?"

"Go ahead Maria, walk through the door." Dom puts as much iron in his voice as he can muster under the circumstances. "It's OK. I'm fine. Just something I gotta do so we can put this all behind us."

Voice aquiver, she asks, "What? What is it you have to do? Dom, where are you? What's going—"

The don yanks the phone back and pushes her onto the front stoop.

"You hear that?" he asks, slamming the door behind her.

Dom releases a breath he wasn't aware he'd been holding. "I'll call you once I get a lead on Worthington."

"You make sure you do that, Dom. And son, don't forget: your father loves you. So does Maria."

Once again, message received: Just 'cause she ain't in the house, doesn't mean they won't have eyes on her.

The line goes dead, and Dom stares through the windshield. Phone still clutched in his fist, he punches the Mustang's steering wheel, his hands shaking.

There's no way around it now. He's got to kill James Worthington. Gotta take his life to save Maria's. And after that, he'll inherit the family. No escaping his father. No escaping his blood.

He's on the verge of throwing up when the Jetta from Worthington's driveway shoots past him. The two girls from the kitchen cruising by in a serious hurry.

Twenty-Eight
The Privilege of Driving

Kyle's slumped against the passenger door of the Olds on some ill-marked road-less-traveled. He's snoring into his own shoulder, a replay of Sunday night's main event with Katie showing inside his head.

When James taps the brake and eases the car off the exit ramp, he notices the frown as the kid sits up. If he knew what Kyle was dreaming about, he'd understand. As it is, he assumes the kid's just dreading the rest of their journey.

God he's kept his boy sheltered.

"Are we almost in Mexico?"

Kid's seen too many movies.

"Mexico's where you go if you're running from cops," James says. "This is Ohio."

"What time is it?"

"Three."

"*A.M.?*"

"No rest for the wicked."

"Are we going to a hotel?"

"Can't crash yet. Not enough distance between us and New York."

"Why are we stopping?"

"We need gas, and I'm starving. Been driving for close to eight hours."

They find a small diner a few miles from the access road, one of those places that did great business half a century ago before interstates became the country's vehicular circulatory system. When the road out front was the only way for travelers to head west through Ohio on a cross-country trek.

Now, truckers stick to the highways.

And any footloose American with a bug to see the country probably wouldn't drive. In this economy, it's cheaper to spring for the bus ticket than the gas.

Thus the place is little more than a shining silver anachronism. Long and thin like a train car, front counter with a dozen stools against one wall, string of booths lining the other. Nothing in between but a space barely wide enough for two men to pass abreast. Matter of fact, James—not a stocky or well-built dude by any means—has to turn sideways to pass one of the only two patrons in the place. They both occupy stools, quietly nurse plates of eggs with a variety of meat on the side. Locals, if James were to judge by the rusted out pickup trucks parked out front.

After he ushers his son into the booth, he takes his time removing his jacket, checking around the place once more before he tosses the coat on the seat and heads off to the bathroom. Making sure he's alone, he removes his shirt before the mirror. Winces as he peels the bandages on his front and back. The stitches are red and raw. There's no obvious sign of infection, but James knows he's gonna need some serious pain meds come morning. The four Ibuprofen he popped in the car are only doing so much.

Despite his concerns, he keeps his time in the restroom brief.

Which turns out to be an especially good thing.

'Cause when he returns to the table he finds Kyle holding James' cell phone, getting ready to send a text. The kid's so engrossed in the activity, he doesn't see his old man walking back from the can until James is right on top of him, snatching the cell from his hand.

"Me throwing your phone out the window wasn't clear enough?"

Kyle huffs indignantly. "How come you get to call Beth but I can't call Katie?"

"That was one time, to warn her. I owed her at least that much."

"I just want to make sure she's all right."

"She's fine." James sinks into the seat opposite his son. The car-worn muscles of his legs and lower back practically cry out in relief, and an abrupt drowsiness sets in.

"How do you know that?"

"She got out of Gower with Beth. They'll be fine for now."

"But you don't *know* she's fine."

James doesn't. But pondering the conditions their girlfriends may or may not currently be in can only lead to two things: absolute helpless panic or a desire to do something stupid. Like turn around and go after them. Which would get them all killed real quick.

"You order yet?"

"Waitress said she'd be back."

When she appears, James orders three eggs, toast, bacon, a short stack on the side.

Kyle orders a bowl of cereal.

"Eat something," his father tells him.

"I'm not hungry."

On the run like this, it could be a lifetime before they get some decent food in their stomachs again. Because he can't explain that with the waitress hovering behind her little pad, James just adds a plate of blueberry pancakes and sausage to their order, tops it all off with two glasses of orange juice.

He'll force it down the kid's throat if he has to.

Kyle's stubbornly quiet after that. Like his father's grounded him for getting a *D* on a Science test.

When the food comes, James makes it halfway through his eggs before Kyle starts poking at his pancakes.

"Eat," James says. "You'll need it."

Though it looks at first like Kyle might put his fork down just to spite him, he slowly starts to shovel hunks of purple-stained pancake into his mouth. Until their plates are clean, the only sound at their booth is the clank and scrape of utensils.

James knows they should move on immediately, but the ages-old booth is like heaven for his ass. Fashioned back when things were still made with care and attention to detail. When the food is gone, they just stare at each other over nearly-empty glasses of O.J.

James feels his eyelids drooping. But they spring wide when Kyle suggests, "How 'bout you let me drive a shift."

"No way."

"Why not?"

"For starters, you're not a legal driver."

"You're seriously gonna lecture me about the law?"

James gives his son a hard look.

"Fine," Kyle grumbles. "I can't use the phone, I can't drive. What *can* I do?"

Kid's just whining because he's a kid—an immature, entitled kid whose life has thus far left him with no concept of the hardness of this world—but he has accidentally stumbled upon a relatively valid point.

All the growing up he should have done in his sixteen years, he's gonna have to do now. And that ain't gonna happen if James continues to treat him like a child.

Still, it's the 442 they're talking about.

James is literally the only person who's ever driven it since he rebuilt her in the '80s.

"Here." James digs a folded map of Ohio out of his jacket pocket, tosses it to his boy. "Navigate."

"Wow." Kyle lets it sit on the table. "Thanks."

Too tired to argue, James pretends not to notice.

After three or four minutes of silent pouting, Kyle admits, "I was thinking about Lacy again while you were taking a leak. That's why I wanted to call Katie. To talk."

James nods, sips his orange juice. Remembering he's the reason Lacy and Kelly are dead, it goes down bitter. He should have split town as soon as he woke up in that hospital, but he was too hopelessly in love with his life in Gower. Instead, he closed his eyes, hoped the whole thing would somehow blow over. Careless. Stupid.

And now two kind and innocent women are dead because he was selfish.

When he gets no response, Kyle flips the map listlessly open, asks his father where they're headed. Shaking his weary head, James says he doesn't know. Just west for now.

"West?" Kyle asks. "That's it?"

"Another day or so on the road, then we'll reevaluate the situation."

"Then what?"

"Took them twenty years to find me in PA. We head farther into the heart of the country, by the time they track me down, all they're gonna find is a tombstone. The words 'Happy' and 'Grandfather' etched in stone."

"You think we're just gonna settle down somewhere, like some kind of do-over? What about your store? What about Beth? What about…Katie?"

James doesn't see any other choice. Besides, he's done it before.

Of course, he was totally and completely unattached back then. No Beth, no Kyle, no job. Nothing more than an accident of birth tying him to the city. And he was a lot younger to boot.

James watches Kyle tense up, take deep breaths like there's something heavy sitting on his chest. Clearly, the mere thought of moving on—away from his hometown, his school, his friends, Katie—devastates him. James wants to tell him it's OK to be scared. That he, James, is scared too. That laying down stakes in a new town, leaving the only life you've ever known, was the hardest thing he'd ever had to do until he was forced to leave Gower. James knows it's what Kyle wants to hear. A little support, a little sympathy.

But Jimmy Pedals knows more coddling is the last thing the kid needs.

He rises, slips into his jacket, tosses a few bills on the table. Walks outside and waits for his son to join him. All the while thinking.

It takes another minute or two, but Kyle finally zips his jacket and drifts out into the cold to stand beside his father in the parking lot. James studies his face.

Sees the fear for sure.

But maybe some strength there too.

Could be it's just wishful thinking on James' part.

Either way…

James stuffs his hand in his pocket, tosses a jangle of keys to his boy.

Kyle plucks them from the air, studies his father with a furrowed brow.

"You drive. I'm fucking exhausted."

James sinks down beside his son, eases the passenger seat back and tells him to stick to the speed limit. "Stay off the highway from here on out. State roads, two-lane blacktop. And for the last time, no phone, OK?"

Still amazed his father's relented and put him in the driver's seat, Kyle nods.

And James leaves their fate in the kid's hands.

Falls asleep figuring it's fifty-fifty odds Kyle finds some way to get them both killed.

Twenty-Nine
Waiting, Watching

When their server places three plates in front of Katie—eggs, French toast with strawberries, biscuits and gravy, grits, two orders of bacon—Beth snarls silently behind her egg whites and mixed fruit.

"Oh my God," Katie mumbles, half-chewed wad of powdered starch tucked inside her cheek. "They're all the way in Ohio."

When Beth doesn't respond, Katie looks up from the laptop, reads the disgusted expression Beth can't hide. Not that she's trying. It screams, *Seriously, you killed a man less than twelve hours ago, and you still have the appetite of a rhinoceros.*

"I eat when I'm nervous," Katie explains indignantly. "How are those egg whites?"

"It's all gonna go to your hips," Beth mumbles. "Sooner or later."

"Goddamn bitch," Katie mumbles right back.

"What did you say?"

With just enough force to produce a good, solid *clang*, Katie rests the fork and knife on her plate. "I said you're such a goddamn bitch to me. All the time. With all your 'Little Miss Mansion' crap—"

"How'd you know we call you that?"

"Oh, *please*. Look, I didn't choose my parents, and I didn't choose my house or any—"

"Gimme a break." Like the suggestion of money being at the heart of Beth's disdain is absurd.

Katie raises her eyebrows. Isn't that what this is about? Isn't it, really?

And, of course, it is. Not that Beth will admit it. Not in a million years. "Forget it. You're just a kid. This is above your head."

"Above my head. That's funny. I seem to remember the only reason you still *have* a head is because I left a bullet where that fat guido's prick used to be."

"I was doing fine before you stepped in."

"Really?" Katie laughs. "With your plunger?"

Beth's leaning halfway across the table, jabbing an index finger at Katie, when she opens her mouth and realizes she's got nothing to say.

You can't really argue that a plunger could have resolved that situation.

"Let me see that." Beth yanks the laptop out from under Katie's fingertips, spins it around to get a look.

Katie's head shakes and her eyes roll, but she says nothing and turns back to her grand feast.

"They should only be a few hours ahead of us," Beth tells the screen. "How'd they get so far?"

Fork loaded, suspended midway between her plate and her gaping mouth, Katie reminds Beth they're following a late-sixties muscle car in an early 21st century Jetta. Souped up and decked out as it is—everything top of the line, every last gimmick and gadget from cruise control to satellite radio—there's no way her car can keep pace with a Detroit classic.

"James drives like my grandmother," Beth says. "And she's been dead since '02."

"You don't think he might be driving a little faster than usual? 'Cause he's, like, running for his life?" Katie looks at her like she's never seen a dumber human being in her whole life.

Beth glares a challenge right back at her. Like, seriously, I'm *that* stupid? You head the cheering squad. Surely, you've seen grander stupidity than this.

But Beth opts not to debate the point. Instead, she considers the fact that James is in Ohio.

Where the hell is he going?

*   *   *

Dom's parked across the lot of the service plaza, watching the red Jetta, grimacing his way through an Egg McMuffin behind the wheel of his Mustang. He's been going, going, going for something like eight hours. This is the first time he's stopped for anything more than a five-minute fill-up.

The girls are probably enjoying the works inside the rest stop diner. But since they've seen his face, he can't very well waltz in and grab a booth beside them. Be like, what's up ladies, you eat here too?

This whole ride, he's been worrying over what to do about the girls. Maria, too. She's smart, knows what's at stake, the kinds of people she's dealing with. But she's outnumbered by hardened professionals, hardened *criminals*. They'll be on her 'round the clock. She's a tough cookie, but against those odds?

If Dom doesn't finish this job, get it done right—get it done *completely*—they'll pick her up again, do more than threaten her this time.

That means James, his boy…the girls…

What was it his father wanted? For him to know what it's like making hard choices?

Mission accomplished, Dad.

Exhausted, Dom grinds the back of his harried skull into the headrest. And while he's not looking, a glob of powder-mix egg—the fast food take-out *garbage* he's stuck eating because of the two chicks currently enjoying a nice filling breakfast of actual food—finds an open space between his legs and the grease-soaked wrapper, drips heavily onto the leather seat beneath his crotch.

Dom hears its *plop-pop* and shuffles through the food and paper. Sees a yellow eyeball of faux-egg staring up at him.

If he were home, he'd be eating bagels and lox, maybe some melon and prosciutto. But instead, thanks to Beth and Katie, now he's gotta add getting his car cleaned to his list of worries.

Who knows? By the end of all this, he might be *eager* to kill those two bitches.

*   *   *

In terms of Maria's current situation, Dom was right. Sort of.

She's being watched all right—a continuous cycle of tan goons in conspicuous black suits sitting inside a dark Lincoln parked across the street from the condo at all hours.

But she's watching them right back.

She caught enough of the phone conversation the don had with his son to know Dom's being forced to complete a job that will forever change him just so the two of them can be together again. Something that will muddy his soul, reduce him to one of the blank, empty animals that works for his father.

Unless Maria can do something about it.

But since the don—who pays the bills for their high-rise—has probably tapped the phones, Maria can't call Dom up, make flight arrangements to some far away place. Her cell's probably safe, but she isn't willing to chance his father intercepting the details.

Best she can do is peer through the window, assess each new watchman as they rotate their way around the clock, and try to sniff out their weaknesses.

Do the shift changes occur at the same times every day?

Which soldier appears least professional, less dedicated than the others?

Do they always park in the exact same spot?

Any of them favor an afternoon nap?

Though she's new to surveillance, Maria takes to it like a lion to a wounded zebra—fucking devours it. For the first time in her life, the tremendous amount of downtime afforded her by her modeling is an absolute blessing. In the past, she'd always found herself going stir crazy if she was between gigs for longer than a week. Now, she's grateful for the extra time she can devote to that window, trying to flip the situation, turn the stalkers into the stalked, the sharks into the minnow.

Watch a little TV, check on the black Lincoln. Make a trip to the laundry on the third floor, check on the black Lincoln. Walk four blocks to the grocery, check the black Lincoln on the way out and the way back.

Sooner or later, one of her admirers is gonna fuck up.

'Cause it's only been two days, and already they're getting a little sloppy.

They sit for five, six hours a clip, waiting, watching, struggling to stave off boredom, huddling under blankets and heavy coats to keep warm because they can't very well run the engine and crank out the heat the whole time they're parked. They get out, stroll to the coffee stand on the corner, looking over their shoulders the whole time, pound java for warmth without realizing the caffeine is gonna jack them up, make sitting even more tedious and unbearable. Call their girlfriends or their buddies or their mothers (seriously, walking to the store, she actually hears one saying, "No, Ma, I don't know when I'll be home for dinner. I'm working."), fiddle with the radio. Anything to pass the time until the next black Lincoln rolls in and she sees their faces glow with jubilant relief.

Eventually, one of them's gonna crack. Go off looking for some place to take a piss, leave an opening for her to slip away. Or she'll overhear him talking about Dom as she walks past to do her shopping, find out where he is, sneak off after him. Whisk him away to Europe before he's scarred irreparably by his own actions.

All she has to do is wait them out.

And in the meantime, she thinks about Dom. What he's being forced to do, what will happen to him if he can't go through with it. What will become of him if he can. She keeps coming back to their conversation from the other day—God, how it feels like a lifetime ago—how Dom took such an interest in the first time they met. His wondering how she was able to just roll with the punches when her pervert photographer had her canned for refusing to suck him off.

The answer is simple, really. She had Dom.

They had her sprawled out on an Irish hillside, pouting as sexy as she could with the lush green grass chafing her bare flesh. Nothing between her and the camera but her arms wrapped around her breasts.

And suddenly, there he was. Some grungy college kid hiking the mountains, no clue where the fuck he was. She couldn't be sure, but she thought the best shot of that day—the one where her expression found the ideal combination of pensive and confident—was taken right at the moment he caught her eye.

But before she could ask for a break and find out more about him, the photographer called for a new setup, and the crew popped out of the bushes, frantically producing props and testing the natural light while two magazine executives in expensive suits reviewed the shots. Maria's assistant threw a towel over her shoulders and hustled her off behind some makeshift divider.

She lost the gig later that night and that was when Dom appeared for the second time, the two of them crashing at the same hostel. As crushed as she'd been, her fascination with the young man who'd appeared like an apparition out of nowhere on that hillside became all she could focus on.

"You gotta be kidding me," he said as they sat down for drinks. "They clear an entire landscape for you and then they give you the boot?

"It's just as well," she tried to sound as though she was over it. "That whole back-to-nature thing's a million years old."

Dom's face dropped like an anchor. "Most beautiful sight I've ever seen."

So getting over her sudden dismissal from the spotlight proved easy. Dom helped her through.

His own moment in the spotlight looming, she only wishes she can return the favor.

But for now, she'll have to wait for that.

And watch.

Thirty
The Night Chicago Died

"We're really gonna let this fucking guy drop the flag?" some leisure suit-clad, *Miami Vice*-wannabe in the stands blurts out. "Where's the brunette with the big tits?"

The driver of the Camaro grins around the toothpick between his teeth, raises his sunglasses, and eyeballs the stacked broad beside him. She may have been dropping the flag last week, but this week she's his. As they say, winner truly does take all.

"Yeah, sit down ya fag!" another voice chimes in.

Jimmy watches from behind the wheel of the 442 as Sonny takes an exaggerated bow—his flowered shirt and shoulder length hair dangling dangerously close to the tarmac of the ancient airstrip—before running full speed toward the bleachers and diving over the fence to shower his hecklers with a flurry of wild blows.

Nervous as Pedals is about the 442's first big run, he can't contain a trill of laughter.

Fuckin' Sonny.

The guy in the Camaro takes his eyes off his woman, revs the engine impatiently as he turns a stony look on the quarter-mile before him. As if nothing exists now but the swatch of white spray paint at the far end.

Another driver—a guy who's not running until later that night—pops out from under the hood of his Thunderbird with a greasy rag and stands between the two cars, hands held high.

Jimmy clears his throat, feels a rush of blood through his temples as his pulse swells and the small world around him—the dashboard, the strip, the Camaro, Sonny in the stands—blurs like streaks on glass. Catching his breath, the horizon becomes clear, the last of the evening sun setting over the Jersey shore in an explosion of bruised purple.

Then the grease monkey's arms fall, and the rag hits the pavement.

The only thing Jimmy remembers after that is the Camaro in the farthest reaches of his sideview mirror as he hits second gear. Next thing he knows he's laying on the brakes, tires smoking and squealing at the finish line, the Camaro barely past the halfway mark.

And Sonny's double-timing it down the stretch, pumping his fists, jumping up and down in triumph, Hawaiian shirt flapping open at his sides. The broad with the big tits is screaming and cursing at the dude in the Camaro, embarrassed to be seen with the loser of the night's very first heat. For his part, the driver's dumbfounded, keeps flapping his gums but doesn't know what to say about how he just got his ass handed to him by some rookie none of them have ever seen before.

Sonny catches up with the 442 just as the girl slams the Camaro door and runs off. He's got his arms spread for a colossal hug, screaming, "You did it, Jimmy! You fucking did it!"

Jimmy's grinning big for a shy kid, and he's all about the love, throwing his arms open to receive the only friend this life's ever allowed him.

Or at least he's trying to.

Seems his arms have taken on a life of their own. As if looking down at another man's body, Jimmy sees his right hand raising a revolver in Sonny's direction. No matter what he tells his brain, he can't stop that hand from coming up, cocking the hammer.

Sonny's wearing an expression of utter confusion.

Jimmy's screaming, "No!"

But his finger pulls the trigger.

*   *   *

James awakens to the sound of some white-trash hippo shouting at her kids in an endless parking lot. Through bloodshot eyes, he sees her stomp past, pushing a cart to which three of her progeny cling, cursing them, their father, Obama, anyone she believes had a hand in reducing her life to the "shit mountain" it's become.

James is pretty sure she should add Entenmann's to the list.

He arches a stretch. Muscles loosen from his calves to his wrists, and he becomes aware of a nagging ache in his lower back he owes to four hours spent napping awkwardly in the passenger seat of the 442.

The passenger seat.

James stops in mid-stretch and stares at the vacant leather beside him, as if doing so will make his boy suddenly materialize out of thin air. Birdlike, his head swivels on his neck, probing the parking lot, craning forward in his seat like the extra six inches will help him see an extra mile or two in front of the car.

Just as his heart falls into his stomach and panic stunts his breath, he spies Kyle walking toward him.

"Rise and shine," the boy says, appearing beside the open window on the driver's side. He's got two tall coffees in Styrofoam cups, and he reaches one through to his father.

Frantically, James searches the car for a cup holder he knows he won't find—not in a '68—as he takes the cup in both hands. "Stay out there," James says.

Watching his father cradle his coffee as delicately as a newborn as he pops open his door and steps onto the blacktop, Kyle tells his old man to relax—he got lids because he knows how anal James is about the Olds.

"These seats were in the frame of this car when it left the factory line," he explains for the hundredth time. "Forgive me if I have no faith in a thin plastic lid."

"We're in Indiana, on the run from the mob," Kyle mutters, "but, you're right, we should be worried about your factory seats."

"Don't be a smartass."

They stand, the car between them, resting their cups on the roof between sips. Looking around, James sees they're in the middle of a busy shopping center in the early afternoon.

"You said we're in Indiana now?"

Kyle nods behind his coffee. "Had to go to the bathroom, saw a Wal-Mart. You ever notice you go into any Wal-Mart you feel like you're home? You know, they're all set up pretty much the same. Once you're inside, no matter where you are, you can sort of pretend you're in *your* Wal-Mart."

James is pretty sure he doesn't have a Wal-Mart.

"I mean, I didn't even know they had Wal-Marts in Indiana," Kyle adds.

"They're like cancer," James muses. "Once they took hold, they started popping up everywhere. What city are we in?"

"Saw a sign said we were fifty miles from South Bend?"

"You didn't happen to notice one that told us where we are *now*, did you?"

Kyle shrugs. "Isn't South Bend where Notre Dame is?"

As if that clarifies their location.

James grabs the road atlas and spreads it across the hood, drinking coffee and squinting at the red and blue arteries crisscrossing Indiana.

"What road are we on?"

"Still on 20."

At least he knows that much.

Kyle watches his father trace a finger across the page, shake his head. No "Thanks for the coffee" or "Appreciate you driving for a while." And really, how big an inconvenience is it that they have to check the map? They've been moving endlessly for two days. Kyle's pretty sure they can spare a minute or two for navigation and coffee.

James can feel his son's frustration—you live with a teenager long enough, you develop a sixth sense for their hormonal ups and downs—but looking up from the map, he sees a bemused grin rather than a stubborn pout.

An expression more "My father's a drama queen" than "Why are you being so mean?"

Maybe it did him some good to drive for a while.

"We just crossed Old 27," Kyle tells him.

"Why didn't you say so?" James taps the map with his finger. "Here"—his forehead forms a tight knot, his voice sounding distant now—"We're in Angola."

"What is it?"

"Nothing," James says absently. "How'd she run?"

"Makes the Accord feel like a tricycle."

"That mean you were speeding?"

"Kept it to fifty-five."

James turns from the map, eyeballs his boy.

"Maybe sixty. Really though, Pop, you've driven the Accord." The name sputters across Kyle's lips like he's spitting out a piece of rotten fruit. "There's a world of difference between the two."

"Can't argue with you there."

Turning back to the hood, James gives the map a muted "Hmm."

"Pop, what is it?"

"Nothing. It's just Angola sounds familiar. Like I've been there before."

Except when the hell would he have been in Angola?

Aside from the Jersey shore, he hasn't been more than forty miles from his home the entire time he's lived in Gower. Before that, if he wasn't racing the 442 or pulling a job, he never left New York. Even the racing circuit was an east coast thing. Maine to Florida. Up and down, not right to left. The only time James can remember *ever* driving east of the city was when he had work for Chicago…

Giving the atlas another look, it starts to come back to him. Indiana, Angola, route 20. He remembers returning home after pulling a job for the Genuardi family, the thought of abandoning the open plains for the concrete jungle of New York resting like a jagged pebble in his brain. Recalls stopping for three nights at a Days Inn.

In Angola.

Turning back a page, he finds Illinois and pokes a finger into the city.

Somewhere far away, Kyle's asking his father what's going on.

James doesn't answer. He's nodding, thinking about Chicago. About the Genuardi family. What little history he has with them is ancient now, probably long forgotten. But it's still a history.

And one thing he's learned from working with Italians, a guinea never forgets.

Asking the Genuardi for help is so obvious, James can't believe he didn't think of it earlier. Probably because the last thing he wanted was to invite more gangsters to the party. Besides, the odds are long against the Genuardi lending a hand. In fact, there's a better than average chance Chicago will opt to simply kill James and Kyle rather than get dragged into a tug-of-war with New York.

But the only other option is the one he suggested to Kyle yesterday: picking up and starting a new life some place neither of them has ever heard of, away from everything and everyone they've ever loved. So if there's even the slimmest of chances he can have his old life back—that he can have *Beth* back—and keep his son safe, he's got to take it.

Of course, If James is fixing to put the two of them in the crosshairs, Kyle should get some say in it.

"I think I found someplace for us to go. It'll be dangerous. More dangerous than what we're doing now. But if it works, we can go back to Gower."

"What's this place?" The words race one another across Kyle's lips.

"Chicago."

"What's in Chicago?"

"Help. Maybe. Or, just more guys with guns. What do you think, you wanna roll the dice? We'll either end up pulling our asses out of the fryer or diving headlong into the flame."

A gray cloud fills Kyle's chest. The thought of steering the 442 *toward* trouble when they could just keep driving and put as much distance between themselves and the fuckers who killed Lacy and shot his old man twists him with shuddery conflict.

Like most American teenagers, Kyle's always wanted his life to be more like the movies. In the movies, a hero offered options like these would smile tough, utter some cocksure catchphrase he seemingly pulls out of thin air spur of the moment.

But now that Kyle's facing a critical decision that requires a big set of balls, he feels a shaky urge to crawl back into the 442 and hide until the storm blows over.

"How?" he asks meekly. "What are we gonna do? Who's gonna help us?"

James opts not to sugarcoat. Talks to his boy like he would a grown man with whom he's about to enter a battlefield. "I can explain a little on the way. But I won't lie to you. These people I have in mind, they're either gonna help us or kill us. And yeah, we could forget all about this option. Find some isolated corner of the world, spend the rest of our lives checking over our shoulders. I can wonder what became of Beth while you wonder after Katie. We'd probably be safe. We'd have our lives. But I don't think it would be much of a life."

James wades through Kyle' silence, knows pushing him now would be a mistake.

"Or maybe we die…trying to live," Kyle says.

"There is also the chance that our gamble actually pays off and we get to go home."

Kyle nods slowly. Though his heart's playing speed-metal percussion beneath his ribs, he forces that movie-character smile, realizing this is the moment for the cool catchphrase.

He knocks on the roof of the 442 with tremulous knuckles. "OK. But if we come through this all right, you're buying me one of these."

As the line settles on the air, Kyle decides it's not too shabby. He wouldn't put it up there with "I'll be back," but his voice was steady enough despite the nerves.

"We survive this," his father tells him, "I'll give you this one. God knows I don't ever wanna see the fuckin' thing again."

Damn, Kyle thinks.

His line was way cooler than mine.

And way more obscene than pretty much anything else he's ever heard his father say.

Kyle wonders, not for the first time in the last few days, who exactly he's sharing this car with.

'Cause James Worthington he is not.

Thirty-One
The Way You Look at Me

Five minutes later, Kyle's pushing a cart through the sporting goods section of Wal-Mart, following as his father scans the shelves.

Somehow, when they settled on a plan, Kyle kind of thought there'd be a bit more adrenaline in their next step. Maybe crank up some hard rock, peel out of the parking lot. Maybe load shotguns, rack the slides in slow motion.

The squeak of the wheels beneath the cart proves a piss-poor substitute.

And Kyle's pretty sure Clint Eastwood never asked a clerk in a Wal-Mart where he could find the men's room.

"What do you want?" James grumbles when Kyle rolls his eyes. "I gotta take a piss."

Bodily functions in check, they stand before a variety of tents and sleeping bags.

"Pop, what does any of this stuff have to do with Chicago?"

"We wanna do this right," James explains. "Don't wanna pull into town exhausted, make any stupid mistakes that could get us killed."

"So?"

"So I don't know about you, but if I have to pass another night sleeping in the Olds, I'm gonna kill somebody. And not in a way that's gonna help us."

"Sure, camping's much better for your back."

"If we're gonna stop, we gotta do it safe. No hotels."

"Pop, you said yourself it took them twenty years to find you in Pennsylvania. We're in Indiana now. It's gotta be like a foreign country to them. I mean, I grew up in the woods, and this place is too country for me."

"Chicago's a big enough risk as it is. We play it as safe as possible until we get there."

"All right, all right. Let's get the one on the end."

"We're not buying a tent. Just sleeping bags."

"This gets better by the second." Kyle laughs. "Let's at least buy a tarp. Bad enough I'm gonna freeze my ass off, I'd hate to get rained or snowed on."

A surprisingly astute point from a kid he's never taken camping.

"Good idea," James says. "We can grab some rope, tie it to the trees like a lean-to."

"See. I'm not a total idiot."

"I never said you were."

"You look at me like I am." Kyle reads the price tags beneath the sleeping bags, talks directly to the stickers. "Sometimes, you look at me like you can't believe I'm actually your son. Like I would try the patience of a saint."

"I do not. You're just being dramatic."

"If you say so."

James exhales heavily. "Go to the next aisle, grab us a tarp, OK?"

When Kyle returns, James takes a look at the massive swatch of blue he's procured. And his face turns painfully dour.

"Twenty-by-Twenty? Why don't we just sleep under a giant flag with our family crest printed on it?"

"Right," Kyle says, grinning. "You never look at me like I'm a moron."

James' lips work to form sentences but emit only incoherent sounds.

Once the cart is loaded with the few camping supplies they need—starter log, rope, thermal underwear, sleeping bags—James surprises Kyle by stopping the cart at the end of the aisle.

In front of the gun counter.

James asks for two boxes of .38 caliber cartridges, looks them over, then requests a third—just in case. The cashier rings him up and places the ammunition in a plastic bag that James adds to the cart. He looks at his son expecting questions, but Kyle just nods as if the purchase makes perfect sense.

In the grocery section, they search for anything that can be warmed over a campfire, come away with hotdogs and a bag of buns. Then James grabs a six pack by the plastic rings, drops it into the cart where Kyle looks at it like his old man just plucked a box of tampons off the shelf.

"Steady our nerves by the campfire," James explains.

"Our?"

His father shrugs. "Keep us warm sleeping outside. Besides, I'd feel guilty drinking it in front of you, all we been through, what we've got planned. I'd say you've earned a couple of brews."

"Wow, Pop, who *are* you?"

"Been asking myself the same thing these past couple days."

Thirty-Two
Double Action

"What time you got?" James asks Kyle.

Since everything in the car is vintage, there's no clock on the dash. There is, of course, the anachronistic splinter of the CD player, but it's such an early model it apparently can't tell time.

Kyle pulls a hand off the wheel, reads 3:30 on his watch. James leans toward the windshield, peers at the sky, gone dark from passing clouds and descending sun, tells his boy they should start looking for a place to stop for the night. Punching a thumb behind them, Kyle reminds his old man of the campground they passed a few miles back.

Though it's a logical suggestion, James tells his boy that would be a good place to get killed. Careful, of course, to control any reflexive facial ticks that might send the unintended message that he thinks his son is stupid. "We need something less obvious."

Kyle's pretty sure a campground (not a hotel) on a state road (not an interstate) when you're running from the New York mob (in Indiana) doesn't qualify as obvious. But he obliges his father, says nothing.

When they pass an old farmhouse on the driver's side—beautiful place, white siding, wraparound porch—James asks Kyle for the odometer reading.

"Thirty-two thousand—"

"Just the last digit."

Squinting through the wheel, Kyle reads the number.

"Good. Keep driving."

Fifteen minutes roll by, during which they pass nary a landmark amid fallow crop fields. "What's the number now?" James asks as they spot a second house on Kyle's side.

"Six."

Eight miles without passing a single building. Not a house or a gas station.

Not so much as an outhouse.

"OK," Kyle hears his father say. "Pull off and turn around."

Heartened by Kyle's obeisance, James indulges his son with an explanation. Tells him the house they passed first was presumably the start of one farm. Somewhere between the two, that farm gave way to the next, marked off on the west by the second house. Nothing but empty space between, which, given the December temperature and the subsequent uselessness of the fields, will go unchecked for the rest of the season.

And they're only looking to crash for one night.

He directs his boy down a dirt path between two unused crop fields that leads to a dense forest of trees. They drive as far as the car can make it, inching along, bumping their way over rocks and ditches, downed tree branches, until the trees reveal a clearing roughly the size of a bedroom a solid mile-and-a-half from the main road without a soul in shouting distance.

James tells Kyle this'll be *their* bedroom for the evening.

Together, they unfold the glossy blue canvas (15' x 10' as per James' request) and tie it at a steep angle to four trees, high as they can reach at the corners of one side, waist-high on the other. They unpack their sleeping bags and lay them beneath the makeshift lean-to. James scrapes the grass from the frozen ground with the blunt corner of a rock, shaping a circle roughly the size of a tire, while Kyle gathers rocks to form a raised edge.

They're nodding at each other, proud of the finished product, when the cannon blast of a snapped twig erupts behind them. Shoulder to shoulder, they turn, James thrusting a protective arm in front of his boy's chest. Feels Kyle exhale a relieved breath to match his own when a squirrel scurries up a tree.

Then they look at one another sharing silently the acknowledgement that the next time they turn in response to an unexpected sound, they could be dead.

But not if James has anything to say about it. "Anything goes down, you know how to fight?" he asks his son.

Kyle shrugs, confident he can throw a few punches. He is, after all, an athlete.

"Let's see what you got."

Unsure what his father's looking for, Kyle squares up, fists cocked, doing his best to channel Jason Statham in any of the countless movies where Kyle's seen him kick maximum ass.

James shakes his head and starts to turn away, shoulders slumping in disappointment. Offended, Kyle drops his hands, takes a step forward, ready to protest.

Which is when James whips around, swings his leg like a place kicker.

Holds up at the last second, the tip of his shoe an inch from his son's balls.

The best defense Kyle has time to offer is a quick crouch into a standing fetal position. When the impact doesn't come, he looks incredulously at his father, James' foot dangling limply between them.

"If you have to fight," he tells his son emphatically, "you *always* fight dirty. This is survival, not sports. Think of the worst thing that could happen to you in a fight, and you do that very thing to the guy standing in front of you, OK? And never let your guard down. Ever. I don't care if you think you've killed the guy, you still keep your hands up."

"You always said I shouldn't hit someone unless they threw the first punch."

"Yeah, forget all that shit. Works OK out in Happy Land, but in the real world you gotta protect yourself. Shit's about to go down, you hit first and you hit hard."

"Speaking from experience?"

"Not saying I'm proud of it, but all it takes is getting your ass kicked one time, you realize there's no place in a fight for manners."

Then, pulling the .38 from the back of his waistband, James ejects the cylinder, spins it with his free hand, flicks it home.

It's all for effect. So he knows he has his boy's full attention

Sure enough, the kid's eyes become dinner plates.

"Fighting dirty only works if there's a guy standing right in front of you. The guys we got on our tail, they're not usually the type to go *mano-a-mano*. More like shoot from a distance, leave the blood and teeth for the cops to sort out later. Do you have any idea how to use one of these?"

Kyle starts to say yes—again, he's seen it in the movies a thousand times—but then he remembers how quick he was to say he could fight. And how swiftly it was brought to his attention that he could not.

"I have an idea how they work, but I've never fired one."

"All the hunters in Gower, I thought maybe you'd fired a rifle or two in the woods with somebody at some point. OK, we're gonna have to fire a few shots in the woods right here."

On the edge of the clearing, James finds a tree with a split trunk, almost like two separate trees planted one on top of another. Counts fifteen paces back toward their camp, then holds the gun up for Kyle to see.

"This is an old-fashioned gun. You got six shots and no safety. So you gotta be real careful with it. Make every shot count, and make sure you don't fire off any shots when you don't want to. Like when you're tucking it under your belt. Could shoot your dick off. Got it?"

"Don't shoot my dick off, right."

"Here, look." James places his thumb on the hammer, tells his son what he's doing as he levers it back, explains how that sets the gun to fire. "That's option one. Once the hammer is back, it's just a quick, easy trigger pull. That's called single-action. You can only fire one shot that way without pulling the hammer back again."

Kyle watches as James puts pressure on the trigger, thumb still in place, to ease the hammer home.

"Now, you find yourself in a situation—and this would be most situations where you'll be firing a gun—where you have to crank out all six shots in a hurry, you wanna go for double-action. Just keep pulling the trigger. Without the hammer back, you'll have to squeeze harder, but you won't waste time setting the cylinder before each shot. Make sense?"

Kyle nods.

"Good. Let's see what you got."

He hands his son the .38 but quickly remembers the pose Kyle struck when asked to fight and doesn't give him the chance to embarrass himself again. Tells Kyle how to hold the piece, legs bowed, firm but don't lock the knees; dominant hand on the grip, finger on the trigger *guard*, not the trigger until absolutely ready to fire; opposing hand cradled beneath the base of the gun. Level your sights over the barrel.

Then he steps back, tells his son to try a single-action shot first.

Kyle points the gun at the left trunk of the tree, aligns rear sight with front, and pulls back on the hammer, surprised at the tension against his thumb.

There's a *crack* like someone dropped a textbook in the school hallway. A murder of crows ascends through the tangle of barren treetops, adrift on the gun's slowly dissipating echo. Kyle and James hear the bullet whip through leafless tree limbs and dry foliage as smoke taints the air. The bark of the tree remains unscathed.

"That's OK," his father reassures him. "Try double-action now. Fire the shots as close to one another as possible. Your hand and eye will automatically adjust after the first shot. Makes it easier."

Kyle fires the cylinder empty. Five more shots, a second-and-a-half between one and the next. When the gray cloud lifts, he sees a chip in the bark on the outer edge, the skinny tree swaying gently from the impact, and he smiles proudly.

"Hey, I landed one. Not bad, right?"

"Yeah, yeah," James says, taking the gun from his boy. "Real good, sure." He's already filling the chambers with six fresh cartridges.

"Now watch," he tells Kyle, the boy still beaming over winging the tree.

Jimmy sets up exactly as he described it for his son.

Six double-action shots and his half of the split trunk is *crying* bark.

When he's done, Kyle squints through the smoke, thinks of how you poke holes in the flesh of a potato before you bake it. That tree's ready for the oven.

James, shakes the shells loose, pulls another handful from his pocket. "You see what I did? Quick shots. Boom, boom, boom, boom, boom. This time, I don't want you to think. Worst thing you can do when firing a gun. Be safe, do it the way it's supposed to be done, but don't think. You think, you might start to consider the fact there's a man at the far end of the barrel."

"Right." Shouldn't be a problem. The last thing Kyle wants to think about is the silly little notion that, you know, he might have to kill somebody.

Like, tomorrow maybe.

He squeezes the trigger as fast as the tension spring allows. Aims like his old man showed him, doesn't consciously consider where the bullets may or may not be going while he shoots.

Two hits this time. More toward the center of the trunk.

"Better," James says, a lift in his voice that lets Kyle know he's not just placating. "See how the second shot hit closer to the middle? That's your eye readjusting. Means you didn't let your brain get in the way."

Hearing himself describe it that way, James shakes his head, unbelieving.

All these years hammering home the importance of grades and homework, going to college, getting smarter, and now the only advice he has for his son is to stop thinking and let his body do the work.

*   *   *

Tucked into their sleeping bags, bellies full of hot dogs, they lay with the fire between them, propped on elbows, drinking beer. With the flames and the bags, the night is serviceably warm, though the cans are icy cold in their palms.

A small price to pay for the numbing effect of the alcohol.

Kyle notices his father grinding his teeth and patting his stomach wound every time he shifts his weight. "Is it bad?" he asks.

"Well, it certainly ain't good. But I don't think it's infected. Hurts like a bitch, though."

James is aware Kyle's already on his second beer. Watching him for signs of drunkenness—won't do them any good if the boy pulls into Chicago hungover—James slides the remainder of the six pack closer to his body, out of Kyle's reach. Base of his can skyward, sucking down a long pull, Kyle doesn't seem to notice.

He does, however, seem somewhat emboldened by the booze.

"Years ago, when you were driving grandpa's car for the mob—"

"It wasn't your grandfather's car."

"What? But I thought—"

"I never knew my father. From what I was able to piece together later, my mother never knew who he was. She was a junkie, discovered she was pregnant and gave me up. I have no memories of her either."

"Shit." Kyle's floored. "So that was all…bullshit? But why? Even if you couldn't tell me about your past, you could have told me the truth about our family."

"They weren't my family. Aren't yours." James shrugs. "I needed a story to go with the car. The grandpa thing was convenient. Explained the 442, took care of the family history, too."

"Coulda just sold the car. Wouldn't have had anything to explain then."

"Are you kidding? I put more time and effort into that car than most men put into their careers. Guess I shoulda figured it would lead them to me eventually, but I couldn't help myself. Had to keep it."

"Anyway," Kyle goes on. "Back when you worked for the mob…"

The kid pauses, struggling with the question—and James knows what's coming. It's the question he's been expecting—and dreading—from the moment he let his son in on the truth.

"Did you ever kill anybody?"

James doesn't hesitate.

"Yeah. But not like you're thinking."

Thirty-Three
The Jimmy Pedals Job

Angelo and Rocky—the good cop/bad cop double act—had required his services for what they explained to him as "transportation to a cemetery."

The Pugliese code being as subtle as that Acme anvil the Road Runner used to drop on the Coyote, Jimmy knows when they stop to pick up another Pugliese goon on the way to the "cemetery" it's lights out for the poor coked-out douche bag.

Part of his arrangement with the Pugliese stipulates that no blood ever touches the interior of his car. A splash or two on the outside, OK. He can wash that shit off. But the 442's nearly a classic, and he fully intends to keep the interior mint. Since a yellow car with fat black racing stripes tattooed from front to back is the antithesis of a mob vehicle, affording the family an almost ironic anonymity as they cruise from job to job, they're respectful of his one request.

The least they could do for such peace of mind is keep the seats clean.

But as their new arrival opens the passenger door, sniffing and prodding his nose as if he fears it might sprout legs and part ways with his face—eyes a glazed red, skin pallid with an icy sheen of summer sweat—Jimmy's pretty sure they won't make it to their destination absent an incident that'll result in his having to scrub the contents of somebody's arteries from the seats.

Sure enough, they're maybe halfway there, Angelo joking with the kid from the backseat, keeping the mood light, the attitude nonchalant, while Rocky—the monosyllabic type—stares impassively through sunglasses, when the dipshit with the swollen nostrils wheels on them, pulling a Saturday Night Special from his waistband.

Their failure to frisk the fuck in an effort to keep him at ease is about to blow up in their faces.

Like, literally.

And Jimmy is gonna have to replace the whole fucking backseat.

'Cause if blood is hard to get out, just imagine what brains will do to the upholstery.

While the guys in the back are going, "Whoa, whoa, whoa, take it easy, take it easy" with their hands in the air, and the guy in the front is all, "Fuck you, you motherfuckers," talking about some dope he *swears* got delivered exactly where and when he was supposed to deliver it, Jimmy does his best to put his leather seats out of mind and concentrate on keeping the car nice and legal, making sure he doesn't punch a red or roll a stop sign in the panic and confusion.

He also recalls the .38 he keeps in the glove box for gigs like this. One of those on-the-off-chance measures a cautious guy takes.

Well, this is an off-chance if he's ever seen one.

But he can't very well reach past this jumpy fuck and retrieve his piece, so a lot of good it does him.

They're out on the avenue where there's a fucking light every two blocks and, as luck would have it, they're timing them out so they hit every fucking one. Not quite bumper-to-bumper traffic, but a lot of stop and go.

While around him three armed killers prepare to shoot it out in a space roughly the size of a closet's asshole.

Then things go from bad to, like, totally fucked.

Jimmy knows at least one of the guys in the back moves for his gun because the junkie starts screaming, "Don't fucking do it, don't even fucking think about it," his voice getting higher and faster, sounding less and less connected to life in this world. Like he's already settled on the fact that they're all gonna fucking die one way or another inside the 442.

And now the guidos in the back are trying to intimidate the guy. Even Rocky, who never says much, starts talking about the boss, how the don's gonna be mighty disappointed at this turn of events. That with the two of them dead, the old man will stop at nothing until the addict in the passenger seat, his whole family, even his fucking dog, suffer for a prolonged period before their untimely deaths.

Yeah, good plan guys. He's got a gun and you go at him with harsh words.

Fucking genius.

So it falls on Jimmy—who's only supposed to be a driver—to end this as bloodlessly as possible, 'cause the others are clearly too preoccupied to consider the sanctity of his seats.

He's sitting at a red light, and there's an off-duty cabbie idling in the lane to their left who must be watching this whole thing go down, 'cause when Jimmy turns in his direction the guy pretends to be watching anything *but* the 442. The cabbie's mouth is hanging open, like, to his knees, but he's a New York guy, and he knows staring at wise guys is a serious breach of etiquette. So he makes like all he's concerned with is the road in front of him.

The light still red, Jimmy takes a quick look left and right down the cross street. So busy with cars he may as well be playing Frogger.

But what the fuck.

He throws the tranny into first and fucking redlines it. The driver of a black Mercedes—some high-fashion stockbroker type probably fresh from a manicure—has to jam his breaks and swerve hard to avoid the 442 as it glides illegally through the intersection. The asshole punches the horn with both hands, pouting like a child.

Jimmy doesn't see any of what goes down in the car after that, but he catches scattered sounds as the speedometer climbs beyond sixty before they even hit the next cross street, closing in on the next stoplight a block-and-a-half away. The dope fiend with the gun is driven back against his seat, his chest striking the headrest so hard it knocks his wind out and the gun falls from his fingertips. Both guys in the back try to jump for it, but the car's sudden change in momentum has pinned their hands at their sides as firmly as if they've been Crazy Glued.

The rear tires finally stop squealing, but the fucking stink of burning radial is enough to make you puke—especially Jimmy, who's thinking vintage tires cost a fucking fortune. As the front tires settle hard on their shocks, Jimmy fights the chassis' sudden desire to jut left and right with a mind of her own.

With Angelo and Rocky both screaming variations of "What the fuck are you doing?" from the back, and the punk fuck who started this whole thing wheezing his own confusion from the passenger seat, Jimmy keeps his eyes locked on the next red light in the rapidly shrinking distance, sneaking a quick glance at the speedometer.

He's got her in third and they're approaching seventy-five.

There's enough room between the 442 and the stoplight to jack her up another gear, so he stands—fucking *stands*—on the gas pedal, waits for the engine to transition from a purr to an uncomfortable whine and throws her into fourth.

She's at about ninety miles per hour when he jumps on the brake with both feet.

Like a refrigerator colliding against the back of his seat, he feels Angelo thump him from behind, figures Rocky's out of control body is doing likewise behind the junkie. Jimmy has to grip the wheel like he's trying to grind it to powder, straining against the force of the 442 with every muscle fiber in his forearms.

And all he can think is *This can't be good for my clutch.*

But here's the important part: As they close the gap toward the red light—the tires billowing smoke, shrieking like a broad in a slasher flick, Jimmy working his arms like a prize fighter to keep her from going sideways—the cokehead flops forward, his unrestrained body careening wildly as he hits the dashboard face first.

And even over the symphony of disaster that has become the car's undercarriage, they all hear a sharp, conclusive *snap*.

As the rubber grips the pavement, bringing the car to an abrupt stop—its front bumper poking meekly into the crosswalk—the light turns green. Nobody in the car moves until they see the vehicles from the previous light catch up and overtake them. The cabbie's head swivels like Linda Blair's as he drives past studying the 442 through the dissipating smoke, all propriety he felt toward the observation of New York City gangsters forgotten in the aftermath of the show Jimmy just put on.

Rocky's the first one to recover. No major damage, but for the next two weeks he and Angelo will be nursing bruises the size and shade of eggplants where they struck the front seats. Silent type that he is, he merely inspects the junkie's limp body and waits for Angelo to make the official pronouncement.

When Angelo finally gets a hand around the guy's neck, feeling for a pulse, he smiles and laughs giddily at their driver, his words coming in a profane, thank-God-we're-alive cadence.

"This guy's fucking dead. You just fucking killed a guy with the pedals of your fucking car! Rocky, get a load of Jimmy fuckin' Pedals over here!"

*　　*　　*

"I wasn't trying to kill him," James says, plaintively. "Last thing on my mind. I just wanted to knock the gun out of his hand, maybe knock him unconscious. If I didn't do something, he woulda killed us all." James cocks his head, as if realizing something for the first time after all these years. "Wasn't more than a few weeks after that I left town. The sound of that guy dying—it was as big a reason as any for me running off the way I did."

Kyle doesn't appear all that surprised.

James supposes his son's had him marked down as a killer since he found out about his past. Would be nice, though, to see some disappointment in the kid's eyes. Some sign that he'd at least been thinking there was a *chance* his old man wasn't a murderer.

Instead, the kid's chuckling.

"Jimmy Pedals," he says. Like it's the goofiest nickname he's ever heard. Learns his old man's taken a life and that's all he has to say.

"Ah, I never liked the sound of it either." James cracks a fresh beer, ponders tossing one to his son, figures what the hell. As Kyle catches the brew between his palms, his father fires a question to go with it.

"Long as we're getting personal, you and Katie been going together a while. Is it serious?"

Kyle flicks at the pull-tab atop his Coors. He knows the answer, but he doesn't want to sound like some starry-eyed kid when he tries to put words to it.

"Well, I mean, we're sixteen," he hedges. "But I love her."

James nods, hopes again he's not making that face his son hates. "Just like that, huh?"

"Yeah. I love her. I just…know it."

James' laughter is soft. "Ah, to be sixteen again."

"Come on," Kyle whines. "You asked me how I felt."

"Sorry, sorry." James raises his palms plaintively. "So if she's the one—"

"I didn't say that."

"—tell me: What do you like best about her? Why's she so special to you?"

Kyle ponders, rolling the beer can between his frigid palms.

"That it would be easy for her to be what everyone expects, but she won't settle for that."

"And what does everyone expect her to be?"

"Come on, look at her. The hair, the house, the cheerleader thing. But she refuses to be that girl."

James' lips turn down and he nods. "Good trait to have."

"What makes it work with you and Beth?"

Before he answers, James laughs—a sound of pride tempered with disbelief. Can't believe he's having this discussion with his son.

"Beth is…a complicated woman. Enough city in her to put me in my place. It was different with your mother. She was very country, and at first I couldn't get enough of it. But I guess you can take the boy out of the city…" It's not a statement that needs finishing. And James would just as soon not admit it aloud. "But that's why Beth and I work."

He chases the thought with a slug of beer. "You and Katie been together a while," he continues. "You two ever, uh—"

Kyle's laughing before his old man can even finish the question. "Jesus, Pop. I know we been through a lot the past couple of days, but you're still my dad."

"Hey, you get to drink my beer, you can answer my question."

"All right, all right."

"So?"

Kyle shrugs, smiles on one side of his mouth.

"No shit. My boy." James crushes his empty. "Didn't think you had it in ya."

"Glad to see I inspire such pride."

"Relax, I'm just kidding around. How long?"

"I don't know, felt like a good five minutes—"

"Jesus Christ, kid, I mean how long have you two been having sex."

Now they're both a little embarrassed.

And more than a little grossed-out.

"The other day. Night after you got shot."

James lowers his eyes, starts to laugh.

"What?" Kyle demands.

"Clever kid."

"What do you mean?"

"She takes pity on you, offers her sympathies, and you take full advantage."

"Come on, it wasn't like that. We were—"

"OK, OK. Whatever the case, we get killed on this road trip, at least you went out with a bang."

When they each pop new beers, James leans his across the flames, taps it against his son's. Kyle's thinking the ways the two of them have changed since the shooting are immeasurable.

"To Jimmy Pedals," Kyle jokes.

James just shakes a dismayed head.

He's always hated that fucking nickname.

Thirty-Four
Spoiled and Old Bitches Alike

Beth had to stop.

Even though Katie argued, logically, that if they took a breather and the boys didn't, they'd end up that much farther behind come morning, Beth didn't give a shit. Two days straight they'd been switching drivers in the Jetta, and the monotony, the exhaustion, it's all about to crash down upon her.

Not to mention the agony of having to look at Little Miss Mansion, whose top brand makeup still clings perfectly to her flawless skin, whose hair has somehow maintained its shape and body.

While Beth smells like a locker room.

But once Katie's in the hotel lobby, she can't believe she wanted to, or thought she could, keep going. All she can think about now is collapsing on the bed after an hour-long shower and sleeping for the next two days.

Which could be a problem because the night clerk tells them the only rooms available are singles.

One king bed.

She and Beth stare one another down, both thinking, *No fucking way.*

"It's fine," Beth tells the guy. She slaps her credit card on the counter. "One of us will sleep on the floor." Her eyes go right to Katie, who doesn't miss a beat.

Pulls *her* credit card—which, let's face it, could run laps around Beth's—says, "Yeah, one of us will."

They argue for close to eight minutes over who's going to pay. Variations of:

"I got this."

"No, *I* got this."

Until the clerk, weary and eager to return to the micro-TV behind the counter, informs them they can split the rate over two cards.

The girls share one last hard look.

"Fine," Beth blurts. "Split the fucker."

Stepping into the room—even if she has to step into it with fucking Beth—Katie feels instant relief. The heat's up high and she loves the thought of pulling those thick curtains across, blotting out the sun when morning tries to rouse them.

But when she drops her clothes on the bathroom floor and steps beneath the steaming spray, the fucking pressure, like, sucks. Wrapped in a robe, trying to scrape out the shampoo and conditioner the nozzle couldn't blast away, Katie warns Beth of the shower's shortcomings.

"Closest I've come to a shower in three days was that patch of rain we hit back in Ohio," Beth says. "It'll be fine." Then she mumbles something about Katie being a "spoiled bitch" and disappears behind the bathroom door.

Katie doesn't reply.

Until Beth emerges from the bathroom, enveloped in a cloud of steam, wearing a meek expression.

And a goddamn nasty bird's nest atop her head.

Then Katie snickers. "Guess the water pressure frowns upon spoiled bitches and *old* bitches alike."

"I'm young enough to be your sister."

If their mother were, like, twelve when she started cranking out offspring.

But still, it's *possible.*

Beth stands reluctantly beside Katie before the mirror. Silently, they brush through their knots. Clad in matching white hotel robes, combing away in similar motions, they *could* be sisters, the clash of one's platinum blond 'do against the other's nearly-purple red notwithstanding.

Once their hair is reasonably terrible as opposed to the astonishingly terrible of their first emergence from the shower, they slather on whatever creams the hotel bathroom has on offer and brush their teeth with their fingers in lieu of the toothbrushes they didn't have time to pack. In unison, they stand back and survey the results.

"Tomorrow—" Beth starts.

"—we stop for makeup," Katie finishes.

"Yeah."

"Hey, wait a minute." Katie remembers something, ruffles through her pile of clothes. She brings Dom's .38 back to the counter by the mirror, shows it to Beth.

"Do you know where the safety is on this? I don't wanna just *leave* it on the chair."

Gingerly, Beth takes it from Katie's hand, tilts it back and forth under the fluorescent lights.

"Does it have one?" she asks, almost rhetorically. Then her eyes go wide. "Oh, wait."

She's back in a flash with Angelo's .45.

"See, I think with this one…" she trails off, fiddling with the red and black switch, unsure which setting puts the safety on.

They may as well be comparing earrings.

Except that earrings don't fire bullets if you're not careful.

Like the .45 does right there beneath their noses.

They feel the sudden thunderclap in their eardrums.

Their shoulders go stiff.

White powder rains over them.

By the time the smoke clears, they're aware of a sharp ringing in their ears.

They're also aware of the hole Beth put in the hotel ceiling. Could just as easily have punched a hole in one of their foreheads.

Beth actually shakes at this realization. Physically shakes as she never has before. A sour bile of inevitability turns her stomach as she prepares for Katie to offer up a verbal beatdown. Braces herself for the tongue-lashing she knows she deserves.

Katie's lips part like the eye of a hurricane. Last moment of peace before she unleashes.

But no words emerge. Just high, girlish shock-laughter that expels the rage and fear of the gunshot and everything else they've experienced over the last forty-eight hours.

It's ludicrous, Beth knows, but it also proves inanely infectious. They fall into hysterics, alternately leaning on one another and bellowing at the gaping wound in the drywall above.

*   *   *

Dom waited to see which room the girls entered before approaching the desk and requesting the one beside theirs, offering up some bullshit about how he'd stayed in that room once before. Then he placed a hard-backed chair with a cushion thin as tissue paper in front of the window and drew back the curtains.

Perfect view of the Jetta. Whenever they decide to depart, he'll see them heading out.

As long as he doesn't, like, need any sleep or anything.

Like, why would he need any of that at this point?

Perched in the uncomfortable chair, his eyelids start sliding down, so he rolls his cell phone around in his hand as a distraction. He knows his father's limited understanding of technology means there's no way he can track a call from his cell to Maria's. But, wanting nothing more than to dial her number, he realizes he couldn't be farther from knowing what to say, and he settles for pleasant recollections of their life together instead.

Her delicate flesh as he settles atop her.

Hair dark as oil upon her porcelain shoulders.

The feel of her breasts against his chest, the heat of her breath when they embrace.

All of it turns to feelings of fear and apprehension over what's next for them. *If* there's a next for them. By the end of this assignment, he'll be an entirely different person, altered in a way that cannot be undone. And Maria's practically been held hostage by his family.

Would kind of make for an awkward Thanksgiving dinner.

Then the gunshot—or something that sounds a helluva lot like a gun's report—chases every last thought and image from his mind.

Dom moves to the wall that separates his room from the girls', presses his ear to the cheap wallpaper, hears overenthusiastic laugher.

Maybe it wasn't a gunshot.

Could have been a car backfiring.

Someone down the hall dropping a heavy suitcase.

A soda can being ejected from the machine outside his door.

Whatever it was, he focuses, listens as closely as he can.

*   *   *

Beth and Katie sit side-by-side on the mattress, propped against the headrest, sharing a pile of candy they loaded up when they last stopped for gas.

Beth's talking about how the thorn bush the low water pressure has left her with is nothing compared to the way she and her girlfriends used to wear their hair back in the day.

"It was the eighties," she says.

"What did it look like?"

"Seriously? Come on, you must have seen the music videos."

"They don't really play those anymore."

"You gotta have some idea. Seen pictures of your mom from back then. What year were you born?"

"1996."

Beth's mouth falls open.

"Jesus, do you even remember 9/11?"

"Vaguely." She takes a generous bite from a Snickers. The rest comes out muffled and distorted. "I was young. Teachers didn't want to scare us."

Watching her chomp away on the chocolate and caramel, Beth can't help herself. "God, I fucking hate girls who can eat like you."

Katie's face turns curious. "You really think it'll catch up with me?"

"Catches up with all of us, honey."

"Still hoping it gives me a big fat ass?"

"I didn't say that."

Katie glares through the tops of her eyes.

"OK," Beth backpedals. "I didn't say that *exactly*."

"You're just like everybody else." Katie crumples the empty wrapper, digs a bag of Peanut M&Ms from the pile.

Beth continues nursing the same tiny packet of Gummi Bears she's been working on since the binge commenced. "What do you mean?"

"Think my life's so perfect 'cause of my family and the way I look."

"Don't you think you've had an easier go of it than the rest of us, Kate?"

"No matter how hard I work—at school, at a job, even with Kyle—nobody thinks I've *earned* anything. Teachers just give the pretty girl her *A*. God forbid she gets anything lower than that, Mommy and Daddy use their clout, call the principal. Real nice boyfriend you got, Katie. Must *love* your in-ground swimming pool and that theater room on the third floor. You try spending your whole life convincing people there's an actual person behind the gated driveway. It's a losing battle."

"Your folks have a theater room?"

"See?"

"Oh, come on. Poor little rich girl."

"Gee, I've never heard that before."

"Well, it doesn't appear to be a battle you take very seriously."

"Excuse me?"

"Like that Jetta you got out there—"

"Hey, those start under twenty-thousand."

"Not when they're brand new with all the extras."

"I bought that car."

"Oh, sure. Daddy shells out a hefty down payment so his little sweetheart can feel all mature making the monthly payments. Really, what do you pay each month? Twenty dollars? Thirty? I'll bet if you come up short he even foots the bill for that."

"I didn't say I made payments, I said I bought it. *I* bought it."

"Didn't realize they offered trust funds you could cash in at sixteen."

"I worked for three years as a camp counselor to earn the money for that car. You try comforting homesick kids all summer long, keeping grade school boys from playing grabass on the playground. You think about that the next time you think you've got someone figured out."

"Well, here's a tip: The next time you try to convince everybody that you're one of the masses, buy yourself a used car like a kid your age should be driving. Might make it an easier pill to swallow."

"I didn't do it for other people. I did it for me."

"Listen, all that stuff you're talking about—having to prove yourself, feeling uncomfortable in your own skin, disappointed your parents aren't perfect—you outgrow that. You grow up, all that changes. You have no idea what it's like to really struggle with stuff that doesn't just go away over time."

"Please, enlighten me."

"Try starting out with nothing. My mother worked two jobs just to put clothes on my back. Girls used to laugh at what I wore to school. Every now and then when I did have something nice to wear—new handbag for Christmas, designer blouse for my birthday—where I grew up in Philly, girls would just smack you around, tear the clothes off your back."

"But you've got a good job now," Katie reasons. "You dress nice, got good taste in clothes. Clearly you're not struggling. Got about the best boyfriend I can imagine. And the whole world knows it wasn't given to you. I could cure fucking cancer and people would still whisper that my boobs had something to do with it."

Beth nibbles a green Gummi Bear. "You really think I have good taste?"

Katie rolls her eyes. "And I don't know why you keep bitching about my figure. You're still in good shape. You're right. I won't be so lucky. Probably blow up like a balloon when I get older. Have you ever seen my mother's ass? Hours a day on the treadmill and she still can't drop those last twenty pounds."

"It takes *marathons* to keep what semblance of a figure I have left. And if we've learned anything these past few days, my boyfriend, he's not so perfect."

"I don't know," Katie reasons. "It's gotta be, like, some big mistake, right? James getting caught up in all this."

Beth is pretty sure it's no mistake. But she's more than happy to push those implications aside for the moment. "Even if it is, he's not perfect."

Katie cocks her head. Like, really? The guy's a saint.

Eyes lighting up with the perfect example, Beth insists, "He falls asleep on his back, he'll snore like a garbage disposal."

"My God. How do you live with such an animal?"

"Wait a minute," Beth says, sleeping arrangements suddenly on her mind. "You don't snore, do you?"

"No," Katie says, as if repulsed by the suggestion. But then, smiling, she adds, "Kyle does." She lowers her eyes, bashful now, expectant.

Beth's not surprised. The kid may have fooled his father, but she and Kyle have a shorthand when it comes to such things. He's always felt more comfortable sharing certain parts of his life with her than James. Not that he's come right out and told her he's boffing Little Miss Mansion, but like a cracking voice or a peach-fuzz mustache, there are some developments a teenage boy cannot hide.

She plays along with Katie anyway.

"So, you and Kyle, huh?"

Tickled by the memory, Katie nods sheepishly.

"Been going on a while?"

"No. It was just once. Day before we left."

"You mean after James got shot." There's a wickedly knowing tone to Beth's voice.

"Why?"

Beth tosses her empty wrapper at Katie.

"Pity Fuck!"

She could just as easily be screaming, "Pillow fight!"

"Nuh-uh." And Katie does actually swat Beth with her pillow.

"Yeah, yeah, yeah. So how many others?"

Katie's shoulders sink beneath an exasperated breath. "Right. I'm a blond cheerleader, so I must have screwed the whole football team."

"No. I was just thinking the quarterback. Maybe the offensive line."

"Oh, fuck you."

"Relax, I'm kidding. I just thought he might not be your first."

"How many blond bombshells have saved your life by shooting a mobster between the legs, huh? You know a lot of ditzy bimbos who could manage that?"

"OK, OK, calm down. I was asking seriously."

"If I'm sharing my number, you're sharing yours."

"That's the way it goes. Jeez, don't you have girlfriends?"

"Most girls hate me for the same reasons you do."

"I don't hate you. I just…didn't know you before all this."

"Didn't stop you from casting judgments."

"Really? And you didn't have any opinions about me?"

Rather than lie, Katie holds her tongue.

"So let's share numbers," Beth says. "It's the great equalizer among women."

"Fine. But you'd still be swinging a plunger at those guys if it weren't for me, so you're going first."

"All right, gimme a minute."

"Oh, don't be a wuss."

"It's not that. I'm counting."

Beth sees Katie's upraised eyebrows and adds, "Ah, look who's judging now." She squeezes her eyes closed, almost in meditation. "OK, got it."

"So?"

"Seventeen."

"*Seventeen!* What are you, a porn star?"

"Gimme a break, huh, I am a few years older than you."

"If you were as old as my grandmother, your number still shouldn't be that high."

"Nobody's grandmother should have a number that high."

"Seriously, you're not old enough to have slept with seventeen guys."

"Why? How old do you think I am?"

"Thirty-five?"

"Nicest thing you've ever said to me."

"Forty?"

"Two."

Katie's mouth turns down, more impressed with Beth's physique than she was before.

"But if you've been with James, what, ten years—?"

"Going on ten, yeah."

"Then that means you had your seventeen by the time you were thirty-two."

"What do you want, I grew up in the kind of place where chastity didn't mean much."

"Does James know?"

"You really don't know guys at all, do you? That's the *last* thing he'd ever wanna know. He's never asked, and I've never offered. Besides, most guys his age have numbers pushing three digits."

"That's disgusting."

"Your turn."

"We're just counting real sex, right?"

"As opposed to fake sex?"

"No, as opposed to...other stuff."

"Meaning..."

"You know." Katie's voice slips into a whisper. "BJs."

"Yeah, honey, the real thing's the only way that counts. Now quit stalling."

"Promise not to laugh?"

"I liked you better when you were acting tough, Kate. I promise no such thing."

"All right, but it's embarrassing."

Beth flaps her wrist in a circle, gesturing for Katie to go on.

"OK. Two."

Her face widening in a parody of horrified surprise, Beth gasps. "You slut! Two different guys at your age!"

"Oh, knock it off."

But Beth keeps laughing.

"Come on, stop it," Katie says. "I feel really bad about it."

"Why? You haven't done anything wrong."

"I mean for Kyle. He wasn't the first, but he should've been."

"Believe me, he's getting what he wants. I'm sure he wouldn't be bothered in the slightest if he knew."

"As long as we're asking questions, Beth, what do you really think James and Kyle are mixed up in? I won't lie, the whole thing scares me pretty bad."

Beth has spent most of the journey turning the question over in her mind. All the miles they've logged, she still hasn't come up with an explanation for the shooting, the gangsters, or the sudden road trip.

She has, of course, entertained a few wild possibilities—situation like this, the mind runs to every last cliché from every last B-movie you've ever seen—but James and Kyle involved in something like that?

Ducking a question she can't answer, Beth tells Katie:

"I think I'm more angry than scared. I just don't know who I'm supposed to be angry with."

"Those two bastards we left bleeding in the kitchen might be a good start."

"We left one of them bleeding, the other one…"

"I don't regret it." Katie downs a handful of M&Ms. "Got what was coming to him."

"It didn't shake you up at all?"

"Not so far. I don't know, maybe once all of this is over it'll sink in. Maybe not."

"Well, if it does, and you need someone to talk to, I'll be around." Her voice loses its usual indignant edge. "I wouldn't be if you hadn't done what you did."

"That sounds a little like a thank-you."

"Well," Beth tells her, after a yawn and a stretch, "that's probably as close as I'm likely to get. Maybe we should call it a night."

"If you say so, porn star."

Shaking her head almost playfully, Beth shuffles under the covers.

And flips Little Miss Mansion the bird.

Thirty-Five
Making His Bones

The sun is just clearing the horizon when James awakens to the barrel of a twelve-gauge poking him in the nose.

"Whatchu doin' on my land?"

James cranes his neck slowly toward the voice, finds a frail old timer in a thick hunting cap, flaps hanging over his ears, and a Carhartt jacket half-zipped over thickly-lined overalls. Guy's face reads like a roadmap of a life lived in the fields, same color and texture as the first baseman's mitt James had as a kid. Lips sucked into the gums as if the teeth have gone missing.

Across the smoldering fire pit, James notices Kyle's empty sleeping bag. Fears maybe the old bastard has done something foolish, but he can't risk asking after his boy if Kyle's off somewhere on his own and this crackpot's got no idea he was ever there.

"Easy, pal. Just crashing for the night. I'll be moving along shortly."

"Surely, you will. I'm 'bout to call the p'lice, have them come git ya."

"No, no, no. You don't need to do that. Just let me grab my things, I'll hit the road."

Old Man River ain't listening. He's got his eyes on the 442's license plate. Plates that Garrett Sanders *might* have put into the system back in PA.

While the farmer tries to commit the digits to memory, James runs his hand across the grass and dirt real slow and silent, feeling for the .38 that had been there when he went to sleep.

"Already took care of that." Lifting one side of his jacket, the old man reveals James' gun sticking out of a pocket in his denim overalls. The shotgun never leaves James' face. "What y'all doin' out here? You poachers? Stalking game on my land?"

"No, nothing like that. Just passing through, got dark sooner than I expected. Had to find someplace to stop for the night."

"And you come all the way out here, mile from the road, through trees and brambles, when there's a perfectly good campground not but three miles from here?"

"Like I said, I'm passing through. Don't know the area."

"That don't explain the shots I heard fired last night."

"Don't know nothin' about that. You see anything killed around here? What kind of poacher sets up camp after a hunt anyway?"

"Goddamn stupid one. Where's your friend? The other sleeping bag, where'd he go?"

"Brought that along as an extra, in case I got cold. It is the dead of winter, you know."

The old man shakes his puckered face. "Been slept in, flattened pillow and all."

"What are you, a detective?"

"Where is he?"

"Before you started waving that fucking gun in my face, I was asleep, remember? How the hell should I know where he is?"

"Getting excited ain't gon' help you here, friend. Don't go doin' nothin' stupid, now." He plunges a weathered hand into his jacket pocket, keeping the barrel of the shotgun close enough James can smell the oil. "Just gon' phone this into the 'thorities, get this sitch'ation fixed up."

Punching numbers on the keypad, he glances around for signs of the other fella.

* * *

Kyle's off taking a piss.

All he drank last night, his bladder feels like it's holding back a waterfall.

He's also new to the whole hangover thing.

Staggered when he stood, fumbled like a human bobblehead.

Didn't want his father to see him that way. Wanted James Worthington to think his son could drink like a man, wake up ready for round two.

So he wandered far enough from the clearing he's got no idea there's a farmer caressing his father's cheek with a loaded shotgun.

Zipping up, he turns back toward camp, feeling somewhat steadier in his gait. He stops when he hears his father's voice along with another he doesn't recognize. At first he figures his father's got the radio in the Olds going, and he's singing along.

Who knows, maybe he managed to dial in some Poison.

As he gets closer, though, he hears no rhythm in the voices, no music in the background. Closer still, he sees through the denuded trees a man hovering above his father, who's still tucked inside his sleeping bag, flat on his stomach.

Pinned that way by the biggest gun Kyle's ever seen outside of a movie theater.

His pulse pounds in his neck, *whooshing* currents of fear explode behind his ears as Kyle flattens himself against a tree. He closes his eyes, tries to force his brain to think. Knows there isn't much time. That it falls on him to be the strong one.

Unfortunately, no feasible plan presents itself.

Mind's a fucking blank.

Of all the mornings to be nursing a hangover.

He tries to focus on the things his father's taught him since leaving Gower. Thinks back through everything his old man's said since he morphed back into the badass he was when he ran with gangsters.

Remembers their conversation about guns and fistfights.

Then Kyle realizes why he sucks at strategizing under pressure.

You're not supposed to think.

And, he recalls, you're supposed to fight dirty.

His eyes open.

And Kyle finds a feasible plan lying at his feet.

*   *   *

"Hello, Lou?" the farmer speaks into the phone. "Waldo here."

"Waldo?" James mocks. "Your fucking name's Waldo?"

Waldo ignores him. "Need you to send out a patrol car, pick up couple'a poachers I found in my fields. What's that? Yuh, two of 'em, I think. Well, one's off walking in the woods. Taking a shit, I dunno. Bet yaw ass I can keep 'em here till he pulls up. Nah, nothing drastic. He comes back, I'll make sure he waits with us. Jus' muh twelve-gauge. The Smith and Wesson. Oh, bull*shit* it could. Right, right, keep talkin'."

They go on like that for a while. The whole time James is calculating his odds if he makes a move for the shotgun. Wouldn't take much to grab the barrel. Old man looks like he died five years ago and no one brought it to his attention. Hand shook with arthritis when he unfolded the phone and struggled to dial. So all James has to do is wrestle the scattergun from his grip, turn it around so it's pointing in a friendlier direction.

Right at Waldo's nutsack would be good.

Only question is whether James can turn that shotgun faster than the crippled old turtle can draw the .38, punch a handful of holes in his supine back.

"They leavin' now, OK. Yup, we'll be here. 'Bout four miles west of the house. Back where I had the corn las' season. Right."

Waldo closes the phone, returns it to his pocket. "That 'us the cavalry. Be here less'n ten minutes. Hope you ain't got too many priors."

"None on record, no."

"Honey of a automobile you got der."

"Built her up myself."

"Interested in sellin' 'er?"

"You've gotta be fucking kidding me."

The old man shrugs, like it's perfectly reasonable to negotiate the sale of an automobile while you're holding the owner at gunpoint.

But it's a point he never gets the chance to argue.

The log shatters over his right ear before he can open his mouth. Sends him to the ground like a sack of quarters.

Getting over the shock of seeing his own son lording over a man he decked with a fucking log, James unzips himself from the sleeping bag.

"Nice shot, son!" Hustling to his feet, he grabs the shotgun.

Kyle's so stoned on the adrenaline he can barely hear his old man. His heart rate's through the roof, like he's ready to bash the next fucker who emerges from the trees. So what if the log busted in two? He'll use his bare fucking hands, man. Hell, bring on a fucking *army* of crotchety old farmers.

He can't believe it fucking worked!

"My .38's in his pocket," James is saying.

Kyle steadies himself, retrieves the pistol. Stepping beside him, James racks the scattergun decisively, aims it at the unconscious old farmer.

The sudden chill in Kyle's blood doesn't mix well with the rush of exhilaration.

Kind of kills his buzz.

"What the hell are you doing? He's out, we're good, we can go."

James shakes his head. "He already called the police. We leave him to describe the car, they'll be hot on our tail. They'll find us."

"We got bigger problems than a couple of cops. Let's just get outta here. We cross into Illinois they can't follow us, right?"

"I'm not talking about the cops. They'll find us."

"Dad, we can't do this."

"Got to. No choice." James sights over the barrel, one eye closed.

As if at this range, such preparations are necessary.

"Yes there is. We can just walk away. Right now. Come on, Pop." Kyle tugs his sleeve, like he used to as a boy desperate for a piggyback ride.

James turns to shout his son down, tell him to grow up, let him do what needs to be done. Except the face staring back at him *is* grown up. It's confident and focused. It ain't fear or naïve sympathy talking. He's pleading for the man's life because it's the right thing to do. Even if it isn't the smart thing.

Jimmy Pedals has never been bothered by right and wrong.

James Worthington on the other hand…

"OK." He lowers the shotgun. "You're right."

Repeating it again as if to convince himself, James nods at his boy.

*   *   *

They're five miles down the road, the pedal pegged to the floorboard, when James hits the brakes, tearing up the grass as they careen onto the shoulder. His hands, slick with adrenaline-sweat, remain locked on the steering wheel.

"Woo," Kyle hollers. "That was great!"

"You did it, Kyle. Helluva lot of guts back there. Helluva lot."

"Did you see me? I cracked that bastard a perfect shot. Bam!"

His father was in trouble and he saved him, but the thrill resonates deeper than that. He broke the rules, struck an innocent man who was merely protecting property that was rightfully his. The kind of thing they throw you in jail for.

And he's being fucking *commended* for it.

It makes the whole experience…

…even more fucking *awesome*.

And in the aftermath, he maybe understands his father's past a little better.

"Bailed your ass out." Kyle laughs.

"Made your bones, kid."

Kyle's jubilation dissolves into befuddlement.

"It's something the wiseguys say," his father explains.

James is almost as gassed as Kyle. Striking first, thinking later, doing something he's been told his whole life he's not supposed to do—it's exactly the type of action for which James feared his boy was woefully unprepared.

But the kid did real good out there. Real good.

"We got any music in this bitch?" he asks his boy.

Kyle searches the glove box, comes up dry just as James remembers he's got a canvas CD wallet on the flipside of his visor. Folding it down, he finds one disc surrounded by fourteen vacant slots.

Silently reading the label, his lips curl into a smile.

"You won't believe this."

"What?"

James hands him the Poison CD.

"Only CD I own that isn't Springsteen, and it's the one we find in the car. Must mean something, right?"

"Yeah, it means I gotta listen to shitty music on the way to Chicago. Woulda preferred the Boss."

Thirty-Six
One of a Great Many Questions

When Beth returns from the continental breakfast, Katie's staring dumbfounded at the laptop.

"Forget your password, Blondie?"

"Yeah, maybe one of the five-hundred guys you slept with knows what it is."

Chewing a dry bagel, Beth waits for Katie to tell her what's really up.

"Where were they when we checked last night?" Katie asks.

"Almost through Indiana."

"That's what I thought."

"Why?"

"How 'bout the time before that?"

"They had just *entered* Indiana. Why?"

"Every time we checked, they were moving fast. Not a lot of stops during the day."

Beth nods quickly. Like, come to the point, kid.

"Far as I can tell, they've been in the same spot since around 9:00 this morning."

"What time is it?"

"Almost 11:00."

"Could just be taking a breather."

Katie checks the red dot's history. "That would mean they woke up at dawn, got back on the road…and needed a two-hour rest after driving for only three?"

"Where are they?"

"Chicago."

Leaning over her shoulder, Beth offers a contemplative grunt. "So you think they've reached their destination?"

"Yeah. But why Chicago?"

"I don't know. But I'll tell you one thing: That's one of a great many questions James is gonna answer when we catch up and I sit him down for a nice, long chat."

*   *   *

Dom slept the whole night in the hard-backed chair. Hadn't planned on nodding off, but his brain just shut down. When he's awakened by voices in the next room, he jumps to his feet, admonishing himself for dozing off, worried the girls have moved on without him.

Throwing back the curtains, he's blasted by the morning sun. Shielding his eyes, he finds the Jetta hasn't moved. Then he listens with his ear to the wall again and realizes he woke up just in time.

When his father calls an hour later, his impatience so potent Dom practically feels it oozing through the phone, he thinks of Maria and, though his doing so will most certainly result in death, he spares no detail. "Dad. Worthington's in Chicago. His girlfriend's leading me right to him, doesn't even know it."

"Gimme twenty minutes, I'll have a crew on their way to LaGuardia."

Right, 'cause when you kill a civilian in middle America, it's always a good idea to do it loud and bloody. That way, the echo reverberates all the way to New York.

And the cops know just where to look.

Fucking inspired, Dad.

"I can take care of this on my own," Dom says.

The don breathes heavily on the other end, clearly unconvinced. "I'll put a call in to Rocky."

"Dad, Rocky got out of the game ten years ago."

"He's in Chicago. And he'll be at your service if I dial his number."

Dom's, like, whatever. All that Sicilian loyalty shit that goes back to the old country? Dom stays out of that. "I'll call you when I know more."

"I'll be waiting."

The line goes dead.

And Dom hopes to God Rocky's easier to work with than Angelo.

Thirty-Seven
A Traditional Guy

Sipping black java from a chipped mug, John Stallone sits within spitting distance of Gino's East and two blocks from the Ritz-Carlton. Where he knows he should pay a visit to Carlo Genuardi, up from Miami to check on his investments before once more ditching the city like it's stricken with plague.

Even if he is the mob boss equivalent of that deep dish crap they serve down at Gino's.

A pale impression of the original back in New York.

When the Chicago guys say there's no more mafia in Chicago, they aren't saying it like the New York guys say it—with a wink and a smug grin. They say it like they've never uttered a truer statement.

There *is* no more mafia in Chicago.

Went on life support in Capone's last days. Limped along until the last of the godfathers sold off their interests in the mid-nineties. Now, all that dirty money's been washed clean a dozen times over in restaurants and jewelry stores and housing projects. Genuardi was the reigning champ when it all finally dried up, and even he's only in town maybe three months a year. Soon as the temperature drops in the early fall, he's got his toes in the sand of some topless beach in FLA.

But he's still the closest thing to a *capo de tutti capo*, and since they're acquainted and they're men of the same profession, it would be considerate and respectful to stop by the Ritz, kiss the overly tanned fuck on both cheeks and welcome him home. Even if he now pledges allegiance to Miami and his legitimate businesses down south and only deigns to grace Chicago with his presence when he needs to check in on the restaurants he started years ago.

Saying hello—maybe buying the guy a fucking fruit basket—would be the traditional thing to do.

And John Stallone is nothing if not traditional.

Which brings us back to the name, 'cause he knows you're dying to ask.

No, he's not related to the actor.

Was a time, though—this would be back in the early '80s—when he got so damn tired of being asked the question, he started to fuck with people a little. He bore a passable resemblance to his famous namesake—no great feat there, three-quarters of the wops on the east coast fit that description—and he decided to play it up. Changed his hair to match the length and style of the guy on the screen as he changed it with each picture. Hit the gym real hard. Not that he was ever a master wordsmith, but he tried to speak as little as possible, and in as deep a cadence as he could muster. Even tailored his workouts to match the guy's latest physique. When the actor slimmed down and toned up for *Rocky III*, John ate nothing but fish, sucked his body fat percentage down into the negatives. Ripped as shit from calves to neck.

OK, so he fucked with people *a lot*.

Figured if they're gonna give me shit about the name, I might as well embrace it.

Now, though, no one in Chicago passes him on the street thinking, "Is that…?" 'Cause John never went in for the face-lifts or the Botox. And fuck that HGH garbage. Might as well be pumping elephant semen into your veins. At fifty-seven, John's body ain't as hard as it once was, but it's years younger than his actual age. His face may have a more lived-in look than his famous counterpart, but he's prouder of the scars and lines than he'd be of a plastic mask he didn't earn the old fashioned way.

He saw the actor on Letterman last week. Face so stretched and pulled, he couldn't blink.

When his phone rings in the coffee shop on East Superior where he breakfasts daily, he takes his time, sipping slowly from his mug before setting it down and checking the call ID. When he sees the number, he sighs, takes one more lingering sip of coffee.

"Yeah, Don Anthony. How are you, Boss?"

"Rocky, I need you."

It was inevitable, when those boxing movies started making bank, he'd be saddled with the nickname. Could have been worse. He remembers—fondly, but for other reasons—a kid they used to call Jimmy Pedals. Fuckin' travesty of a nickname.

"Go on."

The don does, but Rocky's only half-listening. As traditional a guy he is, there's one very *un*traditional quirk about his career in the mafia.

It ended.

Got to a point where he'd had enough and he told Pugliese he wanted out. Pugliese, much to everyone's surprise and chagrin, let him walk. But he was cautious to add a deterrent that would keep the rest of his employees from cashing in a similar retirement package.

The move cost Rocky half his assets.

Enough for anyone else to think better of such pipe dreams, but not enough to dissuade John Stallone, who showed up at the don's place on Long Island with two garbage bags full of green bricks. He left his new phone number and kissed the man on both cheeks.

Not for a second over the last ten years has Rocky regretted leaving. He has, however, on occasion, wished he'd have left the don a bum number. How easy it would have been to change one digit. Or give him the number for a moving company or a bank like you would some skank at a party who just won't leave you the fuck alone.

Instead, he did what a traditional made guy would do: He encouraged his boss to call him if ever he could be of service. Figured, how often can the don use me if I'm all the way in Chicago?

As it turned out, seventeen times over the last decade. Nearly twenty jobs he's had to pull during his "retirement."

As always, Rocky is polite while Pugliese goes through the details—which are unusually cryptic for a gig like this—and he's sure to finish the conversation with a subservient "OK, Boss, I'll see what I can do."

Only after he hangs up does he curse the don and all of his heirs that they may each die of a long and painful bout of gonorrhea.

Of the eyeballs.

Not that he won't follow through. Rocky is and always has been a man of his word, and he's never botched a job. Not as a member of the family and not in his current role as consultant or whatever the fuck the don wants to call it.

This time, though, the job certainly has its peculiarities.

Dominic's coming into town and he's to be the triggerman. Under no circumstances is Rocky to assist in the hit itself. Help the kid pinpoint the target, show him around town, protect him from local law if need be. Any of the characters on the periphery that need to be disposed of, Rocky can lend a hand there. But the primary target is to be touched by no one other than the don's kid. Which means Rocky's been reduced to a glorified babysitter.

From there it gets even weirder.

Because Pugliese doesn't even tell him who's gettin' whacked. Tells him Dom will fill him in on the rest. The boy's been instructed to contact Rocky once he rolls into Chicago. And then, apparently, the don himself is coming to town. Something about wanting to watch his son finish the job.

Rocky asks no questions, offers no opinions or dissentions, just accepts a duty that's technically no longer his.

And then he wonders why it cost him half his assets to keep doing the same shit he'd done before.

Thirty-Eight
What a Cooker

Less than fifteen minutes later, news of Don Anthony's great journey to the windy city has descended the ranks, and more than a few of his underlings are more than a little pissed at the sudden turn of events.

Take, for example, the goon watching Maria's window. He's shouting into his cell phone and waving his arms a solid five minutes when Maria turns to Fernando inside the condo and tells him this is what they've been waiting for.

Fernando's worked with Maria for years. He's a makeup guy who's never even implied Maria should blow him if she ever wants to work in this business again, let alone demanded it. Not that a makeup guy wouldn't do that. It's just that most makeup guys are...

Well, if there *is* a blow job in the equation, Fernando's usually on the other end of it.

So Maria's never felt even remotely threatened by Fernando. All she's ever felt toward him is gratitude and respect, because he's the best fucking makeup guy in the business. Works from a palette that seems to have more colors than nature and science allow.

When Maria calls to him from the window, urgency in her voice, he practically jumps off the couch. Studies her outfit, considers what she's asked of him, and opens the biggest box of materials he's got with him.

Girlfriend's gotta look her best.

*　　*　　*

"Fucking kid ain't even one of us, Paulie!"

The goon screams this loud enough inside the Lincoln that the leggy blond behind the over-sized sunglasses can hear him clear as day through the sealed windows. As preoccupied as he is bitching and moaning, he allows his eyes to wander a bit.

Madonn', she's a looker.

A Marilyn Monroe type—same hair, same sexy sway—but this bitch is even better, right? 'Cause she's got an olive complexion makes it a sure thing she's got at least a little Italian in her. Broad nose, long dark lashes. Lips so lusciously thick it must take her all morning to cover 'em over with that ruby red she's sportin'.

Nothin' like that porcelain doll he's watching up on the fourteenth floor. That bitch is hot, but the *medigan* thing is a real turn off. What's more, she's a model, which means she's probably a total fucking diva. He'd take a real woman like the broad in the shades over that airbrushed twat any day of the week.

Unfortunately, he only has time for a quick look. He'll save the image for later, jerk himself to sleep.

"You know why he's doin' it, right?" he bellows into the phone. "Because it's his fuckin' kid, that's why. And he's fuckin' groomin' him—a kid with no fuckin' experience whatsoever, who doesn't even fuckin' want the big job. You watch, I bet the kid can't even do it. Big man gets to Chicago, he'll have to pull the trigger himself. Junior'll fuckin' soil himself."

Finding it unnecessary to hear what other emasculating descriptions the goon has for her boyfriend, Maria brushes the blond bangs from her eyes and hails a cab. It's all she can do to keep her balance, let alone saunter back and forth in a manner befitting Fernando's greatest achievement in full-body makeover (seriously, the guy deserves a fucking Oscar for the work he's put in), walking in heels *and* lifts, but she makes it to the yellow door and finally flops down inside.

Tells the driver to take her to JFK.

She's got a plane to catch.

Thirty-Nine
Hurry Up and Wait

Tossing the car keys to the valet, James and Kyle step into the cavernous lobby of the Chicago InterContinental on North Michigan Avenue. As James has explained to his boy, if this is to be their last night on earth, they owe it to themselves to get pampered, powdered and plastered.

Kyle's eyes go wide when the lady behind the desk quotes them a four-digit rate, but James plunks his card down and winks at the girl. In a whisper, Kyle reminds him, "Pop, on the off-chance we don't die tomorrow, we're eventually gonna have to pay that bill."

"I told you, I've got some money stashed away."

The suite is bigger than their house.

Three separate living areas, each with its own master bedroom and bath with granite countertops around the sink and Jacuzzi tub. There's a living room in the middle where they could park the 442.

And a bus to her left and right.

Everything shines, sparkles, or fucking gleams. Kyle practically has to shade his eyes against the luminescent glow of gold and silver. When he does, he finally notices the view. Not that the three walls of glass surrounding the living room are easy to miss, but the gratuitous opulence is enough to occupy the eyes for at least a few minutes before one notices the panoramic view of the city and the massive lakes beyond.

It's enough to clear Kyle's head—momentarily—of the disaster zone their lives have become.

James reads the levity on his boy's face and smiles. Go figure. When they hit the road, all he wanted was for his boy to toughen up. Now, seeing his eyes light up in this hotel room, he's glad he gets to be a boy again, if only briefly.

After waiting for the porcelain coffee pot to brew on a countertop that shines like glass, James carries his mug over to the window and stares blankly at the water, lets Kyle run around the place and check it out. He's nearly reached the bottom of his cup when Kyle dives headfirst upon the couch behind him, exhales heavily, and asks what the next step is.

"Gotta walk over to the Ritz-Carlton, try to get a meeting with Genuardi."

"How do you know he'll be there?"

"In the old days, he kept a house in the suburbs and a suite at the Ritz. I imagine he still runs his outfit that way."

"And if not?"

"Let's put out one fire at a time, shall we?"

*   *   *

Shoulder to shoulder, they glide into the lobby of Genuardi's hotel. If this were a movie, Kyle thinks, they'd be moving in slow-motion.

Which is why, when his father leads him to a pair of massive chairs and sinks down like he's ready for a nap, Kyle feels as if he's been kicked in the teeth.

Seriously, they make it all the way to Chicago, and the plan's to wait?

"Pop, what the hell are we doing?"

"Sit down, take a load off. This is how it works."

Kyle searches around, as if there must be someone there who'll share his disbelief. "How what works?"

When James realizes the kid ain't gonna sit, he leans forward, explains how you don't just walk up to the concierge and ask for the room number of a major mob boss. That'd be like asking the tour guide at the White House if the President is available for a quick talk. You know he's in there somewhere, they know he's in there, but neither of you entertain the illusion that he's, you know, actually in there.

"So what do you do?"

"You take a seat"—James nods at the chair beside his—"and keep your eyes open for somebody who looks mafia."

"And then?"

"You talk. Explain who you are, let him know you're a connected guy, not just some schmo off the streets. Ask graciously if you can have a word with the boss."

Ten minutes they wait in the lobby of the Ritz—which, Kyle is floored to discover, is even more glamorous than their digs over at the InterContinental, what with the mammoth statuary in the middle of its pool-size fountain—before the kid stands up and asserts that their approach to this whole meeting deal is totally bogus.

"We're seriously just gonna sit here?"

"Yeah, we're seriously gonna do that. However long it takes."

"Tell me again why we can't just ask at the front desk. I mean, it couldn't hurt to try."

James rolls his eyes so hard they ache.

When he turns back he finds an empty chair, spots Kyle halfway around that ridiculous fountain, shuffling toward the front desk. Groaning, James hustles to catch up, but there's an efficient elegance to the kid's movements from all the running, and James can't reach him in time.

"Excuse me, my good man," Kyle addresses the finely-tailored clerk. "Is Mr. Genuardi currently staying with us?"

James clamps a hand around Kyle's bicep, about to drag him away before he can cause further damage, when the deskman offers a room number.

"And may I borrow the house phone?" Kyle continues, undeterred.

"Certainly, sir."

The clerk produces the requested amenity, spins it to face Kyle and his father before leaving them to their business. Beating his father to the punch, Kyle insists there's no sense reading him the riot act since simply asking for Genuardi turned out to be the smart move.

"Not so smart if he sends a couple of button men down here."

Still, it was a move born of balls his son's never shown before.

"Relax," Kyle says. But then he pauses with his hand on the phone. Faces his father and nods submissively at the receiver.

"Oh sure," James grumbles. "It's your plan, but I get to do the hard part. Shrewd."

Forty
An Offer He Might Refuse

James can tell by his voice that the bloated guido granting them entrance to Genuardi's suite is the same guy he spoke with on the phone. He's thinking the same thing he kept telling his son on the elevator ride to the penthouse.

It's not supposed to be this easy.

Twenty years have passed, and things may have changed, but James gives his name and says he'd like to see the big man, and they invite him right up?

Something ain't right about that.

Could be James is nervous because Kyle refused to wait downstairs in the lobby. But he doesn't think it's *just* that. Feels too much like he's walking into something.

Something you don't walk out of.

"Jimmy, my boy!"

Genuardi's smile is an obscene hole in a solid mass of bronze plating. He's leaner than he was when James knew him, and his hair's now a slick salt-and-pepper pompadour that would be too thin to sweep back if not for whatever work the guy's had done. Could be hair plugs or a transplant, might even be a rug.

And Genuardi's way too tan for December in Chicago.

Looks like a fucking carrot.

Decked out in a silver designer suit that brings out the distinguished gray of his hair, Genuardi looks as though he's made of the glitzy flash he once eschewed as boss of a powerful American crime family. A guy who didn't need his picture landing in the paper.

"Mr. Genuardi, thanks for seeing us on such short notice. I—"

"Jim, how long we know each other? Call me Carlo. Who's this, your boy?" He evaluates Kyle. "Uncanny, kid's the spitting image of his father. You got a name, little Worthington? Or should we call you Pedals, Jr.?"

"Kyle."

"That's a strong voice, kid. Got balls like your old man, I can tell. But, Jim, enough with the *medigan* shit. *Kyle*? Why not just name him Shamus, for Christ sake."

"Fell for a woman without a drop of Italian blood in her."

"Jim, you're supposed to fuck the mutts, not fall for 'em. What can I do you for?"

Kyle's less than thrilled with the don's assessment of his mother, but James shoots his boy a look urging him to keep cool.

Hesitant because he's still waiting on the catch, some unforeseen development that clarifies why it was so easy to score a meeting with the big man, James asks if the two of them can speak in private. As Genuardi throws an arm over his shoulder and leads him to the master suite, James glances one last time at his son left standing in the foyer beside the burly leg breaker who let them in, and he wishes he'd told Kyle to bring the .38.

It's mystifying, but these guys didn't even bother to frisk them.

Genuardi notices James' concern for the boy, calls over his shoulder for Donnie to fix the kid a drink. Anything he wants.

*   *   *

Genuardi takes up position behind the wall-to-wall wet bar in his office.

"Johnny Walker was it?"

Yeah, Jimmy drank Johnny.

James, he prefers Juicy Juice. Developed a taste for it when his boy was young.

Can't exactly ask the boss of Chicago for a fucking juice box, though.

"Black label. On the rocks."

Genuardi shoots him with a finger. "What brings you to Chicago, Jim? Heard you got outta the game a while back." The old man winks. Everybody knows the details of how Jimmy took off on the Pugliese.

After James explains his predicament, Genuardi tells him he's out of the business.

"I know that's the party line," James says. "I've been in hiding, Mr. Genuardi, but—"

"Carlo."

"I've been hiding, Carlo, I haven't been dead. You don't have to spin it for me like you do in the papers. I was never officially connected, but I was an associate, you know that."

"No, Jim, when I tell you I'm not involved, I mean I'm not involved. Really, I'm out. For good."

He can't mean it. Not the way he's making it sound. "What do you mean?"

"We struggled out here in Chicago for decades. Hate to admit it, but we never had the clout of New York. One by one, the families folded. Everybody sold their holdings in anything illegal, started pumping their cash into real estate as the city cleaned up and became a major media and sports market. Bought into restaurants, bought shares in basketball, baseball. Legitimate businesses.

"Me, I got three high-end places couple blocks from here. Swanky establishments where they charge ya forty bucks a plate and there ain't hardly anything on it. Sold my place in Winetka, moved down to Florida. Got half a dozen restaurants in Miami, own a stable where we breed stallions. Training one down in

Sarasota gonna run in the Preakness. You were lucky to catch me here. Just got into town a few days ago. I'm on a flight to Orlando next Monday."

"You're not kidding?"

Carlo sees the startled disbelief in James' eyes, helps sweep his jaw off the floor. "I'm not saying there isn't the occasional situation in town here where I gotta step in, straighten somebody out. But for all intents and purposes, I'm a businessman on the level now. Tell you the truth, I feel great. I mean, look at me. Pushing seventy years old and I still got a spring in my step, nary a wrinkle on my face. If I was still doing what we did back in the day, I'd be a mess, probably dead."

At least that explains why the meeting was so easy to come by.

Genuardi tilts back a vodka tonic, notices James' untouched whiskey sweating on the bar. "I'd like to help ya, Jim. You were always square with me, you know that. But I can't get involved no more. I help you with this, I gotta worry how that's gonna look in New York. Can't go through any of that, you understand? It would compromise my new empire. The clean one."

When James says nothing—just stares at him so hollowly Genuardi can see right through to his terrified soul—Carlo offers a consolation. "Look, I'm on my way out—gotta make an appearance at each of my places. You know, surprise the cooks and the staff, see how they behave when they're not expecting me to drop by. Why don't you and your boy stay here for the day. Enjoy the suite. You believe there's a pool in the next room? Order up whatever you want. Spend the night. You'll wake up feeling better, I'm sure."

"Two hundred and fifty thousand."

"I'm sorry?"

"Two hundred and fifty thousand dollars. Cash. For you to help us."

Genuardi shakes his glass, swirling the ice and booze. Not drinking, just staring into the pale liquid. "I knew you'd taken a little something for yourself before you hit the wind. That'd be two hundred and fifty thousand of Pugliese's dollars. Either he paid very well or you spent very little."

"Both. You interested in helping us now?"

"In this economy? Be lying if I said I wasn't tempted. Got a restaurant in South Beach about to go under. But—"

"So help us."

Genuardi humors him. "What do you have in mind, Jim?"

"Claim us."

"Claim you?"

"Yeah. Tell Pugliese I'm working for you now. Tell him I can't be touched."

Genuardi takes a drink, shakes his head. "He'll never go for it."

Jimmy fires back the Johnny Walker, slams the glass down on the bar. "You're telling me, for two hundred and fifty large, you won't even try?"

"I'll have to think about it. It's no small thing you're askin'."

"I gotta know within the next twenty-four hours. After that, I'll probably be dead."

Forty-One
The Living Stillness

When James gets through the details, Kyle nods silently.

Then he asks his father if he's ever had a White Russian.

Goes on and on about how much he enjoyed the one Donnie fixed him.

James lets him talk, stares at his own warped reflection in the silver of the elevator door. Two hundred and fifty ain't a number to sneeze at—all that's left of his life of crime. But if Genuardi has really pulled out of the business like he claims, he's got a lot to weigh. James wouldn't say it's a stone-cold lock Genuardi's gonna turn them down, but the odds are definitely not in their favor. If there's an underdog in this race, his name is Worthington.

Of course, it's the only tag he's ever worn.

That's how it goes when you go it alone.

But suddenly, as if to remind him—like, duh—that he hasn't exactly *been* going it alone in recent years, he sees a candy-red Jetta as he and Kyle pass through the revolving door.

And a woman that looks a helluva lot like Beth leaning against it.

James tries to blink the vision away—gotta be some kind of mirage. His conscious mind finally buckling under his weary exhaustion. But this illusion of Beth is apparently as obstinate as the real thing, 'cause she's still there no matter how hard James tries to shake her off.

Next thing he knows, Kyle's calling his own girlfriend's name and Katie's beaming and waving, checking for cross traffic before darting across the avenue. James hadn't even realized she was standing beside Beth.

She may as well not have been. Their expressions couldn't be more different.

'Cause Beth ain't beaming. Ain't waving.

Her arms remain folded across her chest, her eyes twin chunks of stone.

And James knows she's fucking pissed.

*   *   *

A graveyard quiet fills James' suite.

No one's whispered a word since James, seeing Beth was about to open her mouth and unleash a fury out on the street, told her in even tones, "Not now." When she cocked her head in a gesture that said, "Fuck that" and waved her hands like she was again readying herself to explode, James said, "Beth, I'm glad to see you. Let's leave it at that until we're inside."

Forcing an enraged Beth into silence made for one fuck of an awkward walk down Chicago's Magnificent Mile.

Once they're in James' room back at the InterContinental, Beth waits for him to close the door behind the four of them before stepping right into his face. She cocks her arm back and wheels a palm across his cheek. The *crack* echoes off the endless sweep of marble and glass.

James just takes it. Offers no physical or verbal defense. Hangs his head and lets Beth do her thing. Whatever she's got for him, he knows he's fucking earned it.

And, boy, has she got a lot.

Slaps him with her other hand, across his other cheek. Pounds against his chest with the bottoms of both fists before dissolving into a hysterical whirlwind of slaps and punches that glance off his shoulders and neck.

More a funeral dirge than an accusation, she growls over and again, "How dare you. How *dare* you!"

The unchecked, unrestrained tension and fear of the last three days burst from the pit of her anxious stomach. "Whatever this is, whatever you've dragged us into. How *dare* you! And that note you left on the fridge. How *dare* you blame me for any of this. We could have died. Katie had to fucking kill somebody!"

Kyle's eyes are soft on Katie, showing her it's OK. She had to do it.

Katie's response is a stern look that screams, "Fuckin' A I did."

Beth keeps rolling. "What the fuck are you involved in, James?"

For the kids, it's embarrassing to watch. As intimate a scene as if they'd walked in on James and Beth making love and Beth kept right on grinding, audience be damned.

Jimmy catches her by the wrists. "You didn't drive all the way here to smack the shit out of me," he tells her. "You're angry and you're confused, but you came because you love me, right?"

"Love you? *Love you?* You son of a—"

"You got a right to be upset. There are a lot of things I should have told you, and I'm sorry I got you involved in this."

A strangled burp of rage escapes her, and Jimmy raises his voice before she can start blathering again. "I know yelling, hitting me like this, makes you feel better, but it isn't helpful. Settle down, take a seat, and we'll talk. If you want to leave me when this is over, you'll leave me. But right now, you need to listen."

Her lips trembling, Beth steps back. Regaining a touch of self-awareness, embarrassment sets in as she sees Kyle and Katie off by the wall. Placing a hand upon her bosom, forcing deep breaths, she sits on the edge of the longest couch any of them have ever seen.

"I don't...I don't..." She's trying to respond to the suggestion that she would want to leave James. Wants to tell him that's not what she wants. But those words simply won't come. "I don't know what I want."

"Pop."

Kyle nods toward the door. For Katie's benefit, they should stay while James explains the situation, their chances of survival, what he's doing to try to protect them all, set things right so they can go home to Gower.

But Kyle can take care of that.

"Here." James tosses Kyle his phone. "Take my cell. And Katie? Look after him for me, will ya?"

Though James manages a smile, his forced jocularity puts no one at ease.

Still, as the kids walk through the door, neither James nor Beth worries for a second they won't be safe.

James watched his boy club an armed man with a log.

And Katie...well, it's been well-documented what Beth saw *her* do.

Once they're gone, it's just James and Beth.

And the living stillness of that giant suite.

Forty-Two
Better Than Therapy

Coffee shakes rack Dom's body.

And he's gotta take a mad dump.

What's it been, three days without any genuine sleep? Three fucking days, and the closest he's come to rest and relaxation was the night he spent in the hotel when he drifted into a restless sleep that actually made him feel worse for the guilt of having crashed while he was supposed to be keeping an eye and ear on the girls in the next room.

The car running, radio off, Dom drums his shoe against the floorboard, staring across two lanes of North Michigan Avenue traffic. His caffeine-wide eyes have the wet look of an addict either withdrawing or flying really, really high.

There's no more delaying the inevitable.

Time for Dom to show what he's made of.

And he's fucking shitting himself.

Wrestling his cell from his pocket, he makes the obligatory phone call.

"Where are ya?" Rocky asks. "I'll meet ya."

Dom explains how he's managed to corner them inside the InterContinental.

"And 'them' would be…?"

Dom's ready with the names, but he falls silent when he sees the kids shuffling through the revolving door. They hand a maroon-vested valet a ticket and hold hands, waiting for the 442 to come around.

"I'm seven minutes away," Rocky tries again in a frustrated bark. "You're out front? Whaddya drive?"

But Dom tells Rocky he'll call him back and abruptly hangs up.

'Cause the kids are alone. And Dom's thinking they might not panic if he were to approach them with his hands above his head professing a desire to simply talk things through.

Could be the three of them would be able to figure a way out of this clusterfuck.

For all of them.

*   *   *

By the time the attendant whips the Olds around, Kyle and Katie have graduated from handholding to expressing how much they missed each other the way only the young can.

Which is to say, the valet has to grunt six or seven times before they finally peel their reddened faces apart to take the keys from the man's grip.

Kyle retrieves a couple bucks from his front pants pocket for a tip. Then he goes for the driver's seat, and Katie's all, what the fuck?

"You can't drive," she tells him.

"Why not?"

"For one, your permit's no good in a different state. And even if it were, you can't drive with just me in the car. I still have a junior license."

"How come everybody knew the out-of-state thing but me?" he asks rhetorically. "I think we've graduated from worrying over traffic violations, don't you? Besides, who do you think drove this tank into town?"

"Your father let you drive this thing? I can't believe it." She climbs into the passenger seat. "Do you even know how to drive stick?"

Sitting beside her, Kyle says, "Sure, Lacy…"

Makes it no further than her name before he's choking back tears.

But, goddammit, he's not gonna cry in front of his girlfriend again.

"What is it, Ky?" Her hand rubs at his shoulder.

"You didn't hear. Lacy…she…they got to her." He struggles to swallow. "She's dead."

"Oh my God." Katie doesn't know what to feel, but she knows Kyle needs her. "Ky—"

"I'm all right," he insists. "I just haven't had much of a chance to think about it. I need a minute."

"Of course.

Steeling himself, he stares through the wheel, blowing big breaths.

And turns the key.

Actually starts nodding as he revs the engine, gets his emotions in check. "You think my father letting me drive his car's a shocker," he goes on, "wait until you hear the rest."

When he spots an entrance ramp for route 41, North Lake Shore Drive, he hops back out on the road he and his father took into town. Running along Lake Michigan, it'd be the perfect route for a romantic drive under better circumstances.

Instead, it provides the scenery for the narrative of Jimmy Pedals.

For Katie, it all comes from way the fuck out in left field.

James Worthington worked for the mob?

What next? Mr. Rogers got his start doing porn?

But that doesn't mean she's letting Kyle off the hook. "Yeah, but you still could have answered my calls. Jesus, I was terrified when you disappeared. Shoulda heard what the kids at school were saying."

"Oh yeah?"

Katie ignores the titillation in his voice. "Why didn't you call me back?"

"Couldn't."

"Don't give me that. I've spent the last three days in a car, too. I had time to call *you*."

"No, I mean I couldn't. My father threw my phone out the window."

"*Your* father?" Katie shakes her head, dumbfounded. Still can't see James in that light.

"What you said, about the guy you shot—"

"Killed, Kyle. I killed him." She says it coldly, looks him dead in the eye when she does. Wants to see exactly how much revulsion he might feel.

"Right. You did what you had to do."

In the way he stares back at her, she knows he means it, which is sweet and comforting.

But who the fuck needs his approval?

"We'll put aside that he was gonna rape and kill me, then do the same to Beth. He looked at me like everybody looks at me. Saw it in his eyes, two seconds and he had me measured up, decided the blond ditz wasn't a threat. The way he was assaulting me made it easy to pull the trigger, but it was that look that made it easy to walk away without a second thought."

Suddenly, Kyle's in the middle of *I Spit On Your Grave*. "That's good" is all he can say.

"Good?" Katie mocks. "It was better than therapy."

"You know, I, uh, hit a farmer over the head with a log."

She manages half a smile.

As if he's three and he used the big boy potty for the first time.

Kyle looks away in total emasculation.

He's shown her his, he's seen hers, and hers is so much bigger.

"Hey, since when do you give a shit about Beth?"

"Been a long three days."

As if on cue, Kyle spies a silver Mustang flashing its lights in his sideview mirror.

Thinks, *And only getting longer.*

Forty-Three
Youthful Indiscretions

"It's bullshit," Beth insists when James is done explaining. "You didn't do those things."

"I'm sorry, Beth. I should have told you. I thought it was all behind me."

"It's not true. You made it up. I don't know why, but you're lying."

She shivers when he sits beside her, and his heart sinks. "Think about it. Is there any other reason that kid took a shot at me? Why Kyle and me are three states from home, running for our lives."

"Maybe there's…I don't know…another woman. Something like that."

"I wish it were that simple."

"How, James? How could you—*you*—have done all that? You go to bed at 8:30, for Christ sake."

"My life was a lot different back then." He sighs. "Listen, I have an idea how I can put this behind us for good. Tomorrow afternoon—"

"Are you a murderer, James?"

He stops talking as if she put a bullet in him, point blank range.

His inability to look her in the eye is all the confession she needs.

"My God. Your hands have been all over me. James, you've been…inside me hundreds, thousands, of times." She looks away, repulsed.

"No. That guy, the one you lay beside at night, he didn't do those things. That was some hard luck kid who wasn't smart enough to figure out a better way."

"No. Uh-uh. Being young and foolish doesn't get you off the hook." She swallows hard. "You didn't know that when I was thirteen I went down on Billy Preston in the boys' bathroom before third period, did you?" She pauses for the visual to set in. "Now that you do, you can't tell me you don't see me a little differently. And that was a blow job. Everybody involved went home *happy*."

"I…it…thirteen, really?"

"Go to hell."

"Beth, I can't change what happened when I was young. Best I can do is fix it so nothing like this ever happens to us again. That's gonna have to be good enough."

"How?" she challenges him. "What are you gonna do?"

James rubs his weary face. "If I'm involved with one crime family, none of the others can touch me. Not without a high-level sit down. Not without approval from the boss. It's an understanding among the families."

"What are you talking about? You're still working for these people?"

"No. There's a man in Chicago that I used to work for a long time ago. If I can get him to tell New York that I'm connected to him in some way—working for him, something—and I'm not to be touched, they'll back down. I'm meeting with him tomorrow."

"Will he do that for you?"

"I promised to make it worth his while."

"And if he doesn't?"

"Either he's gonna help me or he's gonna kill me, Beth. That's what they do."

"*Us*," she forcibly corrects him. "You've put all of our lives in jeopardy. And you bet your ass we're coming to that meeting with you."

James starts to laugh.

Sees not an ounce of humor in Beth's expression.

"Beth, I'm not taking you—"

"And that's the best plan you can come up with?" she plows on. "You say you worked for these guys—that you were a criminal—and all you've got is a glorified coin toss? Tails you live, heads you die."

"Best I can figure. I told you, I'm not that guy anymore."

Beth still ain't buyin' that. Though she can't tell James as much because the ringing of her cell phone interrupts them. When she sees James' number on the call ID, she flips the phone open, hears Kyle's voice.

"Beth, you and Dad better get out of the hotel. Go some place public. I'm pretty sure we're being followed."

Forty-Four
The Kids

Twenty minutes that silver car's been on their ass. The driver's pulsed his headlights a dozen times trying to get them to pull over.

Needless to say, they don't. Not just because there isn't much of a shoulder on North Lake Shore Drive, but that's something you just don't do when you're on the run from the mob and a car you've never seen before takes a sudden, keen interest in you.

The guy keeps on. Rides their bumper, flashes his lights.

Neither Kyle nor Katie says a word. They don't have to. The nervous glances they share in the mirror say enough.

It's not until the Mustang gets ballsy, pulls up alongside the 442 on the driver's side that they get a good look at the guy. Kyle sees the suit and the tan, knows he's one of them.

Katie? She scolds herself for not killing the asshole when she had the chance.

Her boyfriend's eyes become softballs when she leans forward and slips Angelo's .45 from her waistband, pulls back on the slide.

"Holy fuck!"

He ducks as Katie turns his way, raising a fucking hand-cannon beside his ear.

"Watch out," she warns.

Crouched over the wheel, Kyle shoots a glance at the car beside them, sees the driver's expression, dopey and beckoning. Could be a History teacher ready to start a lecture.

The sight of that .45, though, sends him receding into himself with fear.

Kyle's not sure if it's the obscene squeal of those Ford tires as the guy cuts the wheel or the thundering gong of the .45 in his ear as Katie pulls the trigger, but his heart lodges itself in the back of his throat as the gunshot destroys his sense of sound. He has to struggle to keep the car steady.

The shot sends Katie flying back against the passenger door, her gun hand striking the ceiling, knocking the .45 to the floor. Her wind escapes her and she's too disoriented to see the bullet drive a hole through the Mustang's passenger door, an inch beneath the base of the window.

Kyle's window has given way in the center to a quarter-size hole, hub to a countless array of broad cracks that radiate from it like rays of white sunshine. As shocked as he was watching his girlfriend play Annie Oakley, Kyle immediately forgets the surrealism of the moment when he sees the back of her head bounce off the window. Though he knows he won't be able to hear her answer over the dull ringing in his ears, he asks if she's OK, hollering the question loud enough he can just hear the faint echo of his own voice.

Breathless, her hair frayed and wild, Katie manages a nod.

Seeing her like that, Kyle's mind closes around the white-hot glow of the only words he can remember.

His father's voice.

Hit first, hit hard.

And he jerks the wheel to his left.

Swings the edge of the 442's Detroit-made bumper into the Mustang's passenger door.

The Mustang may as well be made of plastic the way it bounces into the left lane, taking with it a dent dug so broad and deep it could have been made with a bowling ball.

As if through a long, dark tunnel, Kyle hears a chorus of car horns as he steers right, lays hard on the brakes and barely manages to guide the 442 to an off ramp just before it whips past.

*   *   *

Working for the old man is bad enough. Mostly because Rocky doesn't actually *work* for the old man anymore. But working for the kid? The Pugliese's discovered a new way to make him their unwitting bitch.

It's fucking amazing. The don's kid calls him up, pays him all the courtesy one would expect from the young ADD-afflicted fuck Rocky's sure he is, then hangs up. Leaving Rocky with the slimmest of cursory details, the kid sounding like he could give a shit if he figures the rest out or not.

Everybody involved—save for the don himself—knew from day one that kid wasn't Pugliese material. He was soft, college-bound. Fit to run a veterinary clinic, not lead a New York crime family.

If a man could be allergic to a life of crime, Dom would itch like a motherfucker.

Still the old man's doing everything in his power to pull little Dominic into a life he wants no part of. On a job like this, that's how guys get dead.

And the number one reason Rocky said *sayonara* to his former source of income was an overwhelming desire to not get dead.

Be that as it may, the boss has saddled him with a task, and he can't get back to his very simple retired life in Chicago until he sees it through. So he exhales a reluctant breath and takes a ride down North Michigan Avenue, hoping he can find where in relationship to the InterContinental the kid is stationed. Does three laps around the block, but since he has no idea what the kid's driving or what the hell he looks like these days, he can't find the little shithead.

He does, however, see a sight so fascinating he nearly jams his brakes in the middle of the busy avenue.

Wasn't it just this morning he thought of Jimmy Pedals?

Now he sees a guy—staring hard in his direction with the same unmistakable, defiant baby blues—hop into a Jetta with some fine redheaded piece of ass.

When the Jetta jumps out of its parking space, its burning tires trailing white smoke, Rocky thinks it might be prudent to follow.

*   *   *

With the hulking headlights of a semi closing in on him, Dom pauses to recap.

He tried to make nice with the kids. Flashed the lights, waved real friendly. Anything to show them he wanted to call a truce and talk this whole crazy thing over. That way, he wouldn't have to kill them or their adult counterparts back at the InterContinental.

And they responded by opening fire and pushing him into oncoming traffic.

Closing his eyes and turning hard right, Dom promises himself he's calling no quarter from here on out if God sees fit to guide him safely through the two lanes of cars and trucks bearing down on him.

The horns cry long and loud, and there's a split-second where Dom's certain he sees the pearly gates glowing against the darkness of his lowered eyelids, but when he peaks out again, he's back in his own lane, unscathed.

Only problem is, he's moving too fast, and he's aimed at the shoulder.

Which is narrow and bordered by a waist-high retaining wall.

Of concrete.

A pickup truck coming up behind him has to brake and cut around as he careens across both northbound lanes, the chipped beige concrete swelling to consume the view through his windshield.

There's nothing to do but brace for impact or go with the momentum, keep the wheel turning, so Dom tugs that fucker as far to the right as he can force it. The back end fishtails until he's facing the cars behind him. Would keep spinning right around—endlessly, forever and ever, it feels to Dom—if not for the concrete border.

The retaining wall leaps out at the Ford, catches the rear driver's side with enough force to crumple the side panel nearly to the tire. The segment of the divider the Mustang's kissing breaks in half, collapses onto the grass beyond the road.

Cars are winging past him, giving the finger, suggesting a variety of acts he should perform on his mother, but at last the Ford comes to a stop. Facing the wrong direction, Dom realizes he's a mere twenty yards from the exit ramp the kids took. As bad as he's shaking from head to toe, his nerves are no match for the infuriated adrenaline swimming in his veins.

He hits the flashers and welcomes another onslaught of horns as he drives down the shoulder—in the wrong direction—toward the exit for Northwestern University.

*   *   *

Kyle and Katie are cruising past what looks like the campus library—bizarrely round interconnected buildings that resemble farm silos—scrambling for a place to ditch the 442 and camouflage themselves among the mass of students walking to and from classes. All at once, they turn simultaneously to one another, their faces twitching with dazed discomfort.

What the fuck are they doing?

Here they are, surrounded by young adults just a few years their senior, whose biggest worry is which Thursday night keg party to attend, and they're looking for a parking lot where they can inconspicuously ditch the world's most conspicuous monstrosity.

Because if they don't, Scott Baio in his silver Ford will run them down.

As he slows the car for a class-bound twenty-something in pleated khakis and a preppie sweater, Kyle doesn't know if he envies the guy or wishes he could rouse him from the complacent slumber of his sheltered life.

The appearance of Dom's mangled 'Stang in his rearview mirror leaves him no time to decide.

At first, Kyle thinks maybe the driver hasn't spotted them, but then he sees the car lurch forward, picking up speed like a hunting dog dragging its owner behind, hot on the trail of a wounded bird.

Fucking yellow-and-black car.

It would stick out like a sore thumb *among* sore thumbs.

Kyle punches the gas, the preppie cursing him as he dives out of the way, stains his pleated khakis on the dirt and grass.

Closing the gap, Dom hits the speed bump before the crosswalk, which sends his unbuckled ass into the air, his skull thumping the headliner. Teeth clenched in a sneer, bleary eyes bulging in their sockets, he grips the wheel as if he's trying to tear it from the dash. If the kids in the 442 could see him now, they'd surmise he just might be angry enough to summon that kind of guttural adrenaline-strength.

All that hesitation—his bullshit insistence that he can somehow be a wiseguy without dirtying his hands—has vanished like blood down a drain. Seeped through his pores in the sweat he bled as that Mack truck threatened to pulverize every bone in his body, leaving only the salty residue of his former cowardice.

An absence of sentimentality.

A blind white-knuckle rage.

He holds the wheel even with the 442's dual exhaust pipes, pushes the pedal to the floor.

Fuck these kids.

*   *   *

If James were in the car, he'd laugh.

One of those "new" muscle cars trying to keep up with a 390-block from the golden age? Thinking it could actually do some damage if it somehow managed to make contact? Please. That Ford "Mustang" is a glorified rice-burner. A cheap-shit knock-off of the Jap variety that happens to bear an American name.

And a classic name does not a classic machine make.

But James isn't in the car, and James doesn't have to contend with the litter of college kids who have decided, en masse, that now is a good time to cross the main drag through campus. The swan dive that preppie kid took when Kyle first hit the gas? Despite Kyle's incessant horn-honking, it's quickly becoming a Northwestern ritual for students and staff.

That's right, staff, too. Right after a young couple, heretofore holding hands and smiling, hit the grass, a tweed-loving professor—thick beard, gray fedora, glasses, the obligatory curved meerschaum pipe—joins the dance as well. It's more a flop than a dive, the old coot staggering back the way he came like a stiff breeze blew him down, but he hits the turf just like the rest of them.

Wearing their lap belts, Kyle and Katie still whiplash toward the dashboard when the Mustang jars into the Olds. As James would have predicted, the collision causes more damage to the attacker than to the victim. The gentle curve of the Mustang's front end, with its tiny round headlights and its lone-stallion logo, fucking *inverts* around the high, angular rear edge of the 442.

Dom loses horsepower, struggles as the torque threatens to force the wheel from his hands, the car skidding across both lanes of Campus Drive, falling three or four lengths behind the Olds. Kyle and Katie watch the Ford's headlights recede, waste no time taking full advantage. Before Kyle can even ask, Katie's got Angelo's .45 in her hand again.

"Think you can handle it this time?"

Katie really isn't sure. Though she'd never admit it to Kyle.

"If you can keep the car on the road."

She thins herself out, squeezes between the two front seats onto the back bench.

"What are you doing?"

As the rear driver's window rolls down, they're blasted with a bitter fucking Chicago wind and Katie rests her forearms on the sill behind Kyle, palms clamped around the butt of the .45 poking through the frame.

The Ford distant in their rearview, they pass a massive parking lot on their left that would have made a great hiding spot for the 442 if they'd found it earlier. Then Kyle sees a line of joggers in hoodies on a bike path through what a campus street sign brands "Centennial Park."

He tells Katie to hold on and slaps the horn.

Katie feels the car slow significantly, the dip in momentum squeezing her against the back of Kyle's seat, her stomach doing back flips as the car turns unexpectedly to the left. The joggers drift to either side of the narrow road as the car glides through, parting them like the Red Sea.

Once past the joggers, the path is empty. It being winter in Chicago, the timing is not ideal for a bike ride. The guys in the hoodies must be members of the track or cross-country team.

Only those crazy bastards would be running in ten-degree weather.

Kyle knows from experience.

As thickets of trees whip past, Kyle peers anxiously into the rearview mirror, hoping the Ford was far enough behind that the driver didn't see them make the turn. But glancing back, he sees a silver blur spin jauntily off Campus Drive and into Centennial Park, missing the bike path at first and kicking up divots of grass like swatches of carpet as it makes its way onto the pavement again.

"This time," Kyle yells to Katie, recalling his father's advice, "try not to think about anything."

When she squeezes the trigger, Katie concentrates on flexing the muscles in her shoulders, even pushing the gun forward as the shots ring out in defense of the recoil that has thus far kicked her ass. She still bounces back with each shot, but she's wedged securely enough against the window frame that there's nowhere for her body to go.

The first few shots fly wide, and Dom breathes a little easier.

Remembering it's a pair of teenage kids he's dealing with.

Until the next three pierce the windshield over his head and he has to duck beneath the wheel and drive blind.

Kyle watches in his rearview mirror as the Ford swerves off the path, first to the right, then the left as Dom struggles to keep her on course. He sees, with disappointment, the Mustang turn just in time to dodge a tree.

Once he thinks he's got her moving in a straight line, Dom hits the gas. Head ducked just below the dashboard, he prays he's heading straight for the car in front of him and not a maple.

The impact is solid, the squealing clap of metal-on-metal unmistakable.

The gun flies from Katie's grip.

She watches as it skips across the pavement into the bushes beside the path.

Hauling herself back through the window, she sees the guy from James' kitchen when she looks through the rear windshield.

He's literally right on their tail.

Like he's glued to their bumper.

Kyle's fully aware of the situation. That continual grind of steel behind him lets him know for sure, as if the widescreen image of the Ford in his rearview mirror weren't enough, that the driver's trying to give the 442 the perfect nudge to one side or the other and spin Kyle out of control into the park.

"Katie, shoot him!"

"I lost the gun!"

Feeling royally fucked, Kyle looks frantically around.

Sees an endless tangle of trees on both sides of the ongoing path.

There's a beach area on Lake Michigan to his left where the Sailing School keeps its boathouse and the crew team does its rowing—all of that on hiatus in the dead of February—but Kyle doesn't think they're desperate enough to risk punching through the trees to reach the open sand. Odds are pretty good they'd end up wrapped around a tree trunk before their rally wheels would find the sand.

Then he sees the guido aiming a revolver through the Ford's driver's side window.

And Kyle figures, fuck it.

The way he's got the 'Stang pinned to their rear bumper, Dom's confident he can keep the car straight while firing the .38. But when the kid in front of him hooks the wheel hard left, hobbles and hops onto the grass, it becomes a whole new story.

Pissed as he is, Dom doesn't think twice before following behind, keeping the Ford right on that 442's ass. Together, they tango around trees, moving slower but far too fast for the topography. More than once, the 442 leaves streaks of yellow on the bare trunks of maple.

Katie's crouched behind Kyle's seat, her hands laced over her head in bomb-drill mode, thinking this is a pretty shitty idea.

Kyle knows how she feels.

If he weren't already feeling less of a man than his girlfriend after the whole she-shot-a-guy-and-all-I-did-was-club-a-farmer-with-a-log thing, he'd be unable to keep from screaming like a three-year-old who wants his mommy.

Though he's nowhere near clear of mind, Kyle's pretty sure the douche bag behind him is so close to his bumper he can't see anything in front of the 442. When Kyle swerves right, the asshole behind swerves right, blindly, it seems. If that's the case, Kyle thinks maybe he can give the guy what he wants.

You want to see a car collide with a big ass tree? Here's your front row seat, asshole.

Kyle finds a maple with a trunk half the width of the 442, aims the center of his hood—right where the dual grilles come together in a point—at the center of its diameter.

The Ford follows, bouncing lightly off his rear bumper with a scratch of metal.

Just as he's about to collide with destiny, his pulse pounding in his ears, Kyle calls out:

"I love you, Katie!"

Her face between her knees, Katie's like, helluva time for that, Ky.

And then she's thrown against the door as the car careens around the tree at the absolute last second, breaking through to the deserted beach, missing the bark by half a breath.

The Mustang?

It ain't so lucky.

Dom's looking at the 442, then all of a sudden he's staring at a big fucking tree.

As the Olds comes to a stop, its tires spraying sand and grit as the back end swerves, Kyle sees the silver Ford running up the side of the tree, the chassis flying like a stunt on *The Dukes of Hazard*.

For a second, it's a thing of beauty.

A land vehicle in flight.

Though, when it crashes against a second tree and slides harshly to the ground, coming violently to rest on its side, that ain't so pretty.

There's no fire. No explosion. But so wrapped around that trunk is the Ford, it almost looks like it's giving birth to a maple tree.

Forty-Five
Retired Life

Beth's behind the wheel of the Jetta, rambling mindlessly in panic-talk. There's a lot of "Where are they?" Some "We shouldn't have let them go."

She's tracked the kids all the way to the campus of Northwestern University, checking Katie's laptop for a GPS signal before they left the InterContintental and then stopping again at a Starbucks with free Wi-Fi. Once they hit campus, they tapped into the school's wireless network, watched the red dot right there in the car.

James is impressed. He knew she was resourceful, but he's never seen Beth work her way through a pinch like this. He's tried Kyle on the cell, but the kid ain't answering, and James finds it impossible to sit still in the passenger seat as they tear down Campus Drive.

Plus, he's worrying over what it might mean that Rocky's in Chicago.

At least it looked like Rocky back on North Michigan.

Sonny described him as "retired," said he hadn't been around New York in a while.

Could that be?

"There they are!" Beth shouts in an impossible mix of terror and relief.

James snaps to attention, sees the kids idling at a corner, catching their breath behind glazed eyes. He tells Beth to pull up alongside, where Katie—back in the passenger seat—rolls the window down so James can shout across both women to Kyle.

"You two OK?"

Kyle nods. "Campus Security's gonna be on us, like, any second. This car fucking glows in the dark."

"Where's the guy that came after you?"

"Kissing a tree."

"Might still be alive," Katie clarifies, an obvious desire to go back and finish the job coating her voice. James would be in favor of that—they've clearly left too many loose ends in their wake already—but with a sound of sirens swelling across campus, he knows they don't have time to check on a job that is likely already finished.

Instead of doubling back, he takes a long indulgent look at the Olds. Realizes what they have to do, but the words take their time finding his tongue.

"Get in," he tells the kids.

"What about Grandpa's...your car?" Kyle demands.

James swallows what feels like a rock. There's a sharp flame inside his chest like his heart's been cut out, filleted and roasted over coals. He can't make the words leave his lips.

"James, come on," Beth screams.

Deep and rough, like he has to vomit the words just to get them out:

"Leave it."

Kyle gives him a gaping look as if he's suggested they abandon a wounded comrade. "Pop—"

"Just do it," his father says through clenched teeth. "There's no time."

Hearing the choked emotion in her boyfriend's voice, Beth groans.

Boys and their toys.

But the 442 is more than that to James. To Kyle now, too. Heartbroken, the kid yanks the keys, and he and Katie pile into the cherry-red Jetta.

*   *   *

Rocky waits until the four of them pull away, then takes the bike path and finds what must be Dom's car on its side, the roof resting against a tree.

Unfortunately, a white cruiser marked "Campus Security" pulls up at the same time.

The security guard—a young guy in a navy-blue uniform with the muscular build of a police force reject—gets out, mouths, "Holy shit," then carries himself toward the wreckage with the erect posture of a detective arriving at a murder scene.

This doesn't make Rocky happy.

He was hoping to get in and out before the authorities descended upon the wreck. Barring that, he'd have been content meeting up with some aging rent-a-cop he could ply with a handful of bills. But a campus cop who sees the crash as his shining opportunity to be all he can be, he's gonna be a problem.

"Excuse me, officer," Rocky calls, stepping out of his sedan.

The guy does a quick one-eighty, extends a palm in Rocky's direction. "Stay in your car, sir. It's not safe for you to be here. Get back behind the wheel and keep moving."

"That's a friend of mine down there. I gotta make sure he's all right."

"It's a Campus Security issue now, sir, please get back in your car."

"Gosh, it looks so bad, officer. Do you think he's all right?"

It's too tempting for Super Cop not to look back at the wreck. When he does, he thinks, yeah, it's pretty bad. Your buddy's fucked.

He turns back to Rocky, intending not to voice his thoughts, but to tell him once again that he'll take care of the situation and Rocky should get back in his car.

Only it turns out the guy's given his first and last order as a wannabe cop.

'Cause Rocky puts two silenced rounds in his chest.

Moving quickly, he approaches the car, hopes like hell Dom's gonna make it. Rocky can't imagine the bitch it would be having to tell the old man his kid bought it.

And Rocky's *retired* for fuck sake.

Forty - Six
A Folk Antihero

Carlo Genuardi enters the pool area wrapped in a blue shag robe, Donnie and another swarthy mountain of a bodyguard clearing all bystanders so the man can have some privacy. What few linger around the Olympic-size pool and twenty-six-person hot tub show immediate deference when they see Genuardi walk in. Even the strays and the stubborns who are thinking, *Who the fuck is this guy that I gotta leave the pool area?* change their tune when their buddies take them by the elbow, whisper persuasive explanations in their ears.

No shit? He's *that* guy?

Genuardi's goons take up position in opposite corners of the hazy football field of a room. Protection that is gratuitous now, the former don knows, but there are certain expectations when he comes to town. That he put on the show, remind people of old Chicago and how things once were.

Though he'd generally consider it beneath him to use a public amenity, the pool in his suite is unadorned with a Jacuzzi. And once he's alone, sinking into 100-degree water that instantly loosens up the old muscles, leaning against jets that blast away the knots of his sixty-eight years, he makes a mental note to talk to hotel management about some renovations. It's bullshit that Carlo Genuardi should have to congregate with the masses if he wants a nice hot soak.

To the common Chicagoan, Carlo knows he represents the sentiment that a man can start with nothing and pull himself up by his bootstraps. And since most choose to overlook the fact that he did so through theft, corruption, and murder, he graciously nurtures his admirers' affections by going through the classic *capo* motions.

Even though he now wields as much power as the janitor at the pentagon.

Sure, it's the pentagon, but the guy's just cleaning up shit for a living.

Still, in exchange for his efforts keeping old Chicago in the forefront of people's minds, they offer him respect like no honest man can achieve. Because he's a folk antihero whose success promises their hard work will someday pay great dividends.

And now Jimmy Pedals comes into his town and tries to bribe him like he's some flatfoot street cop.

It's not that he doesn't want to help Jimmy out, because Genuardi still loves to do favors. And it's not that he doesn't like him, because the kid's got guts and heart, and his leaving the Pugliese in the lurch brought Carlo close to tears of joy once upon a time.

It's just that, even if he hasn't been a full-time resident in twelve, thirteen years, and there hasn't been a family for him to lord over in nearly as long, Chicago still *belongs* to Carlo Genuardi. He need look no further than the faces of its adoring citizens to know that for certain.

And what message would it send to the people who respect him so highly if he were to allow some nobody who was barely connected to some New York family many, many years ago to come into his town and coax him into what could become a foolish war with the Pugliese?

That admiration in the eyes of his constituents? That's based on the *legend* of Carlo Genuardi. The myth. Returning to a criminal life against his will, on Jimmy Pedals' terms, could only tarnish that legacy, humanize him in a way that would open their eyes to the one fact Genuardi refuses to accept.

That he's become just like them.

Some Joe Nobody earning a living like any other sucker.

If it's a choice between that and turning his back on an old associate, Carlo doesn't see much choice at all.

Donnie responds to a snap of the former don's fingers, crosses the room, his spit-shined shoes clacking against the concrete, produces his boss's cell phone. From the soothing waters of the hot tub, Carlo dials Don Pugliese.

* * *

"Banged up," the doctor tells Rocky, "but it's nothing serious. Little bed rest and he'll be in the clear."

Rocky, ever the man of few words, nods his gratitude, peels three bills from his roll and sends the man, a medical expert who got richer than rich serving Carlo Genuardi, on his way.

Rocky waves a hand in front of Dom's face. Aside from a pained grumble, he remains inert on the bed. But Rocky can see by the rise and fall of his chest that, despite his reluctance to take part in the family business, the kid's a fighter with a strong heart and an equally strong will. Doc's right. He'll be fine.

It's a bigger relief to Rocky than when his last prostate exam came back clean.

When he stood atop the driver's side of the crumpled Mustang and wrenched the bent and jammed door free from its housing, he found a rag doll in place of the don's kid. Hustling him, over one broad shoulder, back to his sedan, Rocky may as well have been carrying a sack of busted chicken bones.

The old 442 he saw abandoned on a campus street corner has him pacing the kid's bedside, too. The one to which Jimmy Worthington's trail led him. It could only mean one thing.

Pedals is the target.

So, with the kid likely to be out for the rest of the night, Rocky leaves the room he'd been instructed to prepare for Dominic at the Ritz-Carlton—Genuardi's regular haunt, but Don Pugliese insisted he wanted his kid set up at the best place in town and Carlo Genuardi could go fuck himself if he didn't like it—and dials up the boss.

"Yeah, your kid's gonna be all right."

The don wants to know if it looks like Dominic will still be able to take care of that thing they're all here to see about, and Rocky assures him the kid just needs to rest a couple of hours. Be good as new after that.

"But seeing as how he ain't in much shape to explain all of this to me," Rocky reasons, "I'm gonna need to know—from you—a little more about this thing I gotta coach him through. Maybe start with Jimmy Pedals and what the hell he's doing in Chicago."

Rocky nods along to the details as he takes the short walk down the Magnificent Mile to the InterContinental for a little sit-down with Jimmy Pedals. He's pretty sure the boss wouldn't approve, so Rocky doesn't bother to run the idea past him. It's something he's gotta do for himself. And Worthington.

The way Rocky sees it, he owes the guy at least that much.

Forty-Seven
Some Help

Dom's only asleep for another two hours.

His eyes open, but he still can't see more than a smear of brilliant light. Startled, he shakes an axe-split head until shapes start to solidify. He's in a hotel room, but he couldn't even begin to guess which one or how in God's name he got there. Slapping distraught palms against his forehead, he feels a soft hulk of gauze adhered to his skull.

Frightened and confused, he darts from the king-size bed, past ornate medieval furniture, to find the wall-length mirror above an oaken chest of drawers. He studies the bandage on his brow and the dual medical grade Band-Aids across his cheek. His disorientation swirls, as if his head is a building the rest of his body is suddenly struggling to balance atop his shoulders.

Falling into a chair large enough to swallow him whole, his head swims in anger and self-loathing. A sudden nausea overtakes him, and he drops his head between his knees.

His white-hot pursuit of the kids in the 442 comes flooding back to him. Dom sees what he saw glancing back at him in the rearview mirror. His eyes veiny golf balls, hair a tangle of dark weeds. Sheer fury of hell bleeding through his pores.

Then the tree.

Then…nothing.

At least not as far as he can remember. Hasn't got a clue how he got off campus.

But he remembers the feral intensity in his face as he pursued those kids. He'd exploded, tried to kill them. More his father's son than he knew.

Dom throws up on the three thousand dollar carpet.

* * *

Stepping into the hall, he turns back to the door, rests his head against the cool wood as the lock clicks into place. Breathing deep, summoning a steady foot, he examines the hallway.

Some spread. Broad enough you could run a two-lane down the middle. Classy works of European art from a variety of eras speckle the walls, interspersed by white Etruscan sculptures six feet high, each adorned with some half-naked Goddess Dom can't quite identify lording over a fountain of running water.

It's designed to impress a crowd that's long since grown bored with being impressed.

But the trickling water only makes Dom wish he'd taken a piss before leaving his room.

There's no one in the hall except one tall, elegant stranger with long blond hair and sunglasses the size of headlights— stylish overkill in the hotel's dim lamplight—leaning against the wainscoted wall, checking her manicure. Dom staggers dumbly past, patting himself down in a sudden surge of panic.

Perfect. He can't find a room card anywhere on him.

An exhausting frustration settles in, and he wants nothing more than to pass out right there in the hallway. Even if he'll look like some drunken ass in front of the girl. What does he care? At least maybe she'll call for help.

God knows he could use some.

His hands are on his knees, and he's ready to collapse against the wall, when he hears a chorus of laughter so familiar it stiffens his spine. Still uneasy on his feet, he continues down the hallway, holding onto the paint as if he were a misguided youth and it his counselor. It seems an eternity before he comes to the door, but when he does there's no mistaking who's inside.

He's barely done knocking when Big Bobby Battaglia opens wide, his stone look going soft, face cracking in a mischievous smile. "Hey, Boss," he calls over his shoulder, "somebody here to see ya."

As if in a fever dream, Dom drags his heels as Bobby ushers him into the room, leading him across the main living area of the suite. Passing through the two-story affair—with its spiral staircase, a polished mahogany bar running the length of the wall, endless white marble corridors disappearing into more rooms than his dizzy head can count—everything's so bright and ornate Dom starts to worry that he never made it out of the Mustang, that he's actually arrived at St. Peter's pad in the Great Upstairs.

He passes two lifers—guys who have worked for his old man for, like, centuries—wearing wife-beaters on a couch before a row of oily firearms. They've got each piece broken down on white rags stained black, and they're ritualistically clearing out the barrels and wiping them clean, checking the serial numbers are ground away.

One of them nods up at Dom as he passes. The other's engulfed in a cloud of cigar smoke. He's either too busy to look up from the guns or he holds the opinion that's most popular among the family in regard to Dom and the total abortion of a gangster he's grown up to be.

That's it for the old-timers. There are so precious few left in the family.

Off in the corner, Richie DeRosa and Petey D'Angelo are doggedly cranking out pushups, their skin glistening like caramel. They're stripped down to brightly colored Speedo underwear, their formal attire wonderfully wrinkle-free, draped over the back of a nearby love seat.

Sweating, huffing, crying out with each rep, they may as well be fucking one another in the ass.

Dom wonders if anybody's brought it to their attention that there's probably a state-of-the-art gym down on the first floor.

At a table of swirling marble, Don Anthony sits surrounded by five of his young up-and-comers, throwing down cards and grinning confusedly. They're teaching him some new variation of Hold 'Em, and even though the old man's never played before, he's magically winning every hand.

Imagine that.

When the don realizes Bobby's got somebody with him, he stands in his slacks and suspenders that droop around his weathered frame, waves a hand through the cigar smoke and squints at his boy's disheveled coiffure. The don ambles across the room, offers an obligatory hug and kiss. A by-the-numbers gesture he'd offer any member of the family.

Sure, the kid could have died in that mangled Mustang, but that doesn't excuse the disrespect and negligence that characterize his behavior. Behavior the don's tolerated for far too long.

"You feelin' OK? Rocky said it was some mash-up he pulled you outta."

"Rocky?"

"Yeah. Gave me a call, filled me in. Supposed to be meetin' us here shortly."

Dom looks as if he's forgotten his own name. "Am I home? I'm not finished in Chicago yet."

"*Madonn'*, that crash jumbled your melon but good. We're *in* Chicago."

"What...What are you doing here? Won't this piss off the Chicago families?"

"Chicago." Pugliese says it like there's something on his plate he doesn't want touching the rest of his food. "What families? Only one guy to worry about and worry's too strong a word to waste on that limp dick cocksucker."

"But what are you doing in Chicago?"

Anthony Pugliese slings an arm over his son's shoulder, brings him closer to the group seated around the card table. "This is a big job, Dominic. Your, uh, success so far, the doubt in your voice when you check in—what can I say—you left me less than confident in your abilities. I mean, look what happened to Angelo—God rest his soul."

Pugliese bows his head as do most of the men scattered about the room.

A few shoot harsh looks in Dom's direction.

"The two of you letting some little bitch put him down like that. I mean, Angelo was a big boy, shoulda been able to handle the situation. That's why I sent him along in the first place. To guide you through the rough parts. With him gone, I thought it best to send along some help."

Dom goes woozy trying to count the heads in the room. "*Some* help?"

"Wanted to be certain this time."

"I thought Rocky was gonna be helpin' me."

"He will. He did. But this is such a big deal for you, I wanted the whole crew to make the trip."

"What do you mean?"

Forcing a genial smile, the don slaps his boy's cheek with mock-affection. "Not everyday my boy becomes a man. Wanted to see you finish the job with my own proud eyes. Be good for the other guys to see what you can do."

But those proud eyes dart away.

Because if his boy can't finish the job, then Don Anthony's come to Chicago to be the one who puts a bullet through the coward's heart beating in his boy's chest.

Forty-Eight
A Life to Kill For

Like a swarm of lethargic bees, the cigar smoke follows Dom into the hallway. Walking jelly-legged, motor skills no better than before—probably suffering at least a minor concussion—he wanders after a destination, not wanting to return to his room only to be greeted by the ammonia stench of his vomit soaking into the carpet. Must be some place where he can sit quietly and ponder the doorjamb situation into which his own father has placed him.

Finding her holding up the same wall, Dom wonders if the blond might be a working girl. Top of the line—surely not a streetwalker—but she seems to be waiting for someone, perhaps a client having a hard time giving his wife and kids the slip.

It's odd. Dom's got no experience whatsoever with that sort of thing, but there's an air of familiarity about her. A vibration radiating from her that makes him feel he's been in her presence before today. He realizes he's been staring at her long enough that she probably takes him for a slack-jawed pervert, so he soldiers on.

Then his nerves kick in, because as he passes her, she follows after him. A subtle move, half a hallway in his wake, but he must have been the catalyst for her moving from the spot she's kept warm for the last half hour, right? A friend of Jimmy Pedals'? Perhaps a representative from Carlo Genuardi?

Probably just the concussion talking. Dom tries to shake his delusions away, slides the electronic room card his father gave him into its slot, watches the red light flash green.

Feels her hand on the flat of his back, and he nearly jumps through the roof.

"Missed you, baby." More of a sigh than a statement. Her voice barely more than a whisper, a hush of conspiracy.

But that's all it takes. That baffling familiarity, it's not so baffling anymore.

Dom's about to let Maria into the room when he remembers they're about to step in a puddle of puke. Closing the door, he faces her. Seeing her up close for the first time, he finds a virtual stranger standing before him—broad nose, thick blond 'do, tan she certainly didn't earn the old fashioned way.

Whatever angle she's working, probably a good idea to keep the façade.

"Hey there, beautiful," he imitates—poorly—a man chock-full of cheesy come-ons. "Can I take you down to the bar, buy you a drink?"

She directs him, instead, to her room sixteen floors below. Where she fixes him a drink, and treats him to the story of her escape from New York.

How she left Fernando, hopped a plane to O'Hare, waited out the gangsters, killed a lot of time eating shitty deep-dish pizza—Dom takes it all in, glass of whiskey chilling his trembling palm as he sits on the bed beside her. When she's finished she studies him quietly, and Dom knows from the way her gaze penetrates him, examines his bandages, that she's waiting for an explanation. So, he looks into her eyes—the only part of her face not enhanced or enlarged or painted or plastered, the part he recognized back in the hallway—and tells her everything.

Where he's been. What he's done. What he has to do.

"Been struggling with it half a week now. This whole time thinking I'd find a way out. But there's no time left. My father's here to make sure I do it, even if his *goombahs* have to serve Worthington and the others up on a platter. Like placing a fork in a two-year-old's fist, saying 'Go ahead, Dommie. That's right. *Verrry* Good, Dommie. That's daddy's little guy.' Either I go through with it or I may as well jump out the fucking window right now."

"Wouldn't do you much good. We're on the second floor."

"Yeah. Even if I broke my legs, my father'd wheel me up to the guy, hold him steady while I pulled the trigger."

"Do you still want the life we've always talked about?" she asks. "The villa in the countryside. Our own little garden out back. Naps in the afternoon, love by night. Children, grandchildren. How badly do you want that?"

It's the life they've always fantasized about, trotted out when times were toughest.

Like a couple of grade school kids playing house.

He can see it crumbling to pieces beneath the weight of his father's expectations, and his eyes well to the brim.

"Without that, without *you*," he tells her, fighting back the emotion, "I'd be nothing. There's nothing else in this life that can make me whole. I want that dream more than anything I've ever known. But I don't think it's possible anymore. Not without me becoming my father. And after that…"

He'd rather not envision how the demons will destroy him.

But Maria's nodding. She had a lot of time to think on the plane.

Dom's right. He has to become his father tomorrow. Someone has to die for them to have any chance at that bohemian life overseas. Hell, for any chance at any kind of life for the two of them now.

There's an intense confidence in her voice as she tells him this. Then she talks him through what he must do. How it will feel, how somehow he'll find the strength, she knows he will.

It's all so fucking horrible he dissolves into a weepy mess, collapsing against her chest, blubbering his fears all over her shirt.

"You'll be doing it for us, for the children we'll have. You didn't ask for any of this. Whatever you've been pushed to do, you're doing it in self-defense. If you don't, they'll kill you, and they won't think twice about it. Your own father."

And he knows she's right.

But his tears only intensify.

Forty-Nine
Getting the Message

"Until I meet with Genuardi tomorrow afternoon, nobody leaves this room."

"Until *we* meet with Genuardi," Beth corrects him again.

James shakes a weary head, paces before the three of them on the couch. Kyle's sit-standing on its arm, looking dour despite the adrenaline. Beth's got her arm over Katie's shoulder, the younger woman calm but for a bruise she's nursing on her forearm.

"From now on," James tells the group, "we stay together. Should have known better than to send the two of you off on your own like that." He looks to Kyle and Katie. "You OK?"

Katie nods, but Kyle's too hung up on the 442. Been sulking since they left it in the park.

"What about the car?" he asks.

James' posture crumples, as if his head suddenly weighs a thousand pounds. A quiver in his lip, he tells his boy, "Nothing we can do about that now."

"Will the cops trace it to us?"

"It's never been registered." For fear both he and his son will begin crying like bullied schoolchildren, James turns away. "It's like she never existed."

"What does that mean?"

They both know full well Kyle's wondering what it means for the two of them that the one object they've ever bonded over, however slightly, is gone forever.

"It means," James tells him, "we put it behind us, and we move forward."

"All right." Beth waves her hands like a referee calling delay-of-game. "Enough of this Doctor Phil shit. Are we just supposed to sit here in the hotel room until further notice? They came after Kyle and Katie, James. They know where we are. Won't they be coming for us?"

"I don't think so. They won't want to make a scene in a major hotel. Wouldn't risk it in a city that isn't theirs."

"I don't know, James, they had no problem making one on a major freeway."

James is already shaking his head. "They didn't plan it that way. Thought they could take the kids out quick and quiet. That's why they waited until they were alone." He smiles at both Katie and Kyle. "They just didn't anticipate such a fight."

"And what if—"

The ring of the phone cuts Beth's argument short. After a nervous moment, James inhales a deep breath, pulls the receiver from its marble-faced cradle.

"Yeah?"

His jaw remains firm, eyes unblinking. Without another word, he hangs up.

Three bodies lean so eagerly toward him they're poised to fall off the couch. Each of them dying to ask but terrified of the potential answers.

"That was Genuardi's guy. He said to check with the concierge for a message."

The others glance uncomfortably at one another, hearts pounding within their chests.

Annoyed that nobody else has the balls to ask, Katie blurts out:

"Well, how did he sound? Are they gonna make the deal?"

"Couldn't tell. All he said was to check for the message. I'll be back in ten minutes."

"Whoa." The frustration carries Beth to her feet. "What if it's a trap? You go down there looking for a message, couple guys in suits carry you into the side alley and execute you."

"Yeah, Dad, you said we stay together, right?"

"You said the New York guys wouldn't risk a bloodbath in Chicago," Beth continues. "But what about the Chicago guys?"

"Genuardi's not even in the game anymore. If he wants to kill me, he's gonna find a way to do it so it never gets traced back to him. He's a legitimate citizen now. Gunning me down in the lobby of an upscale Chicago hotel would be too high-profile."

"I'm not letting you go down there alone, Pop," Kyle says.

James exhales slow and angry. "Fine. Katie comes with me. Kyle, you watch Beth."

"For real?" Katie asks. "We're doing the babysitter thing? Making sure the girls are looked after by one of the big strong boys? Do we really have to review the story of the dead mobster I left in your kitchen, James?"

"Jesus," James grumbles. "Kyle, let's go."

*   *   *

The concierge ducks behind the circular mahogany desk and reappears with a piece of stationery, folded and taped at the bottom. James tips the guy a buck, turns toward a row of black leather chairs against the tinted front window, tears the page open as they walk.

"What's it say?" Kyle asks.

"Murphy's Bleachers, 2:00."

"Is that a guy? A place?"

"A bar down by Wrigley. It's on Sheffield."

"That's gotta be good, right? Them setting a time to meet."

James nods, not wanting to alarm his son.

But when it comes to the types of men they're dealing with, there's just no way to know.

Kyle's about to ask how it's gonna work, what their plan is for the meeting, when his father looks up from the note and his expression collapses.

He's looking at a finely-arrayed Italian in a three-piece suit, seated in one of the plush leather chairs.

"Hello, Jim." The guy's voice is the same deep-throated bark it was years before.

When James' hands ball into fists—the note crumpling like crisp lettuce in his grasp—Rocky shakes his head. "Not what I'm here for. Just thought we should talk."

Kyle can tell, when the tension fails to leave his father's face, that James isn't sure whether or not to believe the guy.

"There's a coffee shop down around the corner." Rocky nods in the direction from which he came. "You wanna hear what I gotta say, you can meet me there in ten minutes." He buttons his coat, nods, and walks out.

"Dad, what's going on? Who was that?"

"That was John Stallone."

Kyle almost laughs. "I thought Pedals was a weak nickname."

"Actually, that's his real name. His nickname's Rocky."

Kyle shakes an exasperated head.

James hands him the note, tells him to take it upstairs, let the girls know when they're supposed to meet with Genuardi's guy.

"You're gonna go with this Stallone guy? What if Genuardi sent him to kill you?"

"John's not from Chicago. He's from New York."

"We *know those* guys wanna kill us."

"Not John."

"How can you be sure?"

"He's the guy that gave me the .38. Just before I saved his life that day in the 442."

Fifty
Waking Up

Beth's behind the wet bar, rolling a glass of scotch between her palms, staring through the floor-to-ceiling window. From the couch, Katie sees the sweat beading down the side of the drink Beth hasn't so much as tasted.

"Do you think it'll work?" Katie asks. "What James has planned?"

Beth's eyes remain locked on the skyline.

"Beth?"

As if Katie's interrupted a moment of great significance, Beth snaps, "I don't know, Mansion. Make yourself a drink and don't worry about it."

"I thought we were past that Mansion shit." Katie marches to the bar, lifts a few ice cubes from the bucket, drowns them in cherry vodka. Not because Beth suggested it but because the booze might make the old broad's mood swings more tolerable.

Turning from the window, Beth watches Katie take her first sip, wincing at the uncut alcohol. Lifting her own glass to her lips, Beth returns to the window. "Sorry," she says. "It's not you I'm pissed at."

Katie tries another mouthful, warming up to the taste. "When we get back home, you think you'll leave him?"

Beth sighs. "That's provided we ever get back home. It's hard for me to consider a life with James until I know for sure any of us are actually going to have one. And having to think like that doesn't bode well for a long, healthy relationship with James Worthington."

"You know," Katie says, ice tinkling in her glass as she nurses another sip, "I'll never have a relationship with my parents. Sixteen years old and that's a foregone conclusion because of all the years we've spent living in separate worlds. They'll continue to cut checks and keep up appearances, I'll smile pretty on those rare occasions when the three of us are out together in public, but we'll never be any closer than we are now."

With a tone that says, *So?* Beth tells her, "That's a sad story."

Katie dismisses the contempt in her voice. "It's not, actually. I don't love them—not in any true sense of the word. I mean, they're relatively good people, and I guess I respect their work ethic and the lifestyle they've built for us, but that's not love. And I definitely don't hate them. They haven't done anything to hurt me. They haven't been around enough for that. There's just never been anything there. No emotional attachment. More like a social contract of some kind."

Beth's stare is blank.

"It's easy for me to accept all of this because I'm not losing anything. It would be an entirely different story if they'd ever been there for me. If they'd been model parents and *then* we drifted apart, I'd feel like they'd robbed me of something."

"Kate, I really can't help you with your problems right now. Got enough of my own."

Katie sighs. She's seen doors that weren't so dense. "If you leave James, you'll be losing something great. You get a chance to feel for somebody what you feel for him, you shouldn't give it up without a fight."

Beth exhales into her drink, takes a long sip before responding. "I'm too busy fighting for my life at the moment."

Both their heads jerk toward the sound of the door as Kyle walks in, waving a tiny slip of paper as if he doesn't know what to do with it. When no one follows him in, Beth hurries to the door, peaks down the hall. "Where's your father?"

Describing the note, the wiseguy from the lobby, the way James headed right down the street for a cup of coffee with a professional killer—his words don't sound like his own. As if he's too disappointed in himself for letting his father wander off like that to put any emotion behind them.

Beth locks eyes with Katie.

Offers a frustrated shake of the head to insist her next move doesn't mean what Katie thinks it does.

Then she darts out the door to find James.

"Hey, Beth—" Kyle calls after her.

So much for sticking together.

Kyle looks to Katie, who just shrugs and drinks her vodka.

*   *   *

A steaming cup of milk-lightened coffee awaits James at the same booth where Rocky always takes his morning cup of Joe. He sits there now, raising his eyebrows over his mug as he catches James coming through the door.

His eyes are encased in a pair of teardrop sunglasses—Sly Stallone-style from the '80s—and James can't get a read on the man. His staccato motions at odds with his slumped posture, as if part of him is there for business while the rest is there to see an old friend.

James pulls out his chair but doesn't sit, fairly confident if Rocky had been sent to kill him he never would have made it down the street, but keeping his guard up just the same.

"Cream, two sugars," Rocky says, brushing aside James' trepidation.

Feeling somewhat safer that Rocky cares enough to remember his coffee order from the old days, James sits, slides his chair in. "I just take it with cream now."

"We'll get you another."

James waves him off, takes the mug in both hands. His tongue puckers at the flood of sweetener, but he's thankful for the boost when the sugar hits his blood. "Seems I'm falling into a lot of old habits lately."

"Some of them don't die so hard," Rocky tells him. "Look at me. I live out here now, but if Pugliese gives me a call, I gotta do what I'm told."

"How's that work, living out here? You guys like state employees now? Twenty years and out, nice pension for all your hard work?"

"That what Sonny told you?"

James fiddles with his mug, looks out the window.

"Old man mentioned he turned up dead yesterday. Took two to the body in the office of his auto shop. That'd be you, right?"

James won't—or can't—take credit for the hit. "Yeah, well, he said he thought you were retired, hadn't seen you around the city."

"Got to a point, the family didn't look like the family no more. The boss always took on young start-ups, guys in their twenties, but today's kids, they're nothin' like you or I when we were young. Got to be like babysitting when you'd take one of the new guys out on a thing. They wear the fedoras, proudly refer to themselves as 'guidos.' Fuckin' idiots. Come show time, they're useless. They want the rep but not the responsibility, leave you to do all the heavy lifting. Got no heart."

Rocky pauses for a disgusted breath. "There was already enough blood on my hands for a lifetime, I wasn't about to wear their blood for them. So I told the old man I was out."

"You realize that's the most I've ever heard you say?"

Rocky shrugs. "Must be retired life. You find someone willing to listen to your bullshit, you go off like a geyser. When the old man finally came around to the idea of me calling it quits, I followed one of my *goomars* out to Chicago, got comfortable enough."

"You still with the *goomar*?"

"She didn't take. Pugliese, though, retains my services on an as-needed basis. Like a dog on a very long leash. Just as I start to forget someone's pulling the strings, he gives a good, hard tug. I'm out, but I ain't out. For a while I thought you were the only one pulled that off, with your grand vanishing act. Yet here we are."

"Here we are."

"You been in the same place for twenty years?"

James nods, and Rocky responds with a tilt of the head. "Big risk to take."

"It took them two decades to find me."

"Could've been a lot quicker, you gettin' complacent like that. Musta had a good reason, something to make it worth the chance you were taking."

James remembers what it felt like, his infant son falling asleep on his chest. Sees the boy, years later, falling from the bathroom window at the high school, the two of them making a break for it, and he can't help but smile. Thinks of Beth, soaked with sweat as she leaves their bed for the bathroom. Friday nights cheering for the home team. Detailing the 442 in his own two-car garage, poring over the last remaining trace of a secret he'd long since left behind.

"I lived a dream."

"You know it's the boss's kid got the button on this one?"

James takes a renewed interest in the window. "Last time I saw him he was in diapers."

"May as well still be for all he wants of the life. The young guys I was tellin' you 'bout, the ones with the look but minus the balls? Boss's kid's got neither. Never wanted any part of this. Old man's been forcing it since the kid was born, groomin' him for the top job when he doesn't even wanna be a street guy."

"You're supposed to hold his hand on this one."

"That's what the family's become. It's like that Ford you ran off the road today. Which, by the way, Pugliese's kid was driving."

James kinda wishes they'd tied up that loose end after all. "It was my son ran him off the road."

Rocky's lips form a gesture of admiration. "A kid with some backbone." He raises his mug in salute.

James tries to remember the boy Kyle was four days ago. Can't see anything but the *man* who ran that Mustang into a tree. "Next generation ain't a total wash."

"My experience, the world's gonna go to pieces in their hands." Rocky allows himself a grunt of a laugh. "That Mustang. You believe they give that plastic piece of shit the 'muscle' tag? Looks more like the fuckin' Bat Mobile. I drove past your 442 idling on the side of the road, barely a scratch anywhere on the frame. Tore that Ford to pieces. It's just like those kids. They're the newer, flimsier version of us, you know?"

But James isn't interested in an old thug's philosophy. "What are we doing here, John?"

"Felt I owed it to you, let you know what you were up against. It was a long time ago, Jim, but I ain't forgot what you done for us that day in the 442. Angelo—simple fuck that he was—laughed it off. Until the day he died, he had a knack for letting the important stuff fly right over his head."

"Angelo's dead?"

Rocky pauses behind his glasses. "On this gig. Shot to death by some cheerleader. You didn't know?"

"I'll be goddamn." James grins, sees Katie in a whole new light. Gunning down one of the kids Rocky's talking about would be one thing. Gritty, tough. Certainly something he'd never have imagined she had the capacity for. But taking out *Angelo*, who's worked for Pugliese since Nixon was in office?

Something like fatherly pride tickles James' ribs.

"That kid we was supposed to do all them years ago," Rocky goes on, "that junkie heroin addict, far gone as he was—me and Angelo were dead right there in your backseat. You didn't hit the gas, do what you did, I'm not sittin' at this table right now."

"I just didn't want to get blood on the seats."

Rocky sets his cup down as loudly as he can without spilling his coffee. "Bullshit. The family has its code—honor among thieves and all that—but you and me were different, weren't we? You know I made my bones with that gun I gave ya? The .38.

This Abruzzi guy running snatch in our neck of the woods, the old man gave me a call. My first time. Buried the barrel right in his fuckin' ear. I can still see his right eye bursting out the front of his face."

Rocky drinks his coffee, reverent right up until he shrugs the image off, just one of those things that had to be done. "You with your love of cars, me with the whole movie star thing." The memory forces a smile. "We were unique individuals among a collection of cookie-cutter wiseguys."

It's one way to look at their previous lives.

Another would be to say one of them was a sociopath who got off on the puzzled look on a guy's face when Sylvester Stallone burst through the door and cut his balls off.

And the other was an unfortunate kid who only knew one way to make a living.

But James is more concerned with their present lives than pointing out the inequities in Rocky's analogy. "All right, we're one and the same. So help me out here. I've been talking to Genuardi about giving us a pass—"

Rocky's already shaking his head. "Can't talk about any of that. I'm here on my own. Pugliese finds out I talked to you I'm in deep shit."

But that shake of the head speaks volumes. There's an elegiac defeat about the gesture. Plus, Rocky didn't seem terribly surprised when Genuardi's name came up.

"OK, how 'bout this," James tries. "If I see you tomorrow, what happens? What are you gonna do?"

"You said you lived a dream, right? Something else we have in common. Only two hoods from the old neighborhood who made it out from under. Even if it was short-lived."

"What's that mean for tomorrow, John?"

Rocky rises, slaps a few bills on the table, stares down at the tough street kid he took under his wing a lifetime ago.

"Tomorrow we wake up, Jim."

Fifty-One
No Pity

Beth's waiting for him outside the lobby of the InterContinental. Reddened cheeks, wind-whipped hair, frantic eyes that soften in a way she can't conceal when she sees him walking safely toward her.

Then she tosses up a dismissive hand and turns away.

"Good," she mutters, "you're alive."

"Beth, stop." James steps over the snow-rimmed curb, follows after her. When she doesn't respond, he clutches her shoulder, wheels her toward him.

She plants both palms defensively against his chest, tensing as if she might throw a punch.

"You stood out here for the last half hour in two-degree weather, Beth," he reasons. "Hell, you drove across three states to find me. You can't—"

"I had no choice. You might recall a couple of gangsters tried to kill me and Katie."

"That's the only reason?"

She shrugs free of his grip.

"Either we're a team on this," he explains, "or we're dead."

"As if we're not dead anyway." Sighing, she asks what he was thinking sitting down with someone who's likely been ordered to kill them.

"John wasn't gonna hurt me. We go back a long way."

"Did you at least talk about tomorrow?"

"He's a New York guy, not Chicago." James doesn't have the heart to tell her John's opinion on the matter didn't inspire confidence.

Beth closes her eyes in exhausted dismay. "When we go to that meeting tomorrow, they're gonna kill us, James."

"It's our only chance, Beth. All we've got."

"Jesus Christ."

"Beth, I'd do anything to change this."

When she glares at him, a scornful distrust in her eyes, he practically shouts:

"Do you honestly think it isn't killing me inside that I've gotten you all involved in this? Katie, an innocent kid whose love for my son is gonna get her killed? You, the woman I love so much I can't breathe thinking about what I've done to you. My s—" his voice breaks. "My son! How can you think I'm not dying inside?"

Her voice catching in her throat, her emotional crisis strangling her rage, she tells him simply, "You lied to us, James. For all this time. Nothing but lies."

After a moment that stretches to a lifetime, she looks at him with steady resolve.

And turns wordlessly back into the hotel.

*   *   *

Kyle falls onto the couch, defeated.

Couldn't stop his father from going to meet a gangster. Couldn't even stop Beth from running after him.

"You look beat to shit, Ky." Katie sits upon the cushion beside him.

"Thanks, Katie. You're a doll."

"Kate."

"What?"

"I kinda like the sound of 'Kate' now."

"Where'd that come from?"

No chance Katie's gonna credit the redhead here.

"Heard it somewhere, I guess." She sweeps the hair from his forehead and strokes his scalp at the temple. He closes his eyes. "Being on the run kinda wipes you out, huh?"

He moans a laugh.

"Wanna go to bed?"

She asks it as innocently as if she's asking if he wants to do some homework.

His eyes open, and the smile he sees on his girlfriend's face—an impossible combination of shy and sly—sets his chest afire.

They both know what they're facing tomorrow.

And it breaks his heart in the sweetest of ways that she wants to spend this night with him.

The sensation in his stomach is so fine, he can't even respond.

"Maybe we can do better than last time," she says.

Kyle sits bolt upright.

"What the hell was wrong with last time?"

Katie recoils from her mistake as though it bit her on the nose.

"Oh no, I didn't mean…It's just…"

"Just what? I wasn't good?"

"No, no, no, I didn't mean that at all."

Kyle's wounded pride won't let him believe her.

"It's just—" she works her way awkwardly to the point— "This one won't be a…a…pity fuck."

Kyle's face goes red. "Who said it was a…who said that?"

"Never mind. Come on," she asserts, "let's go to bed."

Kyle gives up the fight. And, boy, is he glad he did.

Turns out she's right.

There's no pity about this fuck.

Not until twenty minutes later when James knocks on the bedroom door.

"Kyle, you in there?"

Instinctively, they both freeze, pull the sheets up to their bare shoulders, stare at each other as if hoping one of them will somehow produce a magic cloak that can render them invisible. When they hear nervous voices beyond the door, Kyle shuffles into a pair of jeans, tells his father he's inside and that he's OK.

Then, after an awkward pause, the inevitable question:

"Katie with you?"

Even after all he's learned about his father—and even though he's confessed he and Katie have been intimate—Kyle can feel his face flush when he tells him she is.

On the far side of the door, Beth looks to James expectantly.

But he just tells his son he'll see him in the morning. They'll need to get an early start.

She gave him the silent treatment the whole way up, and Beth still opts not to say a word. She just trains a bewildered look on her boyfriend, struggling to read him like a book in a foreign language.

"What?" he asks.

"You're not gonna say anything?"

"You think I should?"

"No. I'm just shocked you haven't. The James I know…"

But she stops, hugs herself as if in defense.

Isn't sure she ever really knew him at all.

"Might be the last chance they have to let each other know how much they care. Probably the last chance for all of us."

"Yes," Beth agrees. "It is."

She slips into their bedroom and closes the door in James' face.

Fifty-Two
Watching Over Nothing

"There you are," Pugliese exclaims when Rocky walks into the empty hotel bar

Rocky's eyes do an elevator over Dom—pale, squirrelly, overstressed, underslept—before he nods at the old man, frail of body but firm with determination as he sips whiskey on a barstool.

"This retirement bullshit," he goes on. "I think sometimes you get it in your head it's OK not to answer when I call your cell. Don't forget our arrangement."

If the don expects to see intimidation on Rocky's face, he is sorely disappointed.

"Some things I had to take care of."

"First it takes me three hours to find this one"—he tips his glass in Dom's direction, and the kid wilts like he's been sprayed with acid—"Not in his room, not in the bar. I finally catch him coming through the lobby, he tells me he was takin' a walk, had to clear his head." The don winces around a sip of liquor. "Imagine that, the opportunity of his fuckin' life and he has to wander around the city, think about his feelings first."

"We're here now," Rocky answers for both of them.

"Yeah, you are. So can we finally get set with the details for tomorrow or what?"

Rocky shrugs like why the fuck else would I be here?

"You?"

Dom takes a breath. Maria did a good job building him up for this, but right now, looking the deal dead in the eye, it takes a minute before he can nod consent.

"Good then. Genuardi set the meet for 2:00. Place near the stadium called Murphy's Bleachers. I got directions upstairs. The old faggot wants to make sure his hands are clean of it, no connection to him or his defunct family. Sounded remorseful, like he hated having to do this to Pedals. Seems everywhere I look I'm surrounded by fuckin' softies. Thank Christ he got outta this game."

"So what do we do?" Rocky asks. "Take us through it."

But Don Pugliese notices a certain lack of enthusiasm from his son. Sure, he took a beating in that Mustang, but the kid's white as a fuckin' sheet.

How the fuck could they have the same blood pumpin' through their veins?

"You gonna be able to do this?"

Dom doesn't answer, just stares through the question with empty eyes.

Any other father would be proud of what he sees before him. College man, bright, in good shape, a born leader. But this is a different kinda life altogether. Anthony knows he's only got a few years left. Every day he wakes up a little shorter of breath.

And a little less continent.

If Dom can't lead the Pugliese crew, he's worthless in his father's eyes.

"I didn't think I'd have to remind you we're watching that condo of yours. Ready to call upon Maria whenever I deem it necessary."

Dom stirs at this, sits straighter in his chair, narrows his eyes at his father.

Finally, the kid shows some fucking life, some fucking balls.

Or so it seems.

Really, he's just trying to keep up the façade that his father's threats amount to anything more than a bunch of young thugs watching a condo they don't know is vacant.

"I can do what I have to do."

"Well, good then. Let's proceed."

He walks them through the specifics, but Dom hears none of it.

Like a ghost of himself watching his father's lips move.

He wonders—*agonizes*—over where he's come from.

And what he is about to become.

Fifty-Three
The Cowboy's Sad Song

There's a Blackhawks game on the silent TV over the mirror behind the bar. James isn't sure if it's live or a replay—he doesn't give enough of a fuck for hockey to know if they play the games in the middle of the day or not—but he notices the entirety of its audience in Murphy's Bleachers consists of a local drunk sipping his lunch at a corner booth.

All he can think about, walking in there without Kyle, Beth, or Katie is how he couldn't risk waking any of them with what might have proved a final goodbye. Too big a chance Beth would've stomped her foot, demanded he bring them along to the meeting.

And James knew from the start he'd never let that happen.

Instead, he passed a restless night on the sofa before wandering into the Chicago cold without so much as a last glance at any of them.

Broke his heart more completely than he thought possible.

At the bar James breaks a few bills and pumps a series of quarters into the lifeless jukebox in the corner. Orders a beer and smiles sullenly as the bright acoustic chords shimmer to life.

He's an hour early, but he knows when the phone rings—loud as cannon fire in an asylum—whoever's on the other line is calling about him.

Probably watching the place, put their plan in motion once they saw him walk in.

Nervously, the bartender—an old guy with a paunch and a head smooth as a bowling ball—peeks up at him before offering one-word consent into the mouthpiece and hanging up. He locks the cash drawer, rounds up the lone patron in the far corner. The guy's mildly belligerent, but once the bartender whispers something hoarsely urgent in his ear, he becomes almost impossibly alert.

It's no surprise when they pass through the front entrance and a suit-clad *paison* steps in to take their place.

Squinting through the gloom, realizing it's a somber Rocky coming through the door—face adorned with dark shades that he doesn't remove—James still ain't that surprised. He turns back to the bar, sipping his beer, watching in the mirror as Rocky pulls up behind him.

"Genuardi ain't comin', huh?" James asks the reflection.

"Turned the situation over to us." Rocky tilts his head toward the jukebox. "What's this?"

"Better get used to it, I picked it twelve times over."

"Not exactly the good ol' rock and roll I used to hear coming out of the 442."

"Lay off, will ya," James says. "This song saved my life."

Though with Rocky glaring down at him, it suddenly feels more like a stay of execution.

"If you say so," Rocky says. "Arms up."

Instead of surrendering to a frisk, James turns on his stool, details a proposition. "How's your retirement fund holding up, John?"

Rocky sniffs, rubs at his nose.

"I offered Genuardi a quarter of a million to let me walk away from this. Since he apparently doesn't want it, it's yours. Just go take a piss, tell Pugliese I never showed. Let me slip out the back."

"They already know you're here, Jim."

"Then tell him whatever you have to. Just let me duck out the back, the money's yours."

"Whaddya got? A check in your back pocket?"

"It's in a safe place."

"You thought Genuardi was gonna let you walk on your good word alone?"

"For two hundred and fifty large, I thought there was a chance."

"Still got balls, I'll give you that."

"I can have it to you in forty-eight hours."

Rocky removes his sunglasses. "Can't do it, Jim. I told ya yesterday, I'm out, but I ain't out. I don't make the rules."

"Without me, you're a stain in the back of my Oldsmobile. You told me *that* yesterday too."

James watches Rocky slip his dark glasses back into place, a punctuation mark on his final answer. "Whatever I owed you I paid back in full at the coffee shop. Did everything I could to tip you off. Shoulda run, Jim."

"They're on me now, where am I gonna go?" James takes a long pull on his beer. "What about for my family? Kyle, his girlfriend, Beth. Two-fifty to let them go. The don's kid has the button on me, not them."

"Tell ya what." Rocky sits down beside him. "I can buy you a drink while we wait for the man of the hour to show."

He leans forward, reaches behind the bar in blind retrieval of a bottle. Turns out to be bourbon. He lays a fifty atop the mahogany and twists the top loose.

James stares at the money on the bar.

His offer of two-fifty was the last card he had to play.

As Rocky passes him the bottle, he catches his own reflection in the mirror behind the bar.

Looks something like Sonny did in his final moments.

*   *   *

"It doesn't make sense," Katie blurts, studying the note for the hundredth time. "It is his handwriting, right?"

Fairly certain he would have noticed if it wasn't, Kyle takes another look and nods.

"I don't get it," she goes on. "'Be back soon. I love you.' What are we supposed to do with that?"

It's been the same since they woke, Beth coming into the kitchen first, cursing at the cryptic note as she put on a pot of coffee and sat down to wait for James' ballyhooed return.

Four hours and two pots of coffee later, they're still waiting.

"Look, it's almost two," Kyle tells Beth. "We seriously have to start considering the possibility that Dad's not coming back."

Beth's slouched in a kitchen chair, arms folded across her chest. She says nothing.

"Like he ran off on us, left us to fend for ourselves?" Katie demands.

Kyle shakes his head, his throat swelling as he says: "No. Like he went to the meeting alone. Or...tried to." He feels a powerful shortness of breath, the implications of that thought crushing him.

"But why would he try to do that? That wouldn't change anything. If they want to kill us, they're gonna kill us." And, though she can't picture the James Worthington she knows ever doing such a thing, she asks again, "Are you sure he didn't run off?"

Beth cocks an eyebrow but remains silent.

"He...he wouldn't do that," Kyle tries to insist.

But considering everything he *thought* he knew about his father, he'd have to admit he's not really sure about anything anymore.

"I can't believe this," Katie rambles. "We're supposed to be in this together. *He* got us into it."

Kyle falls back against his seat, slaps the table. "What the hell do we do?"

Finally, Beth says, "You're right."

For all she's said over the past few hours, they'd practically forgotten she was there.

"Who's right?" Kyle asks. "Right about what?"

"He is going to that meeting alone. Just because I insisted we go with him. Stubborn son of a bitch. Probably thinks he's gonna make some big sacrifice of himself. Save us like some martyr. As if that'll erase the shit he's put us through."

"You think so?"

Beth slides her chair back, pulls the note about Murphy's Bleachers from the back pocket of her jeans. "Yes, I do. But I don't intend to make it that easy for him."

Before Kyle or Katie can request an explanation, Beth's halfway to the elevator.

Fifty-Four
An Understanding

The bottle's nearly dry when a car pulls up out front. There's a hustle of voices before the door swings open and four young mafioso lead the old man into Murphy's.

Either the bourbon's hitting James harder than he realized or the guy's half the size he used to be. Once a burly bruiser a la Tony Soprano or Brando's Godfather, he's disintegrated into a dry leaf of a tough guy. Thin, brittle, slow. If the don hasn't officially been diagnosed with something like prostate cancer or cirrhosis, he should definitely get himself checked out.

The muscle scatters around the bar, each man saying nothing and looking on as if the scene doesn't interest him much. But James can see in every facial tick that they're all-too-eager to gun him down like Pacino at the end of *Scarface*.

Fuckin' punk kids, just like Rocky said.

For his part, Rocky caps the bottle and rises from his stool, makes way for the boss, who sits down in his stead, settling tenderly upon the seat.

If he had to, James would guess hemorrhoids.

But the don grins the same cocky smile he has his whole life, and there's plenty of youth left in his baritone. "Have a good drink, Jim?"

James sucks his teeth.

"You remember last time we met, all them years ago, I offered you a permanent job working for me? I told you in this family we got understandings? Well, I need for you to understand something, and we'll sit here all day until you do. If I gotta pull your tongue outta ya fuckin' mouth, you'll answer me. You were nobody. Some street kid on Hot Wheels who'da been dead inside a year when I found you, offered you a life. You run off in the middle of a job, leave one of my guys to get killed right there in the alley, you gotta understand you're a piece of shit deserves everything he's brought on himself."

The boss's hand—surprisingly broad and strong—falls heavily upon James' shoulder.

"Once you do that—once you tell me, 'I'm a piece of shit, Don Pugliese'—I'll make quick work of ya. My kid arrives, I'll have him put the bullet right through your heart, forego the agonizing lead-up I've fantasized about for the last twenty years. Two decades allows for a lot of creative thought, let me tell ya. But, your family—your son, his girl, your girl—I'll kill you all quick, you just have to tell me—"

"You won't touch them." James keeps his eyes on the bar, won't pay Pugliese even the miniscule respect of direct eye contact.

"Take a look around you, Jim. That ain't up to you no more." Then he leans in, speaking in a whisper to make sure Jimmy knows how personal he's taking all this. "And I'd watch my tongue tryin' to tell me who's boss. It's that attitude—balls, balls, balls with no pause for thought—that got you where you are."

James thinks, sure, 'cause patient consideration's *your* strong suit.

Pugliese leans back, satisfied he's made his point.

But there's no whisper about Jimmy's response:

"Go fuck yourself, Mr. Pugliese."

He lingers on the *mister* too. 'Cause fuck these wops and their bullshit concept of respect.

There's a low rumble in the room. Tough guys shifting their weight to their toes.

Though his face is red, strained with furious embarrassment, the don laughs. Like the comment, being what it is—an insult from a dead man—troubles him no more than a sip of water that didn't go down right.

His voice, however, is much coarser than his expression:

"That's the way you wanna play. But you will look me in the eye and tell me what a piece of shit you are before we're through."

But Jimmy's rolling now. Figures, what does he have to lose?

"See, that's why Abruzzi was able to sink your family to the bottom of the heap and take over New York. You know what you gotta do to me, but you've got this bullshit pride thing that's gonna keep you from pullin' the trigger. 'I gotta hear ya call yourself a piece of shit,'" he mocks. "What the hell is that? You wanna kill me, just fuckin' kill me."

"You gotta know you can't disrespect my family the way you have."

"Sure. I'll know it for, like, a minute and a half before you put my lights out. I don't see that as a valuable use of time and resources. *That* attitude, that's why you couldn't hold New York. If the papers are right—and they're usually dead-on the way you hoods toot your own fuckin' horns—all you got left is a few blocks out by Yankee Stadium. Right where I grew up. It was a fuckin' shit hole then, it's a fuckin' shit hole now."

The old man nods at Rocky, and before James knows what's going on, he's being shuffled to the center of the room where two goons prop a chair and Rocky forces him to sit. James' stomach wound throbs and the .38—Rocky's old .38—tucked into the back of James' waistband raps dully against the slats.

James forgot he was even carrying the piece. But he'd swear Rocky flinches, hears the metal hit the wood. Yet for the second time that afternoon, the goombah fails to frisk him.

Could he be so lucky as to have the man make the same mistake that almost got him gunned down by a sweaty junkie twenty years ago?

"Hold him," the don commands.

The weight of Rocky's two meaty palms sinks down upon either side of James' neck. Pugliese steps forward, stabs him with a stare. Defiantly, Jimmy glares up at the man, grins sardonically.

Pugliese's first slap catches him square on the left cheek. It turns his head, but—impotent fuck the old man's become—hurts little more than a snapped towel in a locker room.

"One last chance, Jim. Everything that's gonna happen to you, all we're gonna do to your family, you brought it on yourself 'cause you're a piece of shit coward. Say it."

"Don't talk about them," James says.

A backhand from Pugliese's other side.

"I were you, I wouldn't be so worried about my words, Jim. You make this hard, we're gonna take our time with the girls. Find out what it is about country pussy so enticed you to run out on my crew. Then your boy—Rocky's gonna carve his head off so I can keep it on the shelf in my office. Maybe use it for a fuckin' ashtray, snuff my stogies in the gaping holes where his eyeballs used to be."

James' jaw goes so rigid it feels nailed shut. But he struggles against it. "Better write all this down. The way you work, it could take you another twenty years to track them down."

This time, the boss's closed fist lands on the bridge of his nose.

*　　*　　*

"This is taking too long," Beth mumbles near panic.

She sits beside Kyle in the cab—Katie on his other side—glancing birdlike down every cross street as if she expects to find James standing at the far end, or lying somewhere between. In the places where parked cars obscure the view, she practically leaps from her seat for a better look.

"Guy doesn't know where he's going. Katie, you sure you gave him the right address?"

"I told him the one the guy at the front desk gave us."

"It's right," Kyle says, pointing a finger through the front windshield. Rising in the distance is Wrigley Field, its old-world concrete and pine towering over the much smaller and much younger apartment buildings and storefronts that surround it. Stoic despite the beating its unroofed innards, naked to the Chicago winter, have taken during the off-season.

"This place is supposed to be across the street, right?" Beth asks.

"That's what Dad said."

"Hey," she calls to the driver. "Step on it, come on."

Fifty-Five
Our Sons

The beating's been going on long enough to leave the don gasping, but aside from a sliver of red across his left cheek and a trickle of blood dripping from one nostril, Jimmy's no worse off than if he'd spent the last ten minutes playing with his pud.

He tells Pugliese as much.

"Sure, Jim," he responds between heavy breaths. "I ain't the man I was when I was younger. Happens to us all. Just look at the gutless worm you turned into chasin' after your American pie dream. But it don't matter. When the time comes, it's my son pullin' the trigger, not me."

"Oh, you mean that twerp my boy ran right off the fuckin' road? You see that Ford when my kid was done with it?" Jimmy's laughter pulls painfully at the stitches in his stomach. "So where the fuck is he already?"

"In due time, Jim. Due time."

"And what exactly happens in due time, huh? All I've heard about your kid, he doesn't sound like he's up to the task."

The don ignores the comment. "It's his big moment, Jim. He'll be fine." Though there's barely enough conviction in his voice for the don to fool himself. "Just a shame his first big act for the family gotta be wasted dispatching a guy who sells windshield wipers."

"Hey, my franchise happens to be one of the ten best in the state of PA."

"We'll put that on your tombstone."

"They sure can give you a headache, can't they?"

"Windshield wipers?"

"Sons."

The don doesn't answer.

Save for a sigh that sounds like he's expunging twenty-four years of parental anguish.

"My boy," James goes on. "We're in the middle of this whole thing with you guys and he starts crying about this look I give him sometimes. Like I think he's stupid or something. Even with bullets zippin' past our heads, this is what bothered him." James cocks his head in a thoughtful gesture, sweat running from his hair. "Truth of the matter, Kyle was right. It was like the last thing I wanted was for him to grow up like me, and then I got frustrated when he didn't. Gave him that…that *impatient* look. The city in me dies hard, I guess. That make any fuckin' sense?"

One of the don's standbys—a young guy with burnt olive coloring only found in a bottle or a tanning bed—sees this going nowhere, looks to the boss for an indication he should jump in, rain blows upon the wiseass in the chair.

But the don remains transfixed by James.

"You want 'em to be their own men," Don Anthony says, "but it hurts ya pride when ya don't see enough of yourself in 'em. No matter how successful they become, you're never sure ya had anything to do with it."

"Eloquent." James laughs. "Your kid must be one helluva fuckin' disappointment."

This time the tan douche bag gets his nod, and he doesn't miss a beat.

Takes a running start and sends a hook through James' face.

James' eyes well up, the flesh starts to swell. He tries to sniff back the disorientation that explodes his sinus cavities. Spitting blood, he says, "This is unbelievable. You gotta hold your boy's hand on this and *this* guy's gotta hold yours. Can't nobody in the Pugliese do their own dirty work no more?"

A mirror image of the first punch, swinging in from the other side, jars his other eye.

"Fuck," he moans, blinking away supernovas. "I got more respect for this guy than any of the rest of ya."

"Say it, Jim," the old man instructs. "You're a cowardly fuck and you brought this on yourself."

Licking swelling lips, it almost appears as if James is about to come up with the right words. "You know whose fault this really is? Sorrentino. And his little bitch of a son."

The heavy makes to swing again, but Pugliese stills him with a look. The old man leans closer. "He *was* a little bitch. The father, too. Both of them, useless fucks." He breaks into a husky chuckle. "And that's how little I think of you, Jimmy. I should thank you for snuffin' 'em out, and, instead, I'm gonna feed ya your own intestines. Bad as they were for business, letting little nobodies from nowhere spit in the face of my organization ranks even lower."

Pugliese nods once more at the henchman. And the blows resume. From the right, the left. This one draws blood, the next raises a bruise. One busts his nose wide open. Red, ropy strands of mucus slop down James' shirt.

"Two hundred and fifty thousand," James slobbers between punches.

At the very least, it gives the goon pause.

"What did you say?" the don asks.

"To let my family go." James huffs a breath through the murky mess of his mouth and nose. "Have all the fun you want with me, but let the three of them walk. I'll give you a quarter of a million dollars."

Immediately, the don raises his fingertips to his forehead as if rubbing away a mother of a migraine. "And where exactly would a small town auto mechanic come up with that kind of cash?"

James sidesteps the issue. "I've got it," he gasps.

"No, *I've* got it. At least I will once you're dead and buried. See, that's my money, Jim. Paid out over a five-year period back when you worked for me. Where else would it have come from? The way you run out on us, you got no right to that money. And now that I know it exists, I'm puttin' it back in my pocket."

"You'll never find it," James spits.

Knowing full well the safe behind the counter of his auto parts store does not scream inconspicuous.

"After my son puts you in the ground," the don continues unabated, "and we take care of the rest of your family, I'm gonna tear apart your fuckin' store and then I'm gonna march right into that bank in Gower and persuade the manager to hand over whatever he's holding in your name. Bank accounts, 401K, deposit boxes, whatever. And I think we both know how persuasive I can be."

James smiles. "Yeah. Not persuasive enough to get your boy here on time. I mean, whaddya think happened? Did he piss himself when he lost his nerve or shit himself?"

When the young bruiser starts whacking away again, James feels the .38 tugging against the back of his pants. Between the bourbon and the beating, the world's turning gray, but maybe if junior does finally grace them with his presence, James'll get the moment of distraction he needs to pull his piece.

If only the little fuck would show up already.

Fifty-Six
His Own Worst Nightmare

They hit another red light, and Beth can't take it. Not when they're within spitting distance of the ballfield. Her eyes scramble back and forth, reading the street signs.

"Where are we?" she asks no one and anyone all at once.

Katie reads a sign aloud, "West Newport—"

"—and North Sheffield," the cabbie, clearly miffed at his backseat driver, tells them. "I know where I'm goin', lady. Have ya there in two minutes."

But Beth can't wait any longer.

Kyle grabs for her arm, but she's out the door before he can stop her.

"Hey!" the cabbie hollers.

Panicked, Kyle looks back at Katie. Before she can shrug her confusion, he's hot on Beth's heels, the two of them running down North Sheffield in the shadow of the stadium.

"Son of a bitch!" the cabbie screams. Pivoting in his seat, he glares at Katie, sees her poised to bolt through the open door. "Don't even think about it. Someone's gotta pay this fare, Barbie."

Sighing like she's going to comply, she sits back in her seat. Then, in one swift motion, she flips the judgmental prick the bird and flies through the open door. The cab's horn sounds behind her, but she could give a fuck.

She's got her work cut out for her, keeping up with the two galloping gazelles in her distant sights. Not a prayer she's gonna catch the track star and the marathoner, but she doesn't want to get left totally behind, end up wandering strange streets alone.

Though form is the last thing on their minds, you could cut an instructional video from the side-by-side perfection of Kyle and Beth sprinting down the sidewalk. Fists ear-to-pocket, knees up, springing forward on the balls of their feet. Kyle's squashed what little lead Beth had at the start and now they alternate the front position. Every time one of them draws forward, the other's adrenaline surges—in primal fear—and pushes their counterpart back into second place.

Even though they're both painfully aware it's a race they don't want to win.

Winner gets to be the first to find James lying in a pool of his own blood.

*   *   *

Dom's driver—another barely-legal, fake-bake wop—parks at the curb, comes around to get the door. Dom tumbles from the backseat, his legs going soft beneath him, and the goon has to catch him before he hits the pavement.

"You OK, killer?" The driver can't muffle the amusement in his voice.

Dom shrugs the guy off, pulls at his lapels.

The walk to the front entrance is like a walk through a soap bubble. His vision's warped, flecked with chips of color and a wary sense that he might swoon or vomit. He stands, palm flat against the door before he can bring himself to reach for the handle, his father's goon snickering behind him.

Every face turns his way as he steps inside, and he can see by their stunned expressions just how sickly he must look. In shame, his father turns away. Some of the guys shake their heads, like the don's gotta be kidding giving college boy a shot at the title.

Even Rocky grunts with disgust.

All of which allows James to scramble to his feet.

In front of him, there isn't a single soul who's aware he's even stood up, let alone that he's going for the .38, as his hand closes around the cool, nubbled handle.

But behind him, Rocky sees it go down.

Yanks the revolver from James' grip and pushes him back into his seat as if he's doing a triceps press at the gym. By the time the other heads wheel around, Rocky's tucking the piece into the front of his waistband.

"What the fuck?" the don demands. "Why didn't ya frisk him?"

Rocky shrugs. "He's good."

"Fuck that. Check him."

Rocky squats by James' feet, pats his legs all the way up through the crotch, around the sides, up and down both arms. Standing behind him once more, Rocky repeats, "He's good." Then his eyes, as do everyone else's, fall upon Dominic Pugliese.

Whose face is so pasty green, Kermit the fucking frog would wonder what was wrong with the kid.

He's walked into the very nightmare he described for Maria.

There's Dad and all his buddies, limbering up the mark for him. James beaten too bloody to offer up any kind of defense. Rocky holding him in place so there's no way Dom can miss even though he's standing two feet in front of the guy.

Heeere, Dommie. That's a good boy, Dommie.

Suddenly, he's more pissed than when he tried to run those kids off the road.

When his blind rage brought him to the point where he'd have been glad to disembowel them if that's what his father asked him to do.

His anger makes it surprisingly easy to do what happens next.

What Maria told him he had to.

He raises his .45, trains the barrel right on the man's forehead.

Fifty-Seven
A True Wiseguy

Three strides and she'll have a hand on the door.

But Beth hears the lone gunshot before she makes it, and the realization of what it means hits her as hard as if she's the one taking the slug. She slumps against the bar's brick front, unable to breath. Kyle's face is a contorted mass of disbelief when he catches her.

All Beth can think is that she'd give anything—everything, her own life—if she could have her last night with James back. She can't believe she was so stubborn as to exile him to the couch knowing it was likely the last time they'd be together.

Kyle's young mind goes black, unable to process the implications of that single, perfunctory report.

Her lips quivering, eyes filling, Beth puts a hand on his shoulder and together they force their way through the door.

Because they have to.

James sits in a chair, a shower of blood staining his shirt, coating his jeans, soaking his socks and shoes. His is the only face they can see, for he's the only one facing the door. No one else moves, as if they're as shocked by the inevitable as Kyle and

Beth. The two of them stand gawking, Beth with her palms over her open mouth, Kyle with his hands on his knees.

The worst part is that James' face is such a mess of gore, the only way either of them can tell it's even him is because, well, he's Kyle's father and the love of Beth's life. They can feel it in their bones, their souls. And all the feelings that arise when they apply those terms to the pulpy mess sitting before them buckle their knees and sicken their stomachs.

James, on the other hand, he's shocked, all right, but not so shocked he doesn't spring to his feet and go for the nearest gun. Which happens to be Rocky's old .38.

This time, Rocky doesn't put up much of a fight.

He's too busy staring at the lifeless body of Don Anthony Pugliese on the barroom floor.

The smoking gun's rattling like a pair of castanets in Dom's hand, and though they could overpower him with ease, no one in the room's moving a muscle.

'Cause, technically, Dom's the man now.

After he wipes the gooey chunks of the old man's brain out of his eyes, James turns his gun on the boss's kid, because he's the only other guy in the room with a piece in his hand.

Even if the kid did just kill his old man to save the lowly James Worthington.

It's a confusing moment to say the least.

Their eyes meet. In addition to the fear and disbelief, there's obviously more than a little resentment on Dom's part.

He looks back at James like, seriously, I kill my own father for you and you're thinking about shooting me?

So James raises his palms—gun still snug in his grip—in a gesture of semi-surrender. Sort of bringing it to the kid's attention that they're on the same side now, in case the kid's so rattled he forgets why he decided to plug his old man in the first place. He's also giving Dom a moment to realize every gun-toting thug in the place is theoretically on the *other* side.

And they're probably gonna have a problem with the whole whacking the boss thing.

Sure enough, before Dom can say a word, one of them steps forward, aims his gun at the boss's assassin.

Turns out to be Rocky.

Dom's looking numbly back and forth between his father's prostrate body and the barrel of Rocky's gun, and James can tell that, whatever nerve the kid worked up for this afternoon's events, he shot his wad taking his father out.

So James trains the .38 on Rocky's hulking chest, tells him to put the gun down.

With his free hand, Rocky swipes the sunglasses from his face, sighs audibly.

He's doing what a true wiseguy should do. The boss goes down, you get the son of a bitch that took him out, even if it means you're going down with him. Rocky's got no chance, and he knows it. Knew it the day, forty years ago, when he took his oath. Even after "retirement," he knew this was the only real way out.

Rocky's gun turns lifelessly in James' direction, and their eyes meet.

Better an old friend than some pussy with a B.S. in fucking finance.

Two bullets from his own .38—the one he handed over to a promising young troublemaker so many years ago—catch him in the chest.

The third hits him between the eyebrows, splits his skull down the middle.

As the harsh echo fades, James steps forward, crouches to lower Rocky's gaping eyelids.

But there's too little left of his face for that to be possible.

Standing erect, James asks the stunned crowd, "Anybody else got a problem with the new boss?"

One by one, their guns hit the hardwood floor in a series of coarse, metallic thuds.

It's only then that Kyle and Beth turn to one another in elated disbelief and start breathing again. It's a Herculean effort to keep from running to James, wrapping him in their arms, peppering him with kisses, but there's still an outside chance the gunfire hasn't totally abated, and they wait, holding onto one another instead.

"We're square now," James tells Dom.

It's a while before the don's kid—fighting the spasms in his gut, the shortness of breath—finds his voice.

And, apparently, his balls.

"I just killed my father, and you're gonna tell me 'we're square'?"

James hangs his head, the most respectful gesture he can muster. His freedom—so close now it's as if he's wearing it for a shirt instead of the bloodied rag on his chest—is in this kid's hands. One wrong word and Dom's got every right to snatch it back from him.

"Get the fuck out of here," Dominic grunts.

But James can't leave it like that. "All due respect, kid, I'm not going back to my life if five or ten years from now I end up at the barrel-end of another vendetta."

Dom can't believe the guy's nerve.

"You don't get that promise from me, Worthington. You can't go back to your life without it? Fuck you. I can't tell you we're cool."

'Cause it's entirely possible—hell, *probable* even—that the passage of time will change everything. That Dom will wake up one morning so haunted by his patricide that he can't bear the thought of James Worthington—the catalyst for his blasphemous betrayal—living a normal life somewhere entirely unmolested.

And James totally gets that.

Sees it in the kid's eyes.

He grips the .38, thinks how easy it would be to paint the walls with Dom's brain. Leave him lying lifeless beside his father. Be done with all of this for certain, for good.

But then Katie chooses that particular moment to storm through the door, breathless and wide-eyed. James studies his family, feels their eyes eager upon him. All they want is to walk away with James Worthington.

And even though Jimmy Pedals would press the gun barrel to the little punk's temple and pull the trigger, James Worthington can't do it.

He tosses the .38 atop the body of its rightful owner, throws one arm around his son, the other around the girls and turns them through the door, having never felt a sweeter sensation than the warmth of their bodies in the face of the freezing cold.

There's no destination left on his map but home.

And though it's become a dicey proposition at best after all they've been through, Jimmy finds himself smiling.

Fuck if he ain't getting that good-to-be-out-of-the-city feeling once more.

Acknowledgments

This book honestly would not have been possible if not for my fans. All pie-in-the-sky idealism aside, I simply wouldn't have been able to publish a second book had no one purchased the first one. Without a few sales and a few dollars in the bank, it wouldn't have been worth the time and effort of going to the well once more. So, if you own a copy of *Weekend Warriors* (and if so, I hope you love it; if not, what are you waiting for?) you helped make this book possible.

Though I dedicated the book to him, I have to again thank my father. Anyone who knows either of us will easily spot the bits and pieces of our relationship that have found their way into this novel. And while it would have been quite the thrill to discover he'd once been a driver for a New York crime family (OK, pretty fucking terrifying, too), I wouldn't trade the thrilling misadventures we *did* have over the years for anything.

OK, maybe for the film rights to this book.

I probably owe a thank-you to my daughter as well. I started the first draft around the time we found out she'd be joining the party, and all of my subsequent hopes and fears about fatherhood proceeded to fight their way into the manuscript. So thanks, kid. Someday, we'll read this one together.

But not for many, many years.

There's a lot of dirty shit in this book.